Deadly Deception

Shana Liddell

Copyright © 2024 Shana Liddell

All rights reserved. No part of this book may be reproduced or transmitted in any form or by any means, electronic or mechanical, including photocopying, recording, or by any information storage and retrieval system without permission in writing from the publisher.

Cadence Waves Press —Scottsdale, AZ
ISBN: 979-8-3302-6616-6
Title: *Deadly Deception*
Author: Shana Liddell
Digital distribution | 2024
Paperback | 2024

This is a work of fiction. The characters, names, incidents, places, and dialogue are products of the author's imagination and are not to be construed as real.

Published in the United States by New Book Authors Publishing

Dedication

To all my friends and family who always help me persevere.

Prologue

He carefully inspects the photo. She makes the puffy fuchsia dress look attractive on her slender frame. Pierce's hands are intrusive on her delicate shoulder and he's looming over her, stoic and dominating. Her auburn hair is on fire in the sun, cascading down to her waist in bouncy curls. She is smiling widely, a happiness that would only be fleeting. It's quite a shame because she really is beautiful. But she had plenty of opportunities.

Pierce fills out his tuxedo simply due to random genetics, though dually helped by his egotistical obsession with working out. His face is cut in hard symmetrical angles, which society has inanely deemed attractive, but his skull is hollow. Those smart enough not to be deceived would be able to quickly determine this.

He may stand a full foot shorter, have less pronounced features and nearly no muscle on his frame, but he would ultimately win. His brother started stealing from him right from the womb, stunting his growth, forever mistaking him as the younger, lowly brother. But he would be getting back what should have been his. He would make sure of it. So many times in his mind he had imagined it. Imagination is a powerful thing… until it becomes real.

Chapter 1

Elle woke with a start, her heart pounding. She was gasping for air as if she had been drowning, drenched in sweat. The sheets tangled around her long limbs and her mass of red hair was plastered to her face. She frantically untangled herself and sat on the edge of the bed catching her breath.

She had gone without dreaming of the accident for several weeks. The car accident, almost seven months ago, was as vivid in her memory and dreams, the terror just as fresh, as it was that New Year's Eve night when a drunk driver had come colliding into them on the icy roads. Her best friend, Ami, beside her, clutched her arm so tightly she could still feel her nails digging into her skin. The Uber driver had died instantly, leaving behind a wife and three young daughters.

Elle and Ami had already been hammered upon getting into the vehicle on their way to what was supposed to be the "most epic" New Year's Eve party in the Old Town district. If only they had stayed home. Elle had been content to stay in but Ami had insisted that they go to this party a friend of a friend was throwing with "plenty of single and established bachelors" for Ami and plenty of single and established bachelors and bachelorettes for Elle.

So in support of her best friend's quest for a new man in her life, Elle had reluctantly put on a classic black dress and heels—the last thing she felt like wearing on a freezing Chicago night. But of course, Ami insisted that she put on something more colorful and New Year's Eve-like.

So she ended up putting on the vibrant fuchsia dress she found stuffed in her disastrous closet. She had originally bought it for a girl's trip to Vegas a couple of years ago that didn't end up coming to fruition due to a bad cold she had come down with. One of the most brown-nosing students she had so far in her twelve years of teaching, Billy Fair, had always came to school sick, snot dripping down his face, in his goal to never miss a day of elementary school at the expense of infecting others, including Elle, four times that year.

Thankfully he moved onto middle school last year with undue congratulations for his stellar grades and perfect attendance.

On that New Year's Eve night, she had given herself up to whatever Ami thought was best for her. Ami knew Elle better than herself most of the time. Ami did her makeup like she always had since their first middle school dance, more intensely than Elle preferred, resulting in an escort resemblance when paired with the high heels.

She would never forget waking up in the hospital, the fuchsia dress covered in blood and her makeup smeared everywhere, completely confused. But then she saw the scratches on her arm from Ami and it all came rushing back to her.

She and Ami had once again clung to life together.

Unfortunately, her mind still clung to the accident as well. She had never experienced a panic attack nor ongoing insomnia until that horrific night. She had not realized that the heart palpitations, dizziness and intense sweating that forced her to lock herself in the restroom, with 32 eight-year-olds left to their own devices for 10 minutes the day after an all too short winter break, was in fact a panic attack.

Now this was her new way of life. And the lack of sleep made her feel that she was turning into someone entirely different, irritable or even delirious at times. As an elementary school art teacher trying to get through the day, this was a recipe for disaster. The summer break could not have come soon enough.

Ami, on the other hand, had seemingly forgotten the accident entirely. She had moved on with her life without pause, getting engaged to Clay, whom she had met six weeks later. Just last month she was promoted to partner at her law firm and their engagement soon followed. Elle couldn't have been happier for her especially after her first failed marriage.

So at Ami's persistence, and Elle's gradual desperation, she had found herself in Dr. Berkshire's claustrophobic office on her first day of summer break, what should have been her first thrilling day of freedom. She couldn't help being distracted by the piles of dusty papers and books from who knows when, littering every surface. But the old man's face, so full of concern, drew her back in, putting her at ease enough to retell the story of the accident. Not in great detail as she envisioned countless times, but enough to give him the idea. The reason that she had landed here in his mushy chair, where hundreds of clients had sat before. She could only imagine the horrors that were revealed in this chair and in comparison, her accident felt insignificant. She and Ami had survived. But Dr. Berkshire looked at her with the same intensity and compassion he afforded to all his patients and validated her "trauma response."

He went on to explain that though her best friend had experienced the same accident, everyone processes trauma differently and unfortunately for Elle, her body was still stuck in the "fight or flight" response. However, he felt confident that a little boost from Zoloft for anxiety and Seroquel for sleep would have her back to her old self. Elle had been reluctant to take anything—she struggled to take a Tylenol for a headache as it was—but Dr. Berkshire put her fears at ease in his grandfatherly tone. So this is how she started implementing a new regimen of pills in her life the past couple of weeks. The Seroquel a lifesaver. The first night she took it, she fell asleep within twenty minutes. She slept the entire night, her mind jumping through the craziest dreams but none of which were about the accident thankfully. In fact, she hadn't had a nightmare about the accident since taking the Seroquel until last night.

She peeled herself out of bed and took a cool shower, scrubbing her skin hard, as if trying to wash the nightmare's aftereffects away. Toweling off, she felt a bit better. She wiped the foggy mirror and looked into her bluish green eyes. Today they looked more blue than green. Her unapologetic red hair added to her striking look.

Elle didn't always have red hair though. She had started to lose her hair at nine years old, hair that was such an intricate part of her identity. To this day, she never tired of random people turning their heads and complimenting her.

She would never forget the shock of waking up to find clumps of it on her pillowcase, which was even more devastating than when the pediatric oncologist told her she had cancer. He said it in a tone that seemed to already be sealing her bleak fate. Acute Lymphocytic Leukemia. He nearly whispered the diagnosis while looking at Elle's mother, as if she were the one that would be undergoing the pain and trauma. Elle could remember how her eyes glazed over with tears, one of the only times Elle had ever witnessed her demonstrating what appeared to be true concern for her only child.

The bruises and fatigue had been the first signs. Normally eager to start the day, it took all her effort to just get out of bed. Midway through the school day, she was barely able to keep her head up. Her 4th grade teacher, Ms. Hampton, didn't call her out on this initially, probably because she still somehow managed to keep her grades up. But she had mentioned her concern to Elle's mother at parent teacher conferences, encouraging her to ensure that Elle had a "proper bedtime." This only prompted her mother to incessantly check in on her throughout the night. She knew even then this wasn't out of concern but rather to catch her being up and having something else to reprimand her for.

Elle had always been an avid reader. As a child she would often read with a flashlight late into the morning, riveted by the latest Goosebumps novel she snatched at the school library and could easily devour in a couple nights. But when the fatigue became so intense she stopped reading for fun altogether. She was grateful to dive back into bed right after she finished the burden of chores, homework, and getting ready for bed.

The first sign of her cancer were the bruises. After one of her army showers, (her mother's long showers always stole all the hot water), she had mustered up the energy to slather some lotion on her dry skin. That's when she noticed the splattering of green and yellow marks. She had no recollection of how she got them. She dismissed it at the time, telling herself that since she was so tired lately, she must have been being extremely clumsy.

And then one unseasonably hot spring day, she threw on new shorts and a tank, purchased by her mother's latest boyfriend who had taken them on a shopping spree. She had become so accustomed to the bruises she didn't think twice to cover them. When the principal, Ms. Hampton, called Elle to the office that day, she immediately assumed that she was being called out for violating dress code. Her shorts had been too short; she should have known.

But when she started to question Elle about how things were going at home, adding that she was safe to tell her the truth, Elle sensed where the conversation was going. She immediately defended her mother, envisioning her life at a foster home, with bologna sandwiches for dinner every night and in constant fear of getting beaten with a belt or worse. Even at nine, she was no dummy. Ms. Hampton insisted that Elle get a check -up at least and indicated that she would call her mother. Her mother eventually took her to the doctor's the following month, annoyed that she would be missing her standing hair appointment.

Ms. Hampton probably saved her life that day. By the time she was diagnosed, the cancer had already progressed to stage 3. The chemotherapy was started right away, hours of an IV dripping into her spine. She was able to get used to the discomfort but the confinement in the hospital was near torture. She missed the rest of the school year doing her assignments from bed. Her teacher and classmates sent her a get-well-soon card with a cheerful monkey hanging from a tree. Inside she could clearly recall reading "hang in there!" with a cluster of signatures. She received some personal letters from a few of her friends but as summer came and the last of her hair had fallen out, they stopped. She knew then that she would be spending that summer watching endless cartoons and rereading every Goosebumps and Nancy Drew novel while her classmates swam and went on vacation.

Her mother had basked in the pity bestowed on her, a single mother with a cancer-stricken child. She flirted shamelessly with the oncologist intern, who barely looked like he was out of his teens, breaking down into dramatic tears at one point. After several uncomfortable minutes, he finally drew her in for an awkward hug, her grip on him much tighter than appropriate. Then her complaints started about how exhausted she was shuffling to and from the hospital, though Elle's grandma probably spent twice as much time with her, knitting as she slept or playing cards with her when she had the energy.

Elle spent much of that summer alone, often staring out the window and repeatedly seeing a small bird that quickly befriended her. It came to visit most every morning and evening. She started to attribute its arrival to having a better day or night. There were no great days in the hospital of course. Her immune system had gone to crap and she was getting weird infections left and right. Some days she didn't even see a point in waking up if she was just going to die anyhow.

But she fought back against the negative thoughts when the bird would come. She named her Hope, convinced the bird was a "she" by her pretty, shiny feathers. She would tweet at her in greeting and hop around doing what Elle had coined her "happy dance," trying in earnest to entertain and cheer her up. Elle couldn't help but smile and clap.

And then there was her favorite nurse, Ms. Julie, who worked the morning shift Monday through Thursday. She always brought Elle homemade sweets, which she managed to eat despite her nausea. Ms. Julie was the first person to ask Elle about her dreams and aspirations in the near and distant future, making Elle feel as if her cancer was just a small bump in the road. Dreaming of possibilities filled her with hope and renewed her strength. Her white blood cell count went down and the weird rashes went away.

Ms. Julie's genuine love and acceptance helped her get through those long, tedious days that all blended together. One morning, Ms. Julie presented her with the best present she could receive—an art kit with some drawing paper, colored pencils, and pastels. Elle had never been much into art, afraid that whatever she produced would be inadequate. She would never forget presenting her mother with the picture she had made her for her birthday, a drawing of them together holding hands. Her mother had laughed, commenting on how "cute" her attempt was to replicate her hair and how "interesting" Elle's face was.

Ms. Julie had put the art supplies in a pretty glittery bag on her nightstand. "In case you want to create something," she said. "But by no means do you have to either. I won't be offended." She winked at Elle and then left the room to tend to other patients. That was the first time she drew something just for herself, a thunderstorm clearing up, making way for sunshine and the last time she saw Ms. Julie.

The next day, her new nurse, Ms. Priscilla, informed her that Ms. Julie wouldn't be coming back. Elle's heart was instantly broken. That night she cried herself to sleep, the first time she had cried since her diagnosis. She had been trying to be strong and not feel sorry for herself this whole time but she had reached her breaking point. However, the next morning Hope came and she forced herself to believe that it was going to be a better day.

And that was the first day Elle met Ami. She came into the room in all her red headed glory. The first words out of her mouth were, "well looks like I might as well shave mine and get it over with." She immediately lay down on the bed adjacent to Elle and commented that she would "have to get used to the horrible mattress as well." Then she rolled over on her side, facing Elle like she knew her already, and said, "I'm Ami. Let's beat this crap together." Elle laughed. She liked her immediately.

And from that summer on, the bald-headed duo eventually became the inseparable red headed duo. Ami had just moved to Evanston to receive treatment at Lurie's Children's hospital and they spent the rest of elementary school doing schoolwork from bed, ended up in the same class in middle school and going to the same high school. They lived together in their tiny apartment in Lincoln Park while attending DePaul University and after launching their careers, Ami moved out to live with her now ex-husband, Ryan.

Elle was never a fan of Ryan. She had said her piece early on but eventually Ami became so head over heels Elle simply had to go along with it. Until he hit on her, not once, but twice after their extravagant wedding at the Ritz Carlton.

On the first occasion, he was pretty drunk so Elle excused it, deciding it wasn't worth mentioning to Ami. They had been grabbing drinks together a couple weeks after returning from their honeymoon. Elle had gotten a round of ghastly expensive tequila shots and toasted them a happy marriage for the umpteenth time. Ami immediately looked like she was about to puke and headed to the bathroom leaving her with Ryan. After some awkward silence he made a comment about how it had always been his fantasy to have a threesome with her. Elle had pretended that she was too drunk to comprehend what he was saying and quickly excused herself to the bathroom as well.

When it happened again a couple months later at a party that Ami was hosting in their new million dollar home, he clearly wasn't drunk. Elle had purposefully surrounded herself in the mix of other guests as he toured them around the expansive home, Ami having insisted she go on while she attended to other guests. Remarkably, he still found a way to corner Elle in a remote room. He kissed her before she threw her drink at his face, leaving his disgusting cigarette breath lingering on her mouth.

Telling Ami the next day over lunch she had no appetite for, was definitely the hardest news she had ever delivered. But Ami deserved better and she deserved to know. Elle was so nervous that she ended up blurting it out so quickly she had to repeat herself. Ami's face fell in disbelief and she remained speechless staring at her remaining French fries. Elle had at least let her enjoy her meal. It was the longest pause she ever had with Ami.

After what felt like ten minutes but was more like ten seconds, Ami finally said in her matter of fact lawyer tone, "Well fuck him. I mean you are wonderful and all, and if I got hit by a bus tomorrow, I would certainly give my approval for him to pursue you. But the fact is he married me, and is most likely doing this with other women as well. So it looks like I am back in the dating game with you." More celebratory shots followed.

Elle had been shocked how surprisingly well Ami handled the divorce, which was solidified just a month later with Ami's stellar divorce attorney connections and her desire to leave things clear cut. She did not need or want anything more from Ryan. A girl's weekend to Napa ensued and then things went back to normal—talking every day and getting together for spontaneous meals and gym sessions regularly. It was as if Ryan had never existed, as if Ami was completely unphased by the loss. She never even mentioned his name again.

Things had also moved fast with Clay but their relationship was completely different. Ami finally seemed happy with someone beyond their assessment on paper, the financial security they could provide and their good looks. Clay was down to earth, genuine, and if anything, a bit dorky. He was also a very talented musician. It was impossible not to like him and it was obvious they were completely invested in one another. Therefore, Elle had been sincerely supportive of their fast-tracked marriage plans.

Unlike Ami, Elle was notoriously single. Sure, she had her fun dating men and women and had some relationships that lasted six months or so, but beyond that, she was content being single. Ami always joked that she was jealous that Elle had double the prospects and here she was choosing to be alone. But Ami had eventually given up pressing her about it. And now that she was consumed with an engagement again, she had enlisted Elle to help with some of the wedding planning, which Elle was more than happy to do. The first time around, Ami had ended up spending thousands on a wedding planner who was as unoriginal as Ryan's wedding speech. Plus, she had a feeling she would not be planning for her own wedding—at least anytime soon. The thought of being "stuck" with one person made her feel claustrophobic to some extent and overwhelmed her with a sense of boredom. Ariana had been the closest person that Elle could conceive spending the rest of her life with but her insecurities had eventually become too taxing on Elle. Of course she could never completely voice this to Ami as she did not want to put a damper on her life choices. Ami certainly had never judged her for her bisexuality.

Elle's phone beeped, reminding her to take her Zoloft, and bringing her back to the present. It was already 11:30 a.m. She definitely had slept in. Since the start of summer break, she had been taking full advantage of catching up on her rest after all those sleepless nights. The Seroquel had been a godsend and a curse. It knocked her out cold but made it nearly impossible to get up at a reasonable hour. She knew that she would need to stop taking the meds once school started again, but for now, she would take as much sleep as she could get. She yawned and picked up the phone knowing that Ami would be headed to lunch soon. Ami picked up on the first ring.

"Hey there," she greeted, "I'm heading into a lunch meeting soon but I have a few. How are you?"

"I'm alright. Just starting to get going, to be honest."

"The life of teachers! I definitely went into the wrong profession," Ami teased. But Elle knew Ami knew perfectly well how hard she worked, (and for a third of the pay Ami made), and how much she truly cared about all her students.

"Yeah, that Seroquel certainly helps me sleep, but damn, it's intense. I feel like I'm waking up from a coma most mornings. It's crazy, too, how the other night, I had a small glass of wine and took it like a half hour later. I ended up falling asleep on the couch. In the morning I woke up to wine, luckily just white wine, all over myself and the couch."

"Be careful with the wine, Elle! You aren't supposed to be drinking or at least not drinking like you normally do while taking that stuff, you know that right?"

"I know, I know, but it was just a small glass. You know that's my nightly ritual. I've really cut down, just like a half glass really, just for taste."

"Ok, but seriously be careful with that. I really hate that you're taking anything at all."

"I know. I know it's not sustainable. I will get off of it by the end of the summer. Anyways, just wanted to confirm that you and Clay are still on for dinner tonight?"

"Yep, we will be there. Can't wait. I also can't wait to get this lunch appointment over with to be honest," Ami said, lowering her voice. "It's with that older attorney, the one who could be my great grandfather. I know it will be at least a two hour ordeal, and I have so much work to do, but I can't be rude. He has been referring us so much business. And he is so sweet, I really do enjoy talking to him, just not when my mind is wandering with deadlines."

"Maybe I can call you in an hour and act like I'm a client having an emergency?" Elle suggested.

"That's actually not a bad idea. Yeah, actually do that. Call me in an hour. Oh here he is! Ok, gotta go. Talk soon."

Elle hung up without saying goodbye. Goodbye was not often in their vocabulary with one another as they would be talking sooner than later. Coffee time. She put her thin summer robe on, the one Ezra had bought her, or no wait, was it Ethan? And slumbered to the kitchen to put a pot on. Her heart sank. The coffee was gone. She had forgotten to pick some up yesterday. She opened the fridge to see if there was anything appealing for breakfast besides cold pizza. She eyed the lone pizza box, left open, exposing just one left over slice. That is so odd. She could have sworn that she had left two slices of her beloved Lou Malnati's, which had been becoming a staple for dinner and sadly even for breakfast on a few occasions since the accident. She could have sworn that she purposely left two slices to have today—one cheese and one pepperoni. But here lay just one pepperoni slice. And an open pizza box to top it off.

Oh my God! Could it be the Seroquel?

She had Googled that it could cause some people to sleepwalk before she gave in to taking it. Eating, even driving, while unconscious with no recollection of it the next day. She had mentioned this fear to Dr. Berkshire but he dismissed her concern stating that sleepwalking was very rare and often combined with other factors such as alcohol.

Of course she had her standard glass of red wine last night with her pizza. Her favorite wine, Prisoner, sat on her wine rack with the expected consumption level. My God. She must be the rare exception after all. There was no other explanation. She really had to stop this crap. Tonight she would go cold turkey.

Now back to the pressing matter at hand—her lack of coffee. Though she had cut back on her caffeine intake to help with her anxiety since the accident as well, she still had to have her strong black coffee in the morning as she had since college. Back in her messy room, she retrieved what looked to be clean leggings and a tank top to run out to the store. She swooped her damp hair up in a bun and put some gloss on her full lips; her standard summer presentation.

She grabbed her straw summer bag and keys from the bowl on the console by the door, acknowledging that she was lucky she had only eaten pizza last night and hadn't ended up behind the wheel. The image of her causing an accident was far worse than her as the victim. She shook her head, attempting to erase the images, took a deep breath and stepped into another humid and intensely hot Chicago summer day.

She drove to Whole Foods slightly under the speed limit. Sometimes she would even ride her bike there but she needed to get a few things since Ami and Clay were coming over for dinner tonight. Plus she rather forgo the heat if possible though the air conditioning in her Jeep was pretty weak even at full blast. What should she make tonight? She could get all creative but it had been a while since she had made Ami's favorite lemon butter chicken recipe with green beans, mango salad and angel food cake for dessert. Done.

Elle walked into the familiarity of her go-to grocery store, starting with the produce section. She grabbed four perfectly plump peaches she simply could not pass up. Maybe she would make a peach pie for dessert instead. She certainly had the time today. She could even make the crust from scratch just to say she did. As she searched for a few more of the best looking ones, she sent a couple of innocent peaches to the floor.

"Shit." A few others trailed after them. Suddenly, she felt a hand on her shoulder.

"It's-it's OK," a male's voice stammered, "I g-g-got the-the-them."

Elle turned around, grateful. She did not recognize this new grocer. "Thank you," she said smiling, grabbing her cart to remove herself from this situation.

"No wo-worries," the dark haired man replied. "Any t-t-t-time." His intense blue eyes seemed to intrusively penetrate through her.

She walked on feeling slightly unsettled, then realized she had forgotten the green beans, mango and salad in the produce section. She sighed and turned around to gather the remaining items glad that the man was no longer in the produce section. She couldn't pinpoint it but there was something about their encounter that had given her the creeps. She then moved on briskly, making her way up and down the aisles, crossing off her list of items in her head. Getting ready to check out she stopped, thinking she should also grab Ami some white wine. She went to the back of the store, perusing the wines for Ami's favorite Pinot Grigio. She was about to reach up to grab a bottle of

Cakebread when she heard his stuttering voice again, "le-le-let me help you."

She snapped her arm towards her body instinctively, as the man reached over her to grab the bottle for her with a long, lean arm. "Thank you," she said again, this time not as nicely. She was perfectly capable of reaching the bottle herself.

"My-my pleasure." He stepped even closer to her as he handed her the bottle. She grabbed it, gripping it tightly.

"Ca-ca-can I help you with anything else?" His mouth was so close that she felt a hint of saliva hit her cheek.

"No, I'm done shopping, thanks."

"Ok well if you need hel-hel-help to your car, don't hes-hes-hes-hes-hesitate to ask."

"That won't be necessary," she said more harshly than she would have liked, and added more softly, "but thank you."

He didn't respond but continued to look at her with those X-ray-like eyes, bulging and unblinking, a slim smile on his face, watching her as she made her way to the front of the store.

As she drove home, she told herself to simply dismiss the incident, reminding herself that she was in a "state of constant arousal and prone to interpreting things in a paranoid manner," per Dr. Berkshire. He was just a new employee and trying to be helpful. It wasn't his fault he had a stutter. Fortunately, she was able to park her red Jeep in the same close spot on the street as when she left. As she made two trips up her stairs to unload the groceries, she started to sweat profusely. God, she needed to get back into shape. Before she put the groceries away, she turned down the air and put her face near the coolest vent in her place, in the kitchen by the oven for a couple of minutes. The vents in her bedroom were not nearly as powerful but at least her two fans helped.

She had lived in her cozy two bedroom condo for just shy of three years. When she was looking to buy, it was nearly impossible to find a two bedroom within her budget but luckily this somewhat fixer upper had panned out. She had converted the second bedroom into her prized art studio. In her old apartment, her art had taken over her bedroom and she had felt her creativity stifled without a proper workspace. Plus, she loved the quiet location and old, looming trees that sheltered the complex and marked the turn of the seasons. She also loved the large bathtub that she could extend her long limbs fully out in and her bedroom's beautiful French doors that led out to a small patio garden, which she took advantage of often.

Her kitchen was also pretty spacious, providing ample counter top space to prepare full meals with ease. Not that she cooked every night though. She had to be in the mood to. After a long day overseeing rambunctious children during the school year, she was often too exhausted to even think about putting the ingredients together to make dinner and found herself content with a microwave meal.

Putting away her groceries, she felt a sense of fulfillment as her fridge and cupboards nearly reached full capacity. She left out the pie crust ingredients on the counter. She would get that out of the way first. After she had her coffee of course. She was starting to get a headache from the lack of caffeine. As the coffee percolated, she went on Pinterest to look up a pie crust recipe, selecting the simplest one she could find. Two cups of coffee later and having popped the crust in the oven, she was ready to finish her metal piece for Ami. The rest of the cooking preparations wouldn't take long.

She was excited to give her best friend the "Mr. & Mrs. Richardson" metal piece she had been working on the past few weeks here and there, which she envisioned adorning the couple's wedding dinner table. She was going to wait to give it to Ami closer to their wedding date this October, but she figured she would just give it to her tonight since all she had left were some finishing touches. She grabbed her goggles and got to work.

Ten minutes later the smell of burning pie crust hit her nose.

"Shit!" she said for the second time today, turning off the drill. She ran to the stove, immediately turning it off. It was burned to a crisp. How stupid of her. Of course she wouldn't hear the timer when her drill was going. Then her phone vibrated in her shorts pocket. It was a text from Ami. "Dude, you forgot to call me! Longest lunch ever!"

"So sorry!" Elle texted back, following up with, "I'll make it up to you tonight!"

She shut off the fire alarm, opened the kitchen window to air out the smoke and retrieved the ingredients to make another pie crust. This time she would stay right in front of the oven and enjoy the air conditioning. God, when did she get so spacey? It wasn't like she had a ton of responsibilities to juggle right now. "Be kind and patient with yourself," she could hear Dr. Berkshire say in his gentle voice. "And always find the positive." Well, at least she didn't burn the place down.

Chapter 2

Five hours later, the table looked like it was set for a romantic date. Candles and her best dinnerware adorned the old oak table, handmade by her grandpa, along with her finished Mr. & Mrs. Richardson metal piece. Dinner jazz and the aromas of chicken and peach pie filled the air. At seven o'clock on the dot, Ami and Clay rang her doorbell.

"Hi, hi, hi!" Ami greeted her, in a long black dress and flats, her hair pulled back in an elegant chignon. She leaned in and embraced Elle as if she hadn't seen her in ages.

"Hey there, Elle!" Clay said as Ami backed away, allowing him to swoop in and give her an unexpected peck on the cheek.

"So glad we could finally make this happen," Elle said. "Come in, come in." Ami led the way to the kitchen where she plopped down at the counter stool, making herself at home.

"Thanks for having us! Wow, does it smell great in here!" Clay said, sitting opposite her. Elle could not help but notice that he was wearing what appeared to be Birkenstock sandals, something Ami had formerly always made fun of.

"Yes, it certainly does," Ami agreed, handing Elle over two bottles of wine. "Sorry, I didn't have time to stop and get anything else but I figured you can never have enough wine!"

"True, true," Elle glanced at the bottles. "And Silver Oak? One of my favorites. Thank you so much."

"Of course. So how was your day?" Ami asked, reaching down to straighten the tiny bow on her ballet flat, Clay rubbing her back.

"Oh it was good, pretty uneventful. Just played housewife mostly, minus the husband part. I sure could get used to this summer routine," Elle laughed.

"I bet! I'm so jelly! I feel like work has been so crazy this summer. I know I was opposed to having the bachelorette party, but I honestly can't wait to let loose and just have some fun girl time. No offense to you honey," Ami said, turning to Clay.

"None taken," Clay smiled, a slightly gap-toothed smile. "I know you value your girl time like I value my guy time. I want you to let loose." He appeared to wipe away what must have been an eyelash or a fleck of mascara on her face. "You deserve it, sweetheart."

"Yay! I'm so glad that you realized a bachelorette is necessary!" Elle exclaimed, putting out the hummus, pita and veggie tray in front of them. "So what do you have in mind?"

Ami laughed, reaching for a carrot. "Honestly, I'd prefer just to stick around the city. But you fill in all the details. Oh, and let's shoot for the weekend of July 18th if that works? That would ideally be the best weekend for us if that works for you."

"That sounds perfect," Elle said. "Keep it nice and simple. "Pinot Grigio to start?" she asked as they both nodded. She poured three glasses.

"To an epic bachelorette party!" Elle cheered. All three let out hoots as they clinked their glasses together and then sipped.

"Well, I am excited for you girls! I know you'll have fun whatever you do," Clay gave Ami a quick kiss on the lips.

"Absolutely," Ami agreed.

"So how are all the wedding plans coming along?' Elle asked, sitting down on the third stool.

"Everything is pretty much set actually." Ami took another sip of her wine. "So relieved. I'm just waiting on my dress to get tailored and need to finalize the seating chart but really that's it."

"So you decided on a DJ?" Elle asked.

"Yep! We did!" I'm going with the DJ Angie actually used for her wedding. Of course that was years ago, but that after party always stood out to me with the music being so much fun."

"Oh great, so you guys are really set."

"Yes, we are. I cannot wait to marry this beautiful woman!" Clay grabbed at Ami again, all smiles.

"I cannot wait for you guys, either," Elle said. "So on that note, I will present my early wedding gift to you both, the soon to be Mr. and Mrs. Richardson!" Elle motioned for the couple to follow her into the dining area where the metal work prominently stood on the table.

"Oh wow, Elle!" Ami gushed. "This is so cool!"

"Soooo cool!" Clay echoed, brushing his fingers over the edges of the letters.

"I love it! Thank you!" Ami jumped up and down like a little girl. "I couldn't ask for a better friend!"

"I thought you guys could display it at the wedding on your dinner table," Elle suggested, trying to escape the overly exuberant display of affection Ami gave all too regularly but still made her feel like blushing.

"Of course we will!" Ami said. "And then on the mantel over the fireplace right, honey?" She glanced over to Clay.

'I couldn't think of a better spot," Clay said. "I always forget you have a kickass fireplace you never use."

Ami had moved into a quant but extremely old place just a few buildings down from where she had been living previously at the time she and Clay got engaged. She was having a string of issues with her landlord and Clay had suggested that she just move in with him but Ami vowed that she would not move in with a man until they were married.

Elle had laughed at her, calling her "old fashioned" but Ami had insisted that she was "doing things differently this time around." Ami was determined that she would not let her guard down and would keep her next husband expectantly waiting on her, not vice versa. "I will never bend over backwards for another man unless he is supporting my back" became her new motto.

Also never mind that Clay was not hugely financially successful. As a guitar player and bartender (they had in fact met when Clay served her at Gilt Bar), Ami was definitely the breadwinner. However, this did not appear to bother her in the least given what she had experienced with her ex. Ami found Clay's lack of concern over money "refreshing," and since she would never depend on a man financially it didn't matter anyways. Ami had even quit at her law firm at Ryan's insistence, however, after the marriage quickly dissolved, Ami had returned to the firm with open arms. Besides she worked too hard to become a lawyer and though she complained relentlessly about its demands, Elle knew she loved it.

"You are just the best, Elle," Ami said, squeezing her hand. "Dealing with me and yet another wedding!" she laughed, grabbing Clay's hand as well.

"Yes, thank you. Had I met Ami three years ago I could have saved us all some time and money!"

Ami smiled and kissed Clay on the cheek sweetly. "Damn, I wish you had! But hey, now I am even that much more appreciative knowing what I came from!"

Elle nodded her head. "So true. If you were still stuck with that a-hole I would be miserable, too. I mean he barely even let me see you, he was so possessive of you! I thank you for not being anything like him, Clay, and for letting me still have my best friend."

Clay laughed good heartedly. "Of course, I admire your close relationship and would never want to come between you both. I appreciate how happy you make my beautiful bride to be."

"Okay, okay, enough of the gushiness!" Ami said laughing, "We haven't even finished one glass of wine yet!"

Two glasses of wine later they sat down to eat.

"Wow, this is amazing, Elle!" Ami exclaimed. "You really have perfected my favorite dish!"

"Yes, this really is fantastic, and I am quite a food snob," Clay added.

"Thanks guys, glad you like it! Honestly I don't feel like I can take all the credit for this though; anything with a lot of butter should taste pretty good."

"True, but I have to say this might even be surpassing my mother's recipe this time," Ami said.

"How is your mom doing?" Elle asked, referring to her mom's recent knee surgery.

Ami swallowed before answering. "She is doing OK, best she can. Steve has been such a huge support of course. I hope to get out there to visit in the next few weeks. Take a long weekend. I need the break, too."

"I'm sure she cannot wait to see you."

"Yes, it has been too long again unfortunately. I hate that they moved down south, so far away, but I'm happy that they are happy in their little retirement community."

"It really is quite the spot from the pictures you've shown me. Hell, I'd live there now!" Clay said.

"I'm sure they would love to hear you play at their community events," Elle added.

"Absolutely. I'm all in," Clay said. "I love playing for the older folk."

"You know," Elle said, changing subjects, "I really don't know much about your family, Clay."

Clay carefully wiped his mouth with his napkin. "Ah, well my parents are deceased—have been for almost four years. Car accident. They both went together at least."

"I am so sorry," Elle said aghast. "I had no idea." Ami squeezed his hand across the table.

"Thanks, yeah it was quite a shock but I have come a long way in my acceptance. My mom was a wonderful person, an elementary school teacher for thirty years, and she made the best damn cookies. Man do I miss those!" He laughed easily and Elle and Ami smiled. "And my dad was a very logical engineer. We weren't very close though unfortunately."

"And I have an older sister, Chloe," he continued. "She is a total sweetheart but unfortunately has some pretty serious mental health issues—schizophrenia. She lives in an assisted living facility, even though she is pretty independent. They take good care of her and she enjoys living there, it's become like a family to her."

"Good for her. That must be so tough, though."

"Yes, it has been a rough road. But now that she is older, she is 41, she seems to have stabilized some. I just wish there was more I could do. I have offered several times for her to come live with me but she is so attached to The Bloomtree, the assisted living facility. And she works part time at this amazing little bakery, Sweeties, though I have to say my mother's chocolate chip cookies are still better. Chloe loves working there and has several friends at the Bloomtree. Even when I just call to say hello, she often gets angry or upset as if I am going to take her away from her life there. Part of the paranoia I guess. So I suppose I have stopped reaching out as much as I should."

Elle did not know what to say. For a moment she felt slightly shocked that her best friend would not have divulged this family dynamic to her. "Well I hope she can still make it to your big day!" she said brightly.

"We shall see," Clay said with a sigh. "I hope so, too, but I doubt it."

Ami squeezed Clay's shoulder. "I love you," she said simply.

"Love you too, honey," he said, looking directly at Ami. Elle noticed how intense his eyes were as they gazed into Ami's, how extraordinary, as the candle flames illuminated the golden flints in the green, like a tiger. He was not a traditionally handsome man, he lacked a strong bone structure but he was fit and strong and apparently had some pretty phenomenal eyes. Elle found herself staring and came to.

"So now that we are fully stuffed," she said, eyeing everyone's barren plates, "I hope you still can manage some room for peach pie!"

"Oh my gosh, yes!" Ami clapped her hands in delight "Tis the season! How can I turn down summer peach pie?"

"That sounds perfect," Clay added.

"Fantastic. Allow me to take your plates and I will bring you out your desert. May I also top off your wine?" Elle asked.

"Oh don't be ridiculous," Ami said. "Let us help you!"

"Don't you be ridiculous," Elle retorted. "Just sit here and relax for once. Remember, I've been on summer break!"

"Well then, I guess I will have one more glass, just a small one though."

"And for you?" Elle looked towards Clay. "Oh no thank you, but maybe some coffee if it's not too much trouble?"

"No trouble at all. I was just going to offer. Decaf OK?"

"Either works, caffeine doesn't affect me," Clay said as he massaged the back of Ami's neck, her eyes closed.

That was the thing Elle missed the most about being in a relationship—the physical touch. Not even sex, but just the simple feeling of being touched by another human being; the touch that would linger longer than the brief hug of a hello or goodbye, the comfort of feeling someone next to her in bed and knowing that they would be there when she woke up. Or at least some of the time.

"I really should cut back on caffeine," Elle sighed as she stacked their plates. "I think it heightens my anxiety more than I realize—well, since the accident really." Immediately Elle wished she hadn't referenced "the accident." But Clay appeared to be the perfect amount of concerned yet nonjudgmental as he asked if she had sought professional help.

"Yes," Elle said, letting her guard down, remembering that he had a sister who suffered from schizophrenia after all. "I actually started seeing a psychiatrist I really like at the beginning of the summer."

"Oh good for you. Notice any improvement yet?" he asked.

"I think so," Elle said more emphatically than she really felt. "But I also have been super lucky to have the summer off to work through it all. It's definitely going to be an adjustment headed back to school again in a few weeks. Especially getting up early again." Just the thought of getting up at 6 a.m. made her feel a little panicky.

"Oh you will be just fine," Ami said as Elle placed the dirty dishes in the sink. "Just try to start getting up like twenty minutes earlier each week. And maybe you should consider cutting back on the Seroquel?" she suggested somewhat nonchalantly.

"Oh Seroquel? Yeah no wonder you have a hard time waking up. I tried that stuff one time and man, I felt like I was in a coma for a week," Clay said.

"Yeah, I know you're right. I should just stop taking it before I really do get dependent on it." Elle replied, hoping it could be that easy as she soaked the dishes. "Anyways," she said, getting the coffee going, "as much as I have enjoyed my time off, I am certainly getting antsy to get back into a schedule and have a focus."

"For sure," Clay agreed. "A schedule is key. I find the more hours I work the more productive I am, not only in my music, but just all parts of life. I guess it just makes you realize you only have so much time so you better make good use of it." Ami nodded in agreement as Elle placed their pie slices in front of them. "And the crazy hours this one puts in at her job—well I just don't know how she does it," Clay added.

Ami smiled. "Well, I knew what I was getting into when I signed up for it. I honestly do think I thrive on being busy. When I wasn't working for that brief period of time, I really did feel lost. My work is just such a big part of my identity." She bit into the pie.

Elle always admired Ami's work ethic and the fact that she rarely complained about her job. If anything, she was more apt to complain about her students who refused to try or asked for constant reassurance that their art was "good." Nothing unnerved her more.

Clay bit into his pie as Elle went to retrieve the coffee. "One of the many reasons I love you," he said, poking at Ami's perfect upturned nose, with a small dusting of freckles emanating to her cheeks, like a star spattered country night sky.

Though Elle had the same creamy skin as Ami, she had far less freckles. When they were teens, Ami had become self-conscious about them. She would half joke that she wished she could "give" Elle some of her freckles. And Elle would joke back, "only if I can have a quarter of your ass and boobs!" Ami had been fully formed by thirteen and had only become more refined, while Elle had remained pretty one dimensional and wispy, relying on push up bras and shape enhancing jeans to help her look less like a gawky teen until her mid-twenties.

Clay and Ami whispered and laughed in their intimate way as Elle poured the steaming coffee into some of the only mugs she owned without chips on them. It really was nice to see her best friend this happy. She had never seen her this carefree with another man. In fact, she had never really seen Ami this affectionate either, having treated her ex's more like co-workers whom she was forced to get along with.

"So any weekend plans?" Elle asked as she set the coffee in front of Clay who thanked her.

"Clay is actually headed up north to play at a couple events," Ami responded, "and well, I really have no plans besides finishing up some research I have on this one case I can't wait to be done with. And going to brunch on Sunday with Henry. Actually, would you like to join us? My brother would love to see you!"

"Ah, I don't know," Elle said, searching for an excuse not to join. She sat down again. "Oh that's right, I'm actually grabbing brunch with Ben."

"Oh come on, you are always grabbing brunch with Ben. Come join us! Ben can come, too!" Ami looked at her with her big, pleading eyes that were so hard to say no to.

"Alright, alright," she relented.

It had been several years since she saw Henry. Though it had been a lifetime ago, it still felt like yesterday when Elle found herself trapped underneath his hormone and alcohol enraged body, at Cynde Hall's Halloween party. Ami had gone off with her boyfriend, Rett, at the time, and Elle had been flirting fiercely with Sadie Moore, her sophomore crush who was also openly gay. She was becoming more unrestrained with each sip of vodka and had decided to stay.

Henry had never shown anything more than a sisterly interest in Elle. Once Sadie left, she should have left, too. But instead she found herself locked in Cynde Hall's guest room, Henry ripping off her fishnet stockings and grabbing at her crotch and breasts with unexpected fury. Her fairy wings dug into her back as he grinded his body into her.

She was so drunk by then that she felt like dead weight, unable to move. She cried out, "stop" over and over but Henry ignored her pleas as he unzipped his pants. "You don't get this with a girl," he had growled. She lay there detached from her body until he gave a final grunt and collapsed on her. And then she threw up. All over him, herself and the daisy flowered bedspread, snapping him out of his sexual conquest.

"Hey, I'm so sorry, I didn't mean to do that," he had said, grabbing her shoulder. As he tried to wipe up her puke on the bedspread with his shirt, she managed to unlock the door and ran, not saying goodbye to anyone. She walked home covered in her own vomit, with no shoes, in a trance. She showered in scalding hot water, scrubbing all his skin cells from her body, letting the tears finally release. And that was it. She had never mentioned it to Ami or anyone.

She couldn't put Ami in the position of having to choose her side over her brother's or to tarnish her relationship with either of them. Ami had always idolized her older brother and there was the chance that she would not have even believed Elle anyways. Fortunately she was able to avoid seeing him all but once between periods in the hallway amongst a mass of other students, before he went off to college the following year.

Now, years later, it was still an unspoken secret between them. He was now married with two little twin girls and by all accounts he was an all-star dad and husband. But still she could not forgive or forget, even if it was an adolescent lack of judgement. She could still feel his weight crushing her, suffocating her....

"Perfect, I made a reservation at Merci at 10 a.m., I will just change it to four," Ami said.

"Awesome, thanks." Elle managed to keep her tone upbeat.

Ami gave her a satisfied smile and bit into her last piece of pie. "Wow, Elle, you have really outdone yourself."

"Yes, this is absolutely delicious," Clay agreed.

"Thank you. I worked pretty hard on it," she admitted. "I accidentally burned the crust on the first go around." she shook her head.

"Like I have ever baked anything from scratch in my entire life!" Ami said, placing her fork on the plate.

"And that is where I come to the rescue," Clay said. "Nobody can sustain themselves with frozen meals and salads alone."

"I know, I know," Ami agreed. "Yet another reason I am so thankful to be marrying a man who not only can cook, but who enjoys it so I don't have to feel guilty."

"So what do you enjoy more, cooking or playing music?" Elle asked, trying to make the most out of this time to get to know Ami's soon to be husband better. Sure, they had all hung out before at Ami's and at parties, but never just the three of them.

"Wow," that is a really tough question. I honestly don't know if I could choose. To give up either would be like having to lose a limb. Actually, I'd give a limb before I gave up music or cooking, though I suppose if it were my arm that would be pretty rough. So to clarify I would say that I'd rather give up my leg before I give up cooking or music. They are both as much a part of me as anything else. In fact, I don't feel like myself if I haven't dabbled in some cooking or music for more than a couple days. What about you, do you feel like that with art?" He asked with genuine curiosity.

"I don't think I would lose a limb to give up art, but yes, I do love it and how I can just get lost in it for hours on end. And I do feel like most of my days are better days when I have done some form of art. Teaching also gives me the opportunity to share that passion," Elle answered thoughtfully.

"You work with underprivileged kids, right?" Clay asked.

"Yes, and that makes it that much more taxing but also rewarding."

"Good for you," Clay said emphatically.

"Aw, my Saint Elle, with the biggest heart of gold," Ami said in a sing-song voice.

Elle rolled her eyes. She had not intended to come off as some selfless martyr when in fact she could be plenty selfish. Well, picky she supposed was more accurate. Picky with whom she spent her time with and how. Which wasn't necessarily a bad thing. Life was too short to spend it with shitty people.

"You know, we should have done this a long time ago," she stated. "I feel bad that I hadn't offered to have you both over sooner."

"Don't be ridiculous!" Clay said. "This has been perfect. I really appreciate you going out of your way for us and making this so special."

"Absolutely! It's not your fault that we fell in love so fast!" Ami batted her long eyelashes at Clay coquettishly, pecked his cheek and then used her thumb to smear whatever she had implanted on his skin. He had really good skin, Elle also noted. A baby face in fact. One she was sure he certainly did not work for or worry about. And of course here she was with twenty different anti-aging serums and lotions trying to stave off her own creeping towards middle age decline. She hadn't taken the plunge into Botox yet, as the thought of putting a toxin in her body freaked her out. But she had promised Ami that she would go with her before the wedding and break both of their Botox virginities. It was hard to deny Ami's permanent frown line that were becoming more pronounced as she continued to prove herself as one of the top lawyers at her firm.

"And I could not be more appreciative of all the time and effort you have put into helping with the wedding," Ami continued. "Honestly, it has been a life saver. Three months out now, actually to the date!"

"You're right, it is the 22nd already," Clay said. "June has been flying by."

"It has," Elle agreed.

"When does school start back up?" Ami asked.

"Aug. 25th this year."

"Wow, so early!" Clay remarked.

"Yep, it seems the summers are getting shorter every year," Elle said. "But hell, I'm not complaining," she looked over to see Ami yawning, her entire face contorting, not bothering to cover her mouth.

"Man this week and this wine caught up to me," Ami said leaning back in her chair stretching.

"I'm in a bit of a food and wine coma myself." Clay took his last sip of coffee and before Elle could offer him more he asked Ami, "you OK with me calling the Lyft after we help clean up a bit?"

"Absolutely not!" Elle said "You guys go ahead and call the Lyft now. I got this."

"Thanks, Elle," Ami said. "I owe ya. I got your brunch on Sunday."

Elle did not protest. At least she would get a free meal for spending an hour with her rapist. She got a sudden chill and then reminded herself that it had been years ago. They were both adults now. Instead she said, "Awesome, looking forward to it," as cheerily as she could manage.

Clay announced that the Lyft would be arriving in four minutes. Hugs and goodbyes were exchanged. Clay grabbed the metal piece and they both thanked Elle again for her thoughtful gift and delicious dinner.

"Goodnight, love you girl!" Ami said as she gave Elle one last hug.

"Love you, too!" Elle echoed before she closed the door behind them. She watched through her window, which she noted could use some serious Windex, as they got into the Lyft, Clay opening the door for Ami and taking the time to ensure that she was all the way inside before shutting it. She could not recall the last time a man had done this for her. Then he moved behind the vehicle to the other side to let himself in, greeting the driver cheerily.

It was refreshing to see a man with chivalry still. Who didn't hesitate to help out, even clean. She sighed, not in the mood to clean up. But she forced herself to rinse the dishes thoroughly before loading them in the dishwasher. Her dishwasher had seen better days and most of the time she didn't bother to use it when it was just her few dishes. She wiped down the counter and the table and thought about sweeping the kitchen floor but decided she would do it tomorrow. It had been a long day for having slept in so late. Perhaps she would reward herself for a successful night of hosting with just one more glass of wine. After all, there was only about one glass left of the Pinot Grigio so she might as well finish it off.

She poured herself what turned out to be a pretty healthy glass and plopped down on her couch. She really needed to get rid of it once and for all. It was starting to feel as lumpy as Dr. Berkshire's chair and there were several noticeable scratches from her old cat, Selma, who sadly passed away a couple years ago. Still, it was quite comfortable. She turned the TV on to a rerun of Dateline and watched in removed fascination as a wife detailed waking up to her husband slaughtered beside her.

She woke up to commercials blaring, selling products you never knew you could possibly need. She hadn't made it to the end of Dateline to see if the wife was convicted of her husband's murder, nor had she finished her glass of wine, which sat on the coffee table. She turned off the TV and as she walked to her bedroom, she stripped off her clothes before getting in bed. But there she lay for an hour and checking the clock again, another 45 minutes. Frustrated, she gave in and took half a Seroquel, biting the bitter pill in half with her teeth. Soon she was back in a heavy sleep.

The leaves are especially loud, giving a satisfying crunch with each step. He needs to avoid this, so he trails behind them at a safe distance. He feels invisible most of the time, people only identifying him as the nameless "brother." He is protected from bullying of others as Pierce's brother yet Pierce relentlessly bullies him and has since they were young. He mostly did it in secret but sometimes he did it in front of others. But everyone respects and admires Pierce so damn much that everyone just looks the other way, even his parents. And for what? Because he can catch a football? Because his muscles respond better to protein and strength training?

He watches as Pierce bends down to kiss her on the forehead and then her mouth. She leans back and laughs in that sweet teasing laugh she has. He leans in to kiss her again but she blows a tiny bubble with her gum preventing him from reaching her lips. The bubble grows bigger and then she snaps it back in her mouth laughing uproariously. She then pulls him into her, grabbing his head and working her fingers through his signature tousled hair, kissing him slowly.

He says something inaudible and she says something back, pulling him by the hand down the sidewalk. They are going to her house most certainly. Her parents will still be at work and she is the only child so nobody will be at home at this hour. His brother looks like he is protesting going inside, pointing to his watch. Of course he has football practice starting soon. But she pulls his arm and he relents. How could he even think to say no to her? He would do anything to have an opportunity to be alone with her in her bedroom that still looks like that of a little girl.

She fumbles momentarily with her key as if she is nervous, and then they retreat into the house, an old Victorian, slamming the door. He waits a couple minutes and then opens it softly. He walks down the creaky hallway towards her bedroom on extra light feet. He pauses every few steps to access the numerous photos of her growing up over the years, growing into the beautiful young lady she is, until he is at the end of the hallway.

They hadn't even bothered to close the door. Her canopy bed is fit for a princess. All lacy and pink. His brother is already on top of her, their jeans at their knees. Her gorgeous hair fans out over the bed, He tells himself he will only allow himself five seconds to watch. He counts to five slowly. They kiss each other fiercely and grab at each other as if it was their first time hooking up. His heart races. He feels lightheaded with hunger. He is starving. And willing to kill in order to survive.

Chapter 3

She woke up with a start, feeling as if she were falling. Her heart is pounding. She recalled the last part of her nightmare. She had been falling in and out of consciousness after the accident, as she and Ami were rushed to the hospital, blood and car remnants blaring in her mind. She and Ami had been transported together in the same ambulance.

She remembered Ami's frail touch on her hand and how her weakness paralyzed her ability to hold her hand back.

Could you really call it a nightmare when it was actually an experience she endured? She took long deep breaths and sat up in bed, studying her student's artwork on her walls to distract herself. The picture Rosie drew of her new puppy, the accurate largeness of his paws and head in relation to his body as a developing puppy has, was one of Elle's favorites.

Elle had remembered she had commented to Rosie about the accuracy of her proportions, that most students her age would not notice. She had taken several classes to finish the drawing, and when she had presented it to Elle for hers to keep, Elle had initially declined, knowing the effort she had put into it, but Rosie had insisted.

Her breath finally slowed as she stared at the drawing. She noted the sensation of the sun bathing her face and the chirping chorus of birds outside her window. It was 11:26 a.m. Shit. So late once again. She had the sense she had forgotten something but her brain was too foggy to even think about anything but coffee.

She got up on wobbly legs and walked to the kitchen, not bothering to pee first, and started the coffee maker after thankfully realizing she had already prepped it last night. As it was brewing, she went back to her bedroom bathroom to pee, quickly brushed her teeth and splashed cold water on her face to try to wake up. A heavy line extended from her right temple down her cheek from sleeping so hard on her pillowcase.

Still groggy, she returned to the kitchen and poured herself a cup of coffee even though it wasn't done brewing yet. As the hot liquid touched her tongue she instantly remembered what she had sensed she had forgotten. She had told her friend, Ben, she would spin with him at noon. Shit. She had already cancelled on him at the last minute last week because she felt too sluggish from her (mostly) Seroquel induced hangover. Now here she was again in the same predicament. She chugged the hot liquid aggressively, nearly burning her throat. She could still make it. She needed to be an adult and keep her commitments. She also needed a good sweat. She had vowed that she would not become a slug over the summer especially when she had all the time to devote to exercise.

She hadn't done laundry in almost two weeks and had to dig in her hamper to find a pair of leggings. She pulled them over her slim legs and sprayed them a few times with Febreze to cover up their dank odor. Whatever, she would be sweating soon enough. She grabbed a scrunchy, which Ami made fun of her for wearing, and pulled back her wild mane, not bothering to brush through it. She needed to leave now if she was going to make it on time.

Twenty minutes later her ass sat on the hard bike seat next to Ben who was already in full blown attack mode, having started to train for his next triathlon in November. He greeted her with excitement, his huge smile revealing his blazing white teeth. He was fanatic about whitening his teeth and tanning his skin, the contrast making his teeth look that much more shocking.

And since he started dating Cameron a little over two years ago, he had become fanatic about fitness as well, morphing from the slightly overweight regular looking guy she had originally met at one of her favorite coffee places, Pikes Peak, to one that often received double takes from males and females alike. Elle was happy for him and the positive influence Cameron had on him. But she couldn't help but feel that he was taking his fitness and appearance to a slightly extreme level. It certainly did enhance his image as "your top notch realtor for all of Chicagoland," though. His face was blown up on several signs on the freeway, photoshopped to perfection.

From the day he had graciously traded table spots with her so that she could plug her laptop into the outlet, he had been a consistent supportive friend, the gay friend she had always wanted.

And not that he intended to be judgmental, but she could tell when he was secretly disappointed in Elle's entree choice when they went to lunch or her third glass of wine at dinner. Hence, he was also a good friend to keep her in check. Had she canceled on spin again today, she could only imagine the passive aggressive treatment she would receive.

After adjusting her seat, Elle turned her attention to the instructor, Jane, a sixtyish year old woman with the energy of a 20 something year old, and an ass to go with it. Jane bellowed at the class to "get your mind in the ride!" and "pump up the energy!" inciting hoots and hollers from the class. Elle focused on getting a good pace going as Whitney Houston attempted to take them to "Higher Love." She was already sweating profusely and struggling to breath by the end of the song. She glanced over at Ben who appeared to remain in the same state of comfort.

God damn it. She needed to get her ass back in shape. She forced herself to "get her mind in the ride" because her body certainly wasn't. She challenged herself to keep pace and didn't cheat herself when Jane barked to turn up the resistance. Her hangover quickly dissipated or at least she was in so much pain that she couldn't feel it.

Towards the 40-minute mark, she felt almost exhilarated, and actually joined the class's screams as they went into their final climb before the cooldown. She gave the bike everything she had, displacing all her frustration and disappointment over her mental and physical decline since the accident into the pedals. Her legs were on fire and her nostrils nearly collapsed, she was breathing so hard. When she felt like she could not go on one more second Jane thankfully cheered, "And you are done! Congratulations, you powerful and amazing people! I'm so proud of each and every one of you!"

Ben reached out his hand and Elle gave him a high five. "You did it girl! Aren't you glad you came?!"

"Yes," Elle said, catching her breath. "I really needed that."

After the brief stretch she was able to speak. "Wanna grab a smoothie?" she asked Ben as he delicately patted his forehead with his clean towel. Hers was drenched. She had not had anything to eat yet and now that the adrenaline rush was gone, she was starving.

"Oh I wish I could! I would love to catch up but Cameron and I are actually headed to Wisconsin for the weekend. And we already had a bit of a late start, but I told him, I am not missing my spin with Elle!" he laughed.

"Wisconsin?" Elle asked.

"Yep, I know, right?! Ben's sisters rented a cabin on a lake. We are just staying 'till Monday night, that's about all the camping I can handle!" He laughed.

"Well it's really not camping if you're staying in a cabin...."

"What do you take me for? A survivor in the wilderness with only the shirt on my back kind of guy? No, no, no. A cabin is as far as I will go."

"That's awesome. I'm sure you will all have a lot of fun regardless." Elle felt a tinge of jealousy. She would love to get out of her condo and go anywhere.

"Well Cameron's sisters are a hoot, so it will definitely be entertaining. What do you have going on this weekend?"

"Oh not much. Just brunch tomorrow with Ami and um, her brother. I actually had Ami and her fiancé over for dinner last night finally. We had kind of a late night, so just probably going to take it easy today."

"Oh, nice. Did you give them their gift you had been working on?" Ben asked as he took off his spin shoes. He placed them in a Ziploc bag before putting them in his Hermes backpack, which Elle was pretty certain cost as much as a dozen purses of her own.

"Yeah, I finished it and gave it to them. They seemed to like it."

"Of course they did! Heck when Cameron and I get married, I will commission you to make us one, too."

"Do you think you will propose soon?" Elle asked.

"Hell no!" Ben laughed. "I am not a camping guy nor am I the proposing type of guy. You should know that! I asked Cameron out first, so if he wants to marry me, he best be getting down on his knee."

Elle couldn't help but snort. "That doesn't seem entirely fair that it should all fall on him."

"Would you say that if I were a woman dating a man?" Ben asked.

"Well no, but…"

"Exactly, honey," Ben said resolutely, cutting her off. "Now have a wonderful weekend and wish me luck! Hopefully I will return in one piece." He kissed her on the cheek.

"You will be just fine," Elle said, as he turned away amongst the throng of smelly, sweaty people leaving and fresh riders entering. She may have said this more to herself than to him.

Feeling proud of herself for having gone to spin, yet somewhat deflated that she had another solo day ahead of her, she got into her Jeep thinking of what she would do for food. She decided she would keep her healthy streak going and treat herself to the salad bar at Whole Foods. So back to Whole Foods she went this time determined not to pair her salad with yet another bottle of wine.

She entered the freezing store, her sweat stained clothes gripping her body—whatever, she had nobody to impress. She took her time picking out her salad ingredients, carefully selecting the freshest looking pieces of avocado, tomato and cucumber to go with a sizable chicken breast over a hefty bed of spring lettuce. As she headed to the checkout line she remembered that she had used the last bit of dish detergent last night. She hastily retreated back to the kitchen aisle and grabbed whatever dish detergent was on sale.

She also grabbed some extremely overpriced lavender scented soap that caught her eye as she walked back. Screw it. She deserved a good bar of soap after that ride. The young woman who checked her out, girl really, with her braided pigtails making her look like she could pass for being in high school, greeted her with exuberance, and asked her if she found everything OK.

"Yes," Elle responded. "I know where everything in this store is all too well."

The girl laughed at her joke as she placed the detergent in a paper bag and the soap in a smaller paper bag. She quickly paid, feeling shaky, and wanting to get home ASAP to eat her salad. The girl wished her a nice weekend and Elle smiled as she grabbed her bag and exited the store.

An impossibly put together mother with two twin toddlers in a double stroller entered. The children were screaming and fighting but the woman appeared unphased by it as she spoke into her cell in her other hand. Her hair and makeup looked like they had been professionally done for God's sakes. Elle didn't look like that even on her best days without kids.

For a second she had forgotten where she parked but then she spotted her Jeep, looking dirty and haggard next to all the pristine and expensive vehicles. She would definitely get it washed at some point this weekend.

As she started the engine, the oil change reminder flashed relentlessly, which she had been putting off all summer. She would also make that her first priority this weekend. One of the benefits she missed most about her last boyfriend, Jamie, was how attentive he had been towards her car. Yet, when it came to her, that was a different story.

She sighed as she put the car in reverse, carefully checking her surroundings and back up camera, and nearly screamed as someone rapped on her window.

Chapter 4

"Jesus Christ!" she yelled.

Did she almost hit someone? It took her a few seconds to process that it was the stuttering man who had attempted to help her yesterday. She rolled down her window, completely flustered, as he held out a small paper bag.

"So, so sorry to scare you, M'am, but but but you for-for-forgot your baaag," he stammered as she reached out her hand to retrieve the bag, speechless.

"Thank you," she finally managed, tossing the bag onto the passenger seat.

"It's it's no prob problem." A slight smile formed on his acne trodden face. "I hope you you don't miiind, but I also pppput some free ca-car-wash tic tickets in the the bag. I woooork at a ca-ca-ca-car wash, too."

"Thank you, that was very thoughtful," Elle said, wanting to just get the hell out of the parking lot. "Well, have a good one, see you around," she hurriedly said.

"Buh-buh bye now," he said, holding up his hand in a wave.

She rolled up her window and backed up more quickly than she normally would. She put on her signal to turn left out of the parking lot. Out of her rearview mirror she saw him still standing there, waving mechanically, looking despondent as if he were a child being left by a parent on his first day of kindergarten. Oh my God. What the hell? She flipped her signal to turn right instead. Looks like she would be taking a detour home instead.

She shuddered in her damp clothing. She knew she was overreacting but she couldn't help feeling freaked out by him. It made her feel bad that she was, the poor guy had such a terrible lisp and was only trying to be helpful to her. But she couldn't dismiss her instinct.

Ten minutes later she was relieved to be in the comfort and safety of her home. She placed her salad in the fridge, having somewhat lost her appetite and wanting to shower immediately. She retrieved her new lavender soap which had given her more stress than it was worth.

She languished in the stream of hot water longer than normal. She deserved the water splurge and wasting water this one time wouldn't make a difference. Finally, she forced herself to get out. She rubbed some lotion onto her pale skin, she had given up ever trying to be tan, and put on the last of her clean sweat pants and a U2 T-shirt.

She had not wanted to spend the $40 on the T-shirt, but Ami had surprised her and bought them matching shirts at the end of the concert. It was probably six years ago and she had not been to a concert as fun or memorable since. She was ready to lounge, eat her salad and watch The Bachelor, her secret addiction. Ami didn't even know about her fixation with it.

After finishing every last bite of her salad, she felt rejuvenated. She should incorporate more spin classes and salads in her life. She picked up her phone as a text came through from Ami.

Thanks so much for last night! Clay and I had so much fun! See you for brunch tomorrow! Xoxox.

Absolutely, long overdue. See you both then!

She was not as mushy as Ami and knew Ami understood it was just how she was. But yet she enjoyed watching The Bachelor. Perhaps she was more mushy than she cared to admit. She watched with a pathetic tinge of jealousy as the handsome bachelor kissed an impossibly thin and way too young looking blonde. Britt, 22, vet tech, her caption read. 22? What the hell was she doing on this show at 22? She was taking the spot of an older woman who actually deserved to be on the show.

She averted her eyes and scrolled through her Instagram feed, proliferated by pictures of meals about to be consumed, plump babies and smiling couples. In the midst of all the expected, she saw her metal work, now displayed on top of Ami's fireplace mantel. #Can't wait to marry him! #Lucky to have my best friend by my side.

Elle suddenly realized that Ami was referring to Clay as her best friend. Her heart sank. It wasn't as if Ami had not been married before and it wasn't as if Elle had never been in a relationship. But something felt different now.

She quickly hearted the picture and put her phone down returning to some screaming women in the midst of having a pillow fight. She remembered that she needed to get going on Ami's bachelorette party planning, too. Ami would be more than content with one fun night in the city, crashing at a slick Airbnb and a spa day to follow.

Her first bachelorette party in Miami had set Elle back financially for three months but she never complained once. She picked up her phone again and started scrolling Airbnb for something reasonably priced and spacious enough to accommodate a larger group of women.

She grabbed a random pen and magazine on the coffee table and searched her memory for all the names of the women who had attended Ami's bachelorette party two and a half year ago. Kenzie, Samantha, Brittany, Paige, Kate, Vanessa… and gorgeous Breck with her slender body and big hair. She also added Candance, whom Elle knew Ami had become close with since joining Ami's law firm a couple years ago. She pondered if she was missing anyone.

What about Chloe, Clay's sister? It would be a nice gesture though it seemed doubtful she would come, based on what Clay had described. She wouldn't tell Ami because most likely she wouldn't come, but if she did, it would be a nice surprise. She would make it nonintrusive and just send a letter. Where did Clay say she was living? Bloom something. The Bloomtree! Yes, that was it.

She googled The Bloomtree in Seattle and was instantly brought to their website inundated with happy looking patients engaged in some sort of arts and crafts as friendly looking staff supervised. She scrolled through more photos. It really did look like a nice facility. As she began to read about their "holistic mind and body approach," a notification came in that she had a message on Messenger. It had been so long since someone had reached out to her via Messenger. She opened the message, curious.

Hey Elle! It's Asa. Been a few years, lol. How have you been? I just moved back to Illinois and am living downtown. I thought I'd reach out and say hi. Maybe we could get together for lunch or something sometime if you're interested? It would be great to catch up with you!

Elle's heart skipped a beat. Asa? Asa Follet, from high school? The nerdy loner? She studied his tiny profile picture—wow, was that him? He had certainly aged well. In fact he was far more attractive than he was in high school. She never had given Asa a second thought in high school, acne laden and thinner than she was. She took some time forming her response, erasing and restarting.

Hey Asa! Wow, what a surprise to hear from you! And so awesome you are in Chicago now! I would definitely be open to grabbing lunch. I'm pretty open this week right now so just tell me what you have in mind.

He responded right away.

Fantastic! How does next Saturday sound? You pick the place. I can drive wherever.

That works! I will think of a spot and get back to you!

She noticed she was smiling as she sent her last response. She hadn't felt this excited in some time. It had been almost a year since she and Stella had broken up. Stella was stunning and fun to be around but she had been jealous of Elle's relationship with Ami and that was simply not going to work.

And she had only been on one other date since, a date that she was pretty much forced to go on at the request of one of her fellow teachers. Mark ended up being as boring as his Land's End outfit. He also ate tremendously slowly, cutting his steak into miniscule pieces and even ordering dessert, prolonging his cheesy anecdotes and series of endless questions even more. It had been slightly tortuous.

She texted Ami still in shock.

Guess who reached out to me?

Normally, even if Ami was working, she would still respond to Elle within an hour or so but her phone remained silent. She proceeded to send a group text to confirm July 18th for Ami's bachelorette. All confirmed except for Kim and Kenzie who she had seen on Instagram just had another baby a couple days ago.

Not to be a party pooper but right now all I'm doing is changing poopy diapers if my boob is not being clammored on!

Elle laughed out loud and sent her congratulations. After some research, she also found a sizable but not too expensive Airbnb which she booked on her credit card before it sold out. She cringed as she did so. Hopefully the girls would Venmo her sooner than later since her credit card was nearing its limit. Before she forgot, she dug through her messy desk in search of stationery. Between the thank you notes were a few blank stationary with butterflies and pineapples. She went with the pineapples. She would keep it as brief and simple as possible.

Dear Chloe,

I am your soon-to-be sister-in-law's best friend, Elle. I wanted to invite you to her bachelorette party the weekend of July 18th in Chicago. I know that you are quite a ways away and there is no pressure in coming. However, I wanted to extend the invitation as I know Ami (and I) would love to meet you. If you are interested in coming, please don't hesitate to reach out to me and I will provide you with all the details. I can be reached at 847.302.7041 or at elleemerson@gmail.com.

Best,
Elle Emerson

She read it over; it sounded non-threatening enough. She slid it in the envelope, sealed it with tape in case her paranoia also included germ phobia, and carefully wrote the address of The Bloomtree in the middle-ish along with her return address in the corner. She scrounged for a stamp and then stepped outside into the blistering sun without sunglasses, placing it in the outgoing mailbox.

Feeling a productive streak going, she kept herself busy the rest of the day. She desperately needed to do some laundry, her least favorite chore of all. She made some healthier chocolate chip cookies with a recipe she found on Pinterest as she put in a load. They turned out pretty good for being low sugar. She went out and finally got her oil change and car wash over with. She rewarded herself with a pedicure, choosing a bright blue nail polish which was not like her at all but had stood out to her. Driving home, she gave in to some fast food for dinner. She thoroughly enjoyed her cheeseburger, fries and chocolate shake. She was saving some calories tonight without alcohol at least.

At 11 p.m., she was ready for bed. She set her alarm for 8:30 a.m. to give herself plenty of time to get ready for brunch at 10 a.m. She read the news for a bit and shut off her light at 11:30 p.m. She lay there for 45 minutes, feeling tired yet wired. Reluctantly she reached for the Seroquel in her nightstand but quickly shut the drawer. She would allow herself to have just one glass of wine instead. She ambled into the kitchen and poured herself a generous glass.

30 minutes later she was back in bed, confident that she would be able to sleep now. But she was no better off an hour later. Extremely frustrated, she grabbed for the Seroquel again and swallowed half a pill feeling somewhat like a failure. But 15 minutes later she was finally out.

The snow is a thick fluffy blanket. His tires leave a pronounced trail behind him and the wind bites at his face and the tips of his ears. He forgot his hat but he is already this far. He nearly gets ran over by a car as he crosses the street to the movie theater. He has never been to a movie with a date other than his mother. Pathetic. He sees Pierce's blue Mustang parked in the spot nearest to the theater's door. He even has the best luck with parking. Does he ever have one small difficulty in life?

They got the older Mustang to share for their 16th birthday but did he ever really get a chance to drive it? Of course not. Hence here he is biking in a near blizzard. He locks his bike a safe distance away and walks up to the box office, where he asks to purchase a ticket for just one student. The pocked marked girl still gives him a look of pity, ("look in the damn mirror!" he wants to shout at her), and gives him the discounted student rate of $5. He has enough money left over to buy a medium Coke and some M&M's. He gets there just as the previews are ending and takes a seat in the last row tucked in the corner.

He immediately spots her red hair and his brother's spiked hair in the third row. He watches her as she feeds Pierce popcorn kernels. He can see that Pierce finds this amusing but then he becomes serious as the movie begins. She snuggles into his shoulder and hides her face when the scenes become too violent. He laughs quietly and slowly sucks on his M&M's, dissolving in his mouth until they no longer exist, one by one, until they are all gone.

Chapter 5

Her alarm blazes in the distance. She slowly wakes up, her neck pinched. She is on the couch. A half glass of wine sits on the coffee table. She has no recollection of walking to the couch and falling asleep there. She gets up, dazed, and stumbles to turn off her alarm in her bedroom. 9 a.m. Brunch at 10 a.m. with Ami and her brother.

The thought of eating in front of him makes her vaguely sick to her stomach and she thinks about cancelling. But then she reminds herself that Henry is a different person now, and she will be in a safe public place with Ami right by her side. She had seen him briefly at Ami's wedding a few years ago and had survived.

She steps into the shower, nearly falling on the lavender soap bar that has somehow fallen from the soap dish. Goddamn soap. She quickly rinses off and puts on a conservative long sleeved dress. No makeup. As if she does not want to draw any unnecessary attention to herself. She tousles her hair and puts on a simple pair of earrings. She speaks out loud to herself in the mirror before she heads out. "Everything is going to be just fine."

She arrives at the restaurant exactly on time. Ami and Henry are already sitting with cups of coffee, both of them gesticulating enthusiastically as they talk.

"Elle!" Ami exclaims, standing to give her a hug. "Pretty dress!"

"Thank you, I'm sure you've seen it before though."

"Well you make everything look fresh," Ami winks one precisely eye lined eye at her. She could never get her makeup that perfect.

Henry takes his time rising from the table after their exchange and gives Elle a shockingly tight embrace. His body is firm against hers. His cologne is overwhelming, just as it had been that night. She is instantly nauseous again.

"Henry," was all she could manage, her body stiffening.

"Elle, it's good to see you. You look great. It's been a few years, well, since Ami's wedding I suppose. How have you been?"

"Good, good, can't complain." She was all too eager to sit down. "Still teaching and enjoying my summers off. What about you? How's Arianna? The boys?"

"Everyone is well. Boys are growing faster than we can replenish food and clothing. And Arianna just went back to work part time. She is teaching pilates."

"Oh good to hear," Elle feigned interest. "And the boys must be in what? 4th grade?"

"Going into fifth actually," Henry said, shaking his head in disbelief.

"What can I get for you, hun?" The older yet attractive waitress asked her.

"Just coffee, thank you."

The waitress smiled and leaned over to pour the steaming liquid into her cup. "I'll let you get situated and come back in a few to take your food orders."

"Thank you," Elle said.

"So how was your Saturday?" Ami asked. "Did you make it to your spin class?"

"I did and wow do I feel it today. But glad I went. I'm going to try to go at least two times this week if you want to join me."

"Spinning?" Henry repeated. "Arianna actually just bought us a Peloton bike. It's just so much easier to just have it at home with our unpredictable schedules."

"Oh that's awesome!" Ami said. "I was talking about getting one with Clay once we move in together."

"You definitely should," Henry said. "You know what? That will be my wedding gift to you, my little sister. How does that sound?"

"Oh Henry, you don't need to do that," Ami said, waving her hand away at the idea.

"It would be my honor. There is nothing more priceless than good health. And you know what? I will throw one in for you, too, Elle. As a gift for taking such good care of my sister over all these years especially when I haven't been here to look out for her."

He looked intrusively into her eyes, as she reached her shaking cup to her lips. His eyes told the rest of his insinuation. A thank you for not having said anything to Ami after all these years and a promise to continue to do so.

"You certainly do not need to do that." Elle said after a long sip of the bitter liquid. Certainly she would not accept a rape conciliation gift.

"I do not need to, I want to," Henry said matter of factly, clapping his hands together as if this gesture solved everything.

"Yes! You deserve it, Elle. We both deserve it," Ami said excitedly, taking her clammy hand, which suddenly felt tingly. As if Ami couldn't afford it on her own. "We can do it together! It will be so much fun and we will motivate each other!"

Henry continued reading her uncertainty. "I wouldn't have offered it if I didn't mean it. Business has treated me well. I am in a position to give back. I was actually telling Ami before you arrived that I'm getting an apartment in the city around here. Since I am traveling more to Chicago now, I figured it only makes sense to get a place of my own here. That's part of the reason I came out here this weekend—to furniture shop and get everything ready. It actually doesn't sound that far away from where you live, from what Ami told me."

Elle's heart rate started to elevate. "Oh really?"

"Yay! I can't wait to help you decorate! And it will be so awesome to have you here more often of course," Ami said, clapping her hands. "Don't you think, Elle?"

Elle felt herself getting light headed. The room started spinning. This was all too much. "I'm so sorry but I need to get going. I am not feeling well."

"Oh my goodness! Elle, are you OK?! You look flushed. What's going on? Maybe you just need to eat something?"

"I'm sorry, I just need to go. Get back in bed."

Henry looked at her speculatively. "Let me drive you home at least. I don't want you driving if you aren't feeling well."

"Yes, absolutely!" Ami agreed.

"Oh no, it's totally fine. I will be fine," Elle retorted and forced herself to smile.

"I insist." Henry grabbed his keys from the table.

Elle got up shakily. Ami grabbed her arm and stood up with her. "You poor thing. You go get some rest and I will check in on you later. Take good care of her Henry."

"Of course," Henry said, holding onto her elbow. Elle was so dizzy that she needed the help. The man who once raped her was now guiding her like she was an elderly woman. How disturbingly ironic. Customers looked up at them as they passed, the chivalrous man protecting his frail lady.

He opened the door to his rental Mercedez and reached over her to buckle her seat belt before she could protest. He made sure her legs were securely inside before he closed the door. Just like how Clay had done for Ami last night. He asked her if she wanted the air conditioning on high as he started the car.

"Yes, please," she said wearily. She reached into her purse and popped a Xanax with the water bottle that sat in the console, half drank.

Henry turned the AC on full blast. "Just tell me where to go," he said. She directed him, left then right, straight to the stop sign, the words taking effort to form. He drove slowly as if to assure her but she wished he would just speed up. She craved the comfort of her bed more than anything right now.

He kept glancing over at her about to say something as she kept her gaze fixated out the window. The seven minute drive seemed like an hour but finally he was parked in front of her condo. He undid his seat belt.

"I got it, thanks," she said, undoing hers. "Thanks for the ride. I appreciate it."

"Are you sure?"

"Yes, I'm sure," she said sternly.

He nodded his head. "You take care of yourself, Elle." She simply nodded back and got out of the car with more confidence than she felt. Her legs felt shaky as she ascended the steps. She knew he was watching her. She fumbled for her keys, swearing to herself, and finally opened the door to her reprieve. She did not look back but he honked once and started to drive off as she shut and locked the door. Then she immediately ran to the bathroom and threw up, Lucky Charm marshmallows swirling in the bile.

What the hell? She had not had Lucky Charms yesterday and she had not eaten anything yet today. She wretched again but this time she had nothing more to expel. Her mind raced. When had she eaten Lucky Charms? Oh my God. She had to have eaten them last night of course, sleep walking, or rather sleep eating. She flushed the toilet, disgusted. Overcome with an urge of determination, she then went to her nightstand and grabbed the half empty bottle of Seroquel. She stood with the open bottle of pills over the toilet, but she couldn't do it.

Instead she set the bottle aside and splashed her face with cold water. Her eyes were bloodshot in the mirror. She took a deep breath.

"I am OK. I am just fine," she said to her drained reflection. She should have never agreed to meet Ami and Henry this morning. What was she thinking?

She grabbed a Gatorade from the fridge and forced herself to eat a couple of crackers before she stripped off her clothes and got into her unmade bed. She fell asleep almost instantly, her body and mind succumbing to the emotional exhaustion.

Elle woke a few hours later to Ami's call. The light in her bedroom had dissipated. She glanced at the alarm clock. Almost 5 p.m.

"Hey," she finally answered.

"Hey Lady, how are you doing?" Ami's voice was full of concern.

She yawned. "Better, much better. I just needed some sleep."

"You still haven't been sleeping well."

"Not really and that damn Seroquel is just way too powerful for me. I almost ended up flushing it down the toilet. I'm going to call Dr. Berkshire and see if he can prescribe something else, something not so strong."

"Good for you," Ami agreed. "I can't believe you started taking that crap in the first place!"

"I know, I know but honestly I can't handle a lecture right now."

"No lecture, just a concerned friend. Hey, what do you say I pick up some Chinese for dinner and a bottle of wine and head to your place? You must be starving."

"Ah that sounds really nice but I don't think I will be much company right now."

"Nonsense!" Ami exclaimed. "I got you. I know what you like. We can just sit on your couch and watch TV for all I care. You don't even have to talk."

Elle smiled. "You are too sweet."

"See you in 45!" Ami hung up before Elle could protest.

Exactly 45 minutes later, Elle's doorbell rang. It was quite incredible how timely Ami always was, down to the minute. Stammering to the door, Ami rang the bell again, impatiently, as Elle opened it.

Ami was holding a massive bag of Wok Time Chinese food.

"I got you your favorite! Ginger soup, dumplings, crab wontons, beef and broccoli and chicken pad Thai. Oh and I got you your favorite waffle cone ice cream!" Ami announced, beaming.

"Thank you so much. You really didn't need to get all that though."

"Don't be ridiculous! A girl's gotta eat!"

She bustled past her to the kitchen, placed the ice cream in the freezer and started to take out the foam cartons from the bag as Elle got some clean dishes from the dishwasher she hadn't had the energy to empty.

"So," Ami said. "Wasn't my brother such the gentleman to get you home?"

Elle swallowed hard before she spoke. "Yes, that was very kind of him."

"I'm so happy that he will be spending more time here! I've missed him so much these past few years." She aligned all the cartons in a perfectly straight row down the counter. "He's never been much of a phone person, you know?"

"Yeah, it will definitely be nice."

"We can all go out on the town like in our high school days!" Ami laughed heartily.

Elle forced a smile.

"Well, Clay will be in tow, too, of course. I still cannot believe they haven't met yet. I hope they hit it off. Do you think they will?" Ami asked, wanting to obviously hear only one answer.

"Of course they will, why wouldn't they?"

"Oh I don't know. Henry is still all bent out of shape about Ryan but at brunch I think he realized just how happy I am with Clay. I mean I really talked him up, but not really, because what I told him is all true!"

"You did luck out," Elle agreed as she poured the steaming soup into a bowl to start.

"And you will be next, just you wait!"

"I'm definitely not avidly looking right now. Especially on such little sleep, I can't trust myself to make coherent decisions." She laughed at herself and sat down on the couch careful not to spill the soup. She drank it from the bowl, not bothering with a spoon. Ami copied her.

"Oh, but you know what? Guess who reached out to me on Messenger last night? I texted you about it."

"That's right! I'm sorry, I was so preoccupied with some stupid wedding stuff. Who was it?!" Ami asked excitedly.

"Asa Follet."

"Asa Follet?! The nerdy and awkward guy from high school? What did he say?"

"First off, he is nerdy and awkward no longer. He is moving to Chicago and asked me to give him the lay of the land."

"Along with a good lay," Ami smirked. "Sorry, you were asking for it."

Elle shook her head smiling. "I am not sleeping with him. At least not on the first date and I don't even know if you can call it a date. I haven't seen him since high school for God's sake. I told him I would be open to meeting for lunch."

"That's great! It certainly doesn't hurt to explore. I am proud of you!" Ami took a gulp of the soup like she was taking down a shot.

"Yeah but honestly, he never gave me the time of day in high school so I don't know. I almost find it strange that he would even reach out to me."

"He never gave anyone the time of day. You can't take it personally. And it's not like you took any interest in him. The fact he reached out to you obviously shows you left an impression on him. And look at you now! You still have your figure, are single and childless. I'd say that's a pretty damn good deal." Ami nudged her with her foot under the blanket they started sharing.

"Yeah, I suppose," Elle said, contemplatively. "Anyways what harm can a lunch do?"

"Exactly! So when are you meeting him and where?"

"This coming Saturday, not sure where though. Somewhere fun and lively. Any suggestions?" Elle sipped the last of her soup avoiding the dreaded slurping sound she detested, which Ami made all too easily.

"What about The Alinea?"

"Too fancy."

"The Berghoff?"

"Hmmmm... Maybe. I'll consider it."

"I know! Oriole! Fun, lively, but intimate and sexy. I had one of my first dates with Clay there, remember?" Ami's eyes widened in excitement.

"Yeah, I like that!" Elle nodded her head emphatically. "Classy but not over the top."

"Exactly. So I'm assuming you have Facebooked stalked him already?"

"A bit. He's only on Facebook, not Insta."

"Oh I need to see." Ami took her phone out of her Louis Vuitton and had Asa's profile picture pulled up in less than five seconds.

"Well if this is remotely any sort of recent representation I would say that you will be sleeping with him this Saturday without a doubt," Ami said delightedly. "Wow, did he turn out handsome or what?!"

"Yeah, he looks like he has aged nicely," Elle agreed, "but I don't want to get my hopes up, you know?"

"Just have fun with it!" Elle had always envied how Ami always seemed to be able to have fun in any situation, going with the flow. Sure, Elle had her fun but she much preferred planning and clear outcomes at the end of the day.

"You're right. Just fun, no expectations."

"That's my Elle," Ami squeezed her shoulder. "Now you just sit here while I serve you."

"Why thank you," Elle said, stretching out on the lumpy sofa.

Ami returned with a heap of food on top of a tray and set it on Elle's lap. She dug into the beef and broccoli first. "This is exactly what I needed. Thank you for coming over."

"Of course! I was worried about you!"

"Yeah, like I said, I'm making an appointment tomorrow. I need to get off this crap but I really do need something to sleep. I can't just go cold turkey."

"Is it more because of anxiety or just because you can't sleep?" Ami asked, her mouth full of an entire dumpling. Sometimes Elle couldn't help but be astonished by how almost childlike she could be in light of her professional status. Elle had always thought she would have become a teacher.

"More so that I just can't sleep. But this stuff is not sustainable. Last night I woke up on the couch again with a glass of wine on the coffee table and no recollection of how I got there."

"Yeah, that's not good," Ami said. "You should just try getting up at the crack of dawn like me! Then you will have no issue falling asleep at 9 p.m." She smiled a broccoli toothed smile.

"Ha ha, you know that's not possible." Elle had never been a morning person. And fortunately, she didn't need to be at the school she taught at until 9 a.m. since all the students had their free breakfast at 8:15 a.m.

"Well now that we are going to be bestowed with Peloton bikes we have to ride together and I'm certainly not riding after work."

"And I'm certainly not riding before," Elle shot back, smiling.

"So awesome he's doing that. You know he is a man of his word so he really will do it."

Elle carefully considered her response. "Honestly, it's a super nice gesture but I can't accept a $1500 bike from him. I don't think I would use it all that much anyways."

"Oh my god, just take the damn thing!" Ami exclaimed. "He has the money and he is spot on about you really being there for me, certainly way more than he has this last decade. It will alleviate his conscience."

"Right," Elle said, almost choking on her bite of rice. In more ways than one. "Ok, fine, I accept. But don't you dare expect me to ride with you at 4:00 a.m.!"

"Five then? I can go through my emails first and then get on the bike if I really have to."

"Jesus, you are relentless!'

"Yep, and that's why I'm such a badass lawyer," Ami smiled triumphantly.

"That you are and then some, aka, a pain in my ass." She giggled and Ami pinched the top of her butt check.

"Ow!" Elle almost tossed her plate on the floor. "Who would think that a badass lawyer like you would still be pinching people?"

"Oh would you rather I tickle you?" Ami laughed and set her half eaten plate on the coffee table. "So on a more serious note, ha ha, how's the bachelorette party planning coming along? What can I do to help?"

"Nothing, got it handled, but thank you. I will keep you posted as soon as more details are solidified."

"Well thank you again for planning it. A second time around, nonetheless. And no need to tell me, you know I love surprises and am so patient," Ami grinned mischievously, knowing full well she was the opposite. Elle had always been the one encouraging her to be patient. For example, Elle had to consistently reassure her when Ryan had not proposed soon enough. Or even more dramatic, Elle prevented her from having a complete meltdown when she was waiting to find out if she passed her bar exam, which of course she passed with flying colors on the first try. Elle, though she liked things to be planned, always enjoyed a good surprise. Her level of patience certainly trumped Ami's while Ami's level of determination certainly trumped hers. This balance had served their friendship well.

"So Clay and I are thinking of Paris for our honeymoon!" Ami chirped excitedly. "I know it is so cliche but honestly I can't think of anything more romantic and Clay has never been."

"Aw, that will be amazing!" Elle said, dismissing a tinge of jealousy that she and Ami would not be taking this trip together as they had always talked about doing "one day."

"Yeah, I think we will wait until November though. Just so we can focus on the wedding first."

"Absolutely. Paris is not going anywhere," Elle agreed.

"But obviously I just want to go, so I don't know. Clay is the one who really suggested we wait," Ami sighed with exaggeration.

"Sounds like Clay and I are on similar levels when it comes to patience," Elle remarked. "And come to think of it, we are both easy going, artistic and not hugely motivated to make the big bucks…"

"Yeah, he's kinda like the male version of you actually!" Ami said seemingly to have come to an ah-ha moment. "I never saw it like that before, but wow, you are so right! I was trying so hard to find someone opposite of A-hole and it ultimately landed me with someone just like you!"

Elle laughed. "Who woulda thought?"

At that moment, Ami's phone binged with a text and she leapt for it in her purse. Naturally, it was a text from Clay and Ami's face lit up in delight as she responded quickly to him, her two thumbs fluttering over the keys like a frantic hummingbird.

"I just love how he checks in with me. It really is refreshing. Ryan would go hours without responding to my texts but if he texted me and I didn't respond right away, that was a different story. God, why am I even talking about him?" She dropped her phone back into her purse, with a sound of disgust and stood up, retrieving her empty plate from the coffee table along with Elle's.

"Well, I best be getting on to bed, I actually have a big disposition tomorrow that I haven't prepared much for."

"Of course. Thanks so much for coming by and feeding me on top of it. You always know what I need," Elle said as she started clearing the counter.

"You know it!" Ami exclaimed. She gave Elle a brief hug, their red hair becoming one huge mass, and a kiss on the cheek. "Take care of yourself and don't forget to call that doctor tomorrow," she said, her face dropping into a serious expression.

"I won't," Elle promised, walking her to the door. "And good luck with the disposition tomorrow. Obviously you will kill it."

"Thanks, Elle, love you!" Ami winked at her and breezed past, her mind already off on her next mission.

Elle closed the door, locked it and headed back to the kitchen to put the rest of the food away. She cleaned the few grains of rice from the counter, thankful she did not have many dishes to do. She wanted to just sit back on the couch and watch TV but this desire filled her with instant guilt. She needed to do at least something productive today.

So she flicked on the light in her art room and went to her closet of paints and art supplies, retrieving random colors that she thought looked pretty together to start on a new canvas. She had no idea what she would paint, but she would just let her brush lead her as she often did. She set up her easel and paints, turned on some reggae music, donned her painted laden smock and was instantly lost.

Three hours later, she came out of her painting reverie. It was 1 AM. She stood back from the canvas and stared at the painting she had so far. It was of a girl floating on a cloud with her golden locks pouring out from her tiny head, asleep, while her dreams encircled her. She had finished the giraffe and started the bowl of ice cream. She wanted to keep going, but she was determined to have some good dreams of her own tonight. She closed the lids on the paints tightly, washed her brushes and hung her smock back in the closet. She stopped to stare at her painting one last time and then retreated to her bedroom praying she would sleep easily tonight.

He could see them making out on the boat, the waves slightly swaying their tan bodies. They had no regard for anyone else watching them. She was wearing a strapless bathing suit top that looked like it was about to fall down at any moment. His brother groped her selfishly. When he had the chance, he would be gentler, would relish in the moment and traverse each inch of her body—not just her ass and tits.

His brother's greed and impulsiveness infuriated him. But the fact that she just went along with it without hesitation, infuriated him more. She deserved so much better. He knew exactly how to treat her like she deserved. He would go out of his way for her and make her feel special every single day, not just on Valentine's Day or her birthday.

His brother wouldn't even allow her to pick out the restaurants or movies they went to. He always had a disparaging remark to make about her weight or her intelligence, which he always followed up with his haughty laugh. And his lame second thought flowers and chocolates. Or that stupid ring he gave her from the gumball machine that she never took off. It was tie dye pink and purple, for a little girl but she flaunted it like it was a 3 carat diamond.

He got away with all of this because of his good looks and the fact that he could catch a fucking ball. Like a parasite, he continued to suck the life from him. Now it was finally his turn.

Chapter 6

She woke up screaming. A vivid replay of the accident swarmed in her mind but this time the driver had survived and Ami had died. Elle had watched in useless horror as she bled out next to her. 2:30 AM. She commanded herself to take some deep breaths and after getting up to pee, she lay back down trying to get comfortable.

But the nightmare had been too unsettling. She got up and splashed cold water on her face. Made some Chamomile tea. It was too late to take any sleeping meds but an hour later she bit off just a tiny bit of the Seroquel. She was out again and woke eight hours later on the couch, her sweatshirt on the carpet.

God damn it.

Well at least she had slept.

She brewed some coffee and told herself that as soon as she had her fix she would call Dr. Berkshire. She rinsed her mug of the remaining coffee from yesterday and poured fresh, steaming coffee in it. She savored the first few sips and then drank the rest as quickly as she could without burning her tongue, wanting to get this phone call over with.

She had expected to leave a voicemail but surprisingly, Dr. Berkshire answered on the second ring. His pleasant voice greeted her.

"Good Monday morning. This is Dr. Berkshire. How may I help you?"

"Oh hello, Dr. Berkshire. This is Elle, Elle Emerson. How are you?"

"Elle, it's good to hear from you. I am well. Just came back from a camping trip with my grandsons. It was a bit exhausting keeping up with them, but otherwise I am very well. And how are you my dear?"

"That's wonderful," Elle replied, smiling. She couldn't help but imagine Dr. Berkshire, normally dressed in his suits from the '80's, in the wilderness. "I'm doing OK but still having a lot of trouble sleeping. I was wondering if there could be something else you could prescribe for sleep."

"Ah, what seems to be the problem with the Seroquel?"

"Well, it appears that I've been sleepwalking quite a bit and I wake up very groggy every morning. And I'm still having very vivid dreams."

"I see, I see," Dr. Berkshire said in his doctorly tone. "And are you mixing alcohol with them at all?"

Elle bit her lip. "I've really been trying to cut back."

"And what does that entail, dear? How many alcoholic beverages would you say you are consuming a day?"

"A couple, I would say," Elle responded.

"Ok, well let's try to eliminate the alcohol completely first. Can we give that a go? The alcohol will only exacerbate the side effects, even just a couple drinks. And then if the side effects still persist, we can try something else. How does that sound?"

"That sounds good," Elle forced herself to say. Eliminating all alcohol sounded terrible.

"Ok, great, it's a plan then. It looks like I am scheduled to see you at the end of next week. Let me know if you need anything in the interim, OK?"

"Ok thank you, doctor," Elle said.

"You take care now, Elle."

"Thanks, you, too," Elle hung up, feeling slightly deflated. She eyed the wine sitting on her counter and immediately thought of pouring it out. But that would be so wasteful. She considered returning it but that sounded ridiculous. She would give it to someone she decided. The permanent scowl on her neighbor's face, Mr. Jensen, came to mind. Having that party that had gotten a little out of hand over a year ago, had not helped his already obvious dislike of her. Yes, why not try to get on his good side?

She showered quickly, noting that her bar of soap was still in its place, and got dressed in something other than loungewear, eager to start the day. But as she finished getting ready, she realized that besides delivering the wine, she had nothing on her agenda today. She felt a surge of loneliness.

She started to text Ben to see if he wanted to grab coffee with her and then erased it, remembering that he was still in Wisconsin. She sighed out loud and plopped on her unmade bed, sighing again as she realized the sheets desperately needed to be washed. Had it been two weeks or three?

Restless, she started scrolling through her Instagram and then

Facebook. She went to Asa's page again and stared at his profile picture. Her heart skipped a beat in excitement. Screw it, she was bored and did not want to wait until this weekend to see him. There is no better time than the present, she heard herself mimicking Dr. Berkshire. She quickly messaged him.

Hey! Hope you had a nice weekend. My plans for lunch actually got canceled today and I was wondering if you would like to grab lunch somewhere near your office that's convenient for you?

She sent it even before reading it over, before changing her mind. She could see his response forming back immediately and her heart jumped again.

Hey! Good to hear from you. Yes, I'd love to. How does JT's at noon sound? It's just down the street from my office and has a variety of food.

She smiled, a rush of excitement flooding her body.

That sounds perfect. See you soon then!

Asa hearted her message and sent a happy face. Without hesitation she sent a happy face back. At 11:15 a.m. she left her apartment having finally decided on one of her newer summer blouses, dark jeans that highlighted her minimal curves, and a pair of sandals, the perfect in between height. She wore light makeup and decided to wear her hair down in all its red glory. As she walked to her car she texted Ami.

Headed to meet Asa for lunch at JT's. Wish me luck!

She put in the address of the restaurant, calculating her arrival at 11:40 a.m. Perfect. She did not need to rush. Actually, she had plenty of time to drop off the wine at Mr. Jensen's. She wanted to just get it over with and to get it out of her place before she would be tempted to drink it. She unlocked her door and retrieved the bottles, placing them in the last couple wine bags she found underneath the sink. Tissue paper was unnecessary.

She locked up again and went down the two flights of stairs to his unit. He had no doormat nor one plant on his porch. The only object that marked his unit was a "no solicitors" sign on his door. She knocked tentatively. She could hear his TV blaring in the back room so she knocked louder. She waited a couple minutes and just as she was about to leave, he opened the door, holding a large and very fat cat like a baby, their faces equally unamused.

"What do you want?" he barked.

Startled, Elle lost all her words. His pin drop eye glared at her, the other clearly fake eye gazing over her shoulder.

Elle glanced down at the cat, feeling more at ease, and spoke directly to it instead.

"I just wanted to drop off this wine to you. I, um, thought that you might enjoy it." She suddenly felt extremely foolish and had the urge to just run from his terrible one eye death glare.

"I don't drink wine," he said with a snicker, as if she were a stupid child who should know better. His one eye gaze moved down to her chest, where small beads of sweat had already started forming between her cleavage. She completely forgot she was wearing a more revealing blouse. Oh no, he must think she wore this to impress him. Oh God.

"Looks like it's another hot one out there today, eh?" he said, now full blown smiling, exposing rotten looking teeth. "You know, why don't you come in and have a glass with me? Perhaps I have been missing out this whole time and haven't even realized it." He smirked again as the cat yawned.

"I'm um sorry but I actually have to get going," she stammered. "Um, I um, will just leave the wine in case you change your mind."

"I will save a bottle in case you change your mind," he replied, winking.

Elle dropped the wine and left as quickly as she could without tripping over herself, humiliated and disgusted. What was she thinking? She should have known better. Creepy old man. She cursed him and his fat cat as she got in her Jeep, blasting the AC on her face. God, she could be the biggest idiot sometimes. She took a few deep breaths and then told herself to forget about it. She was determined to enjoy her lunch date with Asa.

She arrived at the restaurant exactly on time, choosing to valet so she wouldn't start sweating again. She thanked the young man who took her keys, who barely looked old enough to drive. She thought of the girl at Whole Foods the other day. As she got older everyone else was starting to look younger and younger. She sighed. But then she saw Asa through the window immediately and they smiled and waved in unison. Wow, he looked better than his picture, that was for sure. She felt slightly self-conscious as she walked through the door but she was immediately put at ease as he stood up and took her in his insanely buff arms.

"It's so good to see you, Elle," he smiled, showcasing perfectly white teeth. She wished she could hold onto him a bit longer.

"You, too, Asa. It's certainly been a long time."

"It certainly has, but yet you look just about the same," he said.

She was about to deny this statement but decided against it. "Thank you. Well, and you don't at all. You really grew into yourself." Whoops, she was already flirting with him.

"Why thank you," he said, his dimples flashed, adding that sweet boyish touch to his face. "I was quite the late bloomer in high school. Thanks for even giving me a chance."

She waved his remark away.

"So what brings you back to the Windy City?" she asked changing subjects, as he pulled her chair out.

"A job opportunity I couldn't pass up. Financial advising with Goldman and Sacks."

"Good for you."

He laughed. "I'm joking," he said. "Don't get me wrong, I feel fortunate to work for them, but honestly, I just needed a change after living in Wisconsin for so long. Megan, my ex-wife, and I got divorced last year. No kids, so really no ties since we moved there for her family. Her family has a toffee business—Amy's Toffee—the best toffee on a side note. I worked for myself for years but decided that I needed the security of working for a stable company. Plus, I missed Chicago. So that is my complete answer."

"Gotcha," Elle said, placing her purse on the back of the chair. "I'm sorry to hear about the divorce."

"Ah it was just a matter of when. Honestly, it was never right from the start. And after years of trying to have children and no success, adding even more frustration and fighting, there was just really nothing to keep us together anymore."

Elle nodded. "Well, welcome," she smiled and took a large gulp of her ice water, nearly spilling the ice all over herself. Fortunately, he didn't seem to notice as he continued.

"Thank you, I am happy to be here. Really. I'm super excited for a new venture. And I'm happy to be here with you. I'm glad you were able to meet me sooner than Saturday." He smiled and took a sip of his water as well.

"Me, too," Elle replied. "I'm glad you reached out." She could feel herself blushing.

"Absolutely. You were always the sweetest in high school. And of course one of the prettiest. So I was super pumped to find out that you were single on Facebook."

"Oh wow, cutting right to the chase I see," Elle laughed.

"Sorry, sorry, I don't mean to come across so aggressively. I just, well, I guess I can be too honest sometimes. And coming out of a marriage like mine, I'm thankful I can just be myself when I felt like I couldn't for so long. My ex was so damn sensitive."

"No, don't change that," Elle said. "I definitely appreciate that."

"So tell me about you—what are you doing with your life?"

"Well," Elle said, "I am single as you know…"

Asa laughed. "And dating?"

"And not dating, but was starting to think about it recently,"—not really—"so it was perfect timing that you reached out."

"That's great then." His beautiful blue eyes seemed to penetrate her. She had never noticed them in high school, his face was so covered in acne. Fortunately, he had perfect skin now. No scars or pock marks even.

"And I've been an elementary school art teacher for the past decade and live a pretty simple life," she added, wishing there was more to say. Her life was definitely not glamorous but she wouldn't change it. Well except for a possible partner to enjoy it with but the right partner, who also had the potential to be an invested dad to their children…

"That's amazing! Good for you" Asa exclaimed with slightly more enthusiasm in his voice than she thought was warranted.

"I enjoy it. I feel lucky to be able to teach my passion."

"And do you paint and draw a lot in your free time?"

"Right now, since it's summer and I have a lot of free time, yes. Next year I think I will need to get a summer job. During the school year, not as much."

His piercing eyes gazed so intently into hers it was almost as if he could read her thoughts, causing her a slight level of discomfort. Fortunately, the waiter approached and asked if they would like anything else besides water.

"Just an iced tea, please," Elle responded.

"Make that two," Asa said. The waiter nodded and walked away briskly.

His eyes refocused on hers. "I started to get into metal work this summer though, which was completely foreign to me," she continued, feeling the pressure to keep the conversation going.

"That's so cool. I wish I had artistic talent. My mother is a gifted painter and yet my art has not improved since kindergarten."

Elle smiled. "Maybe you can join my third grade class this year," she said teasingly.

"I would love to see you teach."

She smiled. "So what do you do outside of helping the wealthy become wealthier?" The blunt remark surprised herself as soon as it crossed her lips and she wished she could take it back.

"Ouch!" he feigned getting shot in the heart.

"I'm totally joking. Well, it's kinda the point of the job though, right?"

"It is, it is. But I also like to think that I offer security to families, so I try to focus on that. And outside of work I also helped to coach hockey for my nephew's team in Wisconsin. A bunch of twelve to fourteen year old punks. I do miss that. And him of course. Great kid."

"Well I'm sure you could get into that here, too," Elle said.

"I would like to in time, for sure. You're right on that—there's nothing like teaching your passion. If I could be a full time hockey coach, I would."

"Hockey was always your sport, then?"

"Yep, hockey all the way. I started playing in middle school. I was never that great until college. I was so scrawny until I turned 18. And then bam, I just seemed to grow overnight. And my athletic ability with it. I somehow managed to get on the team at DU—the best four years of my life."

"University of Denver?"

He nodded. "And you? Where did you go?"

"Here, the Art Institute. The best four years of my life as well," she sighed with reminiscence.

"So you never left Illinois?"

"Nope. I lead a pretty boring life." She definitely wasn't talking herself up. She needed to up her game a little before he lost interest.

"Nothing wrong with that," he shook his head. "I'm wanting to simplify my life now that I'm on my own."

At that moment their waiter set their teas down and asked if they were ready to order.

"Oh, we haven't even had a chance to look at the menu," Asa said.

"Take your time, I'll be back in a few," she responded.

"Have you been here before?" Asa asked.

Elle nodded. "Several times actually. My best friend used to work around here and we would meet for lunch here often."

"So what's good then?"

"Well, what are you in the mood for?"

"I'm open as long as I can have you for dessert," he said quickly followed by a cough.

Elle felt herself starting to blush again. Did he really just say that? God she had been out of the dating world for so long it felt like. Or maybe she just cared about the impression she gave off with him.

"Ha ha, well, we shall see about dessert," she laughed, "but I would recommend their apple and goat cheese salad and their filet mignon sandwich. Those are probably my top two favorites."

"Done." He looked for the waiter and nodded politely to her, suggesting they were ready to order.

"Two orders each of the apple and goat cheese salad and the filet mignon sandwich please," Asa stated.

"Great choices!" the waiter exclaimed and turned away again, briskly.

As they waited for their food, the conversation flowed easier than she anticipated as she and Asa joked back and forth. Elle no longer felt like she was watching herself but simply enjoying herself. Not only was Asa extremely good looking, but he was witty and charming and didn't seem too overly into himself, despite his obvious dedication to the gym and his work. And of course it was not necessarily a bad thing that he actually made money—he could definitely take care of her, too, by the looks of it. She was getting way ahead of herself though. Wait, was that a Rolex on his wrist? Elle tried to not look like she noticed but he caught her.

"This old thing?" He smiled and looked at the watch appraisingly. "It belonged to my grandpa. And then my dad. He gave it to me right before he passed away from cancer three years ago."

"Oh wow, I'm so sorry," Elle said, taken aback by her own judgement.

"Thank you. Yeah it was definitely the most difficult thing to see him suffer like he did for three long years. His passing was not actually as hard as I thought it would be. I was just so glad he was no longer in pain. At first I was mad at him for not doing this experimental trial that seemed really promising. But then I realized having him live any longer would have been purely selfish. It would have been more pain and more time in the hospital." His eyes glistened with a sheer layer of tears, their blueness becoming even more piercing.

Automatically, Elle reached over the table and grabbed his hand. She held it firmly as if trying to contain his grief, to prevent it from overwhelming him. He squeezed her hand back, his ocean eyes gazing right into hers again. But this time, she did not flinch, and she held his gaze steady.

And she held his gaze steady that night as he made love to her, so gently and tenderly that she felt as if they had been lovers for years. He was skillful and patient, exploring every part of her body until she ached to have him inside her. She felt so free—free from any fear or anxiety and so fully present. He told her repeatedly how beautiful she was. She grabbed his body in disbelief that this body was real, or rather, that this specimen was having sex with her right now. When she could tell he could not hold on any longer, she started kissing his neck and instantly she felt him jolt and then collapse on top of her. She laughed a laugh of glorious satisfaction. He joined her laughter and then started kissing her wide smile.

"Oh that was sooo good," he whispered. "You are so good." He kissed her collar bone tenderly. "I hate to bail out so soon but I should probably get going. I have to be in the office early tomorrow."

Elle felt a surge of disappointment. She was not ready for him to leave so suddenly. "Stay a little? Please?" she asked in an innocent voice, hoping she didn't come across as desperate.

He sighed dramatically but teasingly. "Ah, OK, just a little bit."

"Thank you," Elle whispered and kissed his cheek. He stroked her forearm and she closed her eyes, exhausted yet so comfortable that she fought to stay awake for just a few minutes longer.

He slipped the Antifreeze into the beer Pierce snuck into the bathroom as he showered, getting ready for his senior prom. As he got ready to get laid. Again. Prom, which his brother had attended since he was a freshman, the date of a senior girl nonetheless. He hadn't even been to one—at least not yet.

This morning, in desperation, he sadly overheard his mother attempting to find him a date. He was coming to her room to ask her if she would like some coffee, always the thoughtful and caring son.

"I completely understand. I just thought I would ask. Heather is such a lovely girl but I understand how nerve racking it would be for her to go with a near stranger especially with her... um.... disability."

He nearly lunged at her and smacked the phone out of her hand. She was going to sabotage his plan. And Heather? Seriously? His mother thought that Heather was on his level? She couldn't even form a complete sentence. In middle school, she had developed a sort of fixation on him, and when she wasn't in her retard class, she was constantly trying to touch him and giggling incessantly. The teacher even had to ask him to move seats. He was the laughing stock of the grade. It was beyond embarrassing.

He dreamed of killing her when she presented him with a Valentine's card in front of the entire class. They were in fucking 8th grade for God's sakes. His name was misspelled and half the letters were backwards, all circled in her pathetic attempt at a heart. He had thrown the envelope at her face, so ugly it bordered on disfigured, and ran from the class, resulting in his first ever visit to the principal. His mother was called and showed up in a frantic state, as if he had actually touched her.

Did this incident completely escape his mother's mind? How could his mother think that he was on her level? She was just a desperate creature who would go through life without even knowing how to wipe her own ass?

"Oh yes, I would love to grab lunch soon," his mother continued snapping back into her singsong character, pulling on her freshly curled hair. "Great, let's chat next week then.... Ok, you, too, bye now." She hung up with a small sigh.

Deep exhale. His opportunity would come to fruition. He retreated from the bathroom as silently as he came in and carefully placed the Antifreeze back in the garage where he found it, the lid securely tightened. He went to his room and dove onto his perfectly made bed, his heart rate elevated.

His older sister passed his room, immersed in music shooting from her new Discman so loud he could hear it. Twenty years old and borderline pretty if she actually tried. But more often than not she had her face in a book than in the mirror. He had always felt indifferent towards her. She was like ketchup to him, which he could go with or without. He counted to fifty before the shower turned off. He shot up in bed with excitement, knowing exactly what would happen next.

Chapter 7

She woke up and rolled over to find that he had left. She grabbed for her phone, which she fortunately still had remembered to plug in. 7:01 a.m. Damn, she had slept through the entire night and was waking up at a decent time without the freaking Seroquel. She had one text and it was from him.

Sorry to leave without saying goodbye but I didn't want to wake you. I had an absolute blast in more ways than one. Let me take you on a proper dinner date soon ☺

She grinned and kicked her feet underneath the sheets like a little girl. She thought about responding but decided to wait, wanting to give him some element of mystery. She went to the kitchen and chugged a full glass of water, completely parched, and then retreated back to her messy bed, the sheets still smelling of him, to replay the night in her head. She could not wait to tell Ami all about it. But for now, it was nice to have this private moment all to herself.

When she could think of no other detail, she grabbed her phone again and started trailing through her Instagram feed. After perusing through and mindlessly liking several photos, she forced herself to get up. She studied her face in the mirror, inspecting the fine lines around her eyes, the sun spots on her cheeks. She did not feel beautiful. She never had considered herself a beauty. Pretty, attractive, somewhat striking due to her bright red hair but never beautiful. Boyfriends and girlfriends had told her she was but it never meant much to her.

She thought they were obligated to say it. And Ami, well Ami was her best friend. But coming from Asa, it felt true. She smiled in the mirror, considering that perhaps she was beautiful after all. And really she should enjoy her looks now as they certainly wasn't getting any younger. She needed to be kinder to herself. Screw the Botox. That could wait. Plus, on a teacher's salary getting into something as potentially addictive as that was not feasible. She would tell Ami she would need to wait a few more years if she still wanted to lose her Botox virginity with her.

As she started to brew her coffee, she got a text from Ami.
How was it?!
She smiled. Oh where to begin?
It was... awesome! He really is so attractive and such a gentleman.
Yay! So glad to hear. Did you guys kiss.... or anything?
Yep... and then some, lol.
Good for you!
Ha ha, thanks. Yeah, I will definitely be seeing him again soon I hope.
So exciting! I'm sure you will! Well got to run, but congrats! I am so happy for you! Xox
Xox :)

Elle felt a surge of excitement she had not felt in a long time. But she knew she shouldn't get ahead of herself. It was only the first date. But he did seem pretty into her, right? Probably not as much as she was into him but still there was definitely an undeniable chemistry. And he had reached out to her after all.

She sipped her coffee slowly, enjoying the moment. The caffeine added to her excitement, to the point where she did not know what to do with it. She needed to work out or something. She glanced at her phone. She could make the 8 a.m. spin class. She texted Ben.
Spin at 8?
Already planning on it! See you there!

Ben was in serious form the entire ride of course, amping up her own intensity. Focusing on thoughts of Asa instead of the pain made the class go by surprisingly fast. Exhilarated, she was eager to tell him all about Asa. Ben indicated he had exactly 45 minutes before he had to get back to work. They walked down the street to one of their favorite coffee spots, Boss Coffee, sweaty and accomplished.

There were only a few studious patrons but otherwise it was barren. They both ordered iced Americanos, Elle insisting she pay as Ben paid for her 99% of the time. He relented as a text came in from Cameron. Since she was also paying, she couldn't resist ordering a piece of their zucchini bread as well, sitting all by its lonesome self. She didn't bother to offer him a bite as they sat down in their usual corner, knowing that he would flinch at the thought of sugar and wheat contaminating his body.

"So how was your trip?!" Elle chirped.

"Ah well it was good minus the mosquitos and my near death experience attempting to water ski."

"Oh my God!"

"Let me tell you, never again will I give into peer pressure like that. I work too damn hard for this body for it to all be crushed instantly."

Elle knew he was actually serious. "Of course." She resisted the urge to smile.

"No joke, it was pretty traumatizing. This little kid was coming at me completely out of control on her water skis. Luckily, I was able to make myself fall to avoid hitting her. Thank God for my quick reflexes." He paused dramatically and Elle murmured her empathetic disbelief.

"Yeah but other than that, it was pretty relaxing. We did a lot of hiking and yoga. Played a lot of cards and all the typical campy stuff. Glad to be back to my routine though. And service was not great out there, so I lost out on a great opportunity from a seller wanting to list his $2.2 home, but hey, it's all good. It was all worth it." His face appeared to contort in what would have been anger had his Botox not prevented the full effect.

"So sorry to hear that but you do deserve to have a break now and then like everyone else, you know. And I'm sure it was so nice to have some quality time with Cameron."

"Of course. Having uninterrupted time with Cammy was definitely the best part. And getting to know his sisters better. They really are such a hoot. We should all go to dinner sometime. Ami and Clay, too."

"Yes, I would love that. And maybe I can bring Asa as well." She gave him a mischievous smile.

"Asa? Now who the heck is Asa?" Ben laughed, coming out of his reverie.

"Well, currently we have only been on one date but it was the best time I've had in a long time."

"Oh do tell!" Ben exclaimed, allowing her to have the stage, often not an easy feat. Though Ben was extremely kind and thoughtful, it was simply his personality to talk about himself. A lot. And Elle was OK with this. Ben was still capable of listening when it mattered.

"I actually know him from high school but we never got to know each other then. He was... kind of a loner I guess, just doing his own thing. He moved away after college, was married for several years and just recently got divorced. And now he's back, living in the city. A financial planner. He messaged me on Facebook over the weekend and asked if I would be interested in grabbing lunch with him. So we met up yesterday near his office and ended up having nearly a two hour lunch. And he looks nothing like he did in high school... in a very good way," she clarified.

"Wow, so a good looking, successful guy who can manage a two hour conversation while keeping your interest the entire time? Now this is sounding promising."

"Right? I mean at first I was a bit nervous of course. It's been a minute since I've been interested in someone right off the bat. But then I said screw it and just let myself go and the conversation flowed so easily. He seems like such a great guy. He's been through a lot between his wife's multiple miscarriages and his father's death a couple years ago. But those losses also make someone realize what's really important and what they want without wasting time, you know?"

"So you guys had sex, then?" Ben asked, missing her entire point.

Elle sighed, annoyed. She wasn't ready to divulge that part to Ben, but there was no way of getting around it with him. "Well actually, yes, we did in fact have sex. And because I know that this will be your next question, yes, it was great, mind blowing actually—like nothing I've ever experienced with a man."

"Good for you!" Ben held up his hand to high five her. "You so deserve some mind blowing sex, especially after the dry streak you had," he said referring to her seven months of abstinence. "I was worried about you there for a minute!"

"Thanks." Elle relaxed and laughed. "Yeah I guess I was just... not really thinking about dating or sex, well, since Stella and then the accident."

"Well, I am so happy for you. So what's the next move?"

"He texted me this morning that he was sorry that he took off without saying goodbye—I was sleeping and he had to get to work—but that he had a really good time and can't wait to see me again."

"Aw, so sweet. So you haven't responded yet, right?"

"Nope, but I want to soon."

"Perfect. You already know my feelings about timing. Always maintain a little suspense and make sure the person knows just how valuable your time is."

"Believe me, I know," Elle rolled her eyes, knowing just how calculated Ben was in his availability, even with his boyfriend of two years.

"So show me some pictures before I make my final judgement. Just kidding, obviously I will make my final judgement in person."

Elle brought up his Facebook page and handed him her phone.

"Wow, you really weren't joking! That is some serious beauty. Are you sure he isn't gay?"

"No, absolutely not. Sorry."

"Those eyes!" Ben admired a while longer as Elle took the opportunity to fork a hefty piece of zucchini bread in her mouth. It was definitely worth the calories. Plus, didn't you burn like 500 calories in a spin class?

"And he obviously works out—like a lot." Ben continued to stare at her phone with a look of disbelief.

"Yep, and he is even better looking in person."

"Damn. Well let me know when I can meet him. I promise I will be able to keep my composure now that I am prepared."

"Of course. Maybe after one more date we can do a couple's thing. Ami and Clay, too."

"I can't wait!" Ben said as he handed her ringing phone back. It was her mother.

"Go ahead if you need to. I actually need to get going. So happy for you, Elle," Ben said sincerely. He stood up and bent down to kiss her cheek before leaving as she waited until the last second to answer. She really wasn't in the mood but then again, she never was. Might as well get it over with.

"Hey," Elle greeted, waving at Ben as he swaggered off in his air of importance, which she had also grown to accept. He was a money making salesman after all. There was an element of acting with these types of professions, or exaggeration at least. But that did not take away from who he really was.

"My Elle! How are you?!" Her mother crooned in her exaggerated English accent. She had moved to London just a year and a half ago with her boyfriend, Walter, whom she had met on a cruise specifically for divorcees. After her third divorce nonetheless. And only after two months of dating long distance, she went to visit Walter and had not returned since, except for a four day visit after Elle's accident, relishing in the role of martyr once again.

But most importantly, she relished in all her American indulgences that she had been "so deprived of," ensuring that every meal and shopping spree was from one of her beloved restaurants or stores. Elle was already in physical pain from the accident, but the worst part of her recovery was dealing with her mother, and her attempts to pretend that she was invested in Elle's recovery. She couldn't even make it the full week she was supposed to stay, changing her flight back to London when Walter had hinted at "growing lonely without her."

Elle could not have been happier to see her mother go and her mother could not have been more obviously eager to get back to Walter, who "had been going through a difficult time in his business and needed her more than Elle." She left with a third suitcase stuffed to the brim with all her purchases, "mostly for Walter," and leaving Elle with a refrigerator of random leftovers, makeup smudges in her bathroom, and endless strands of her dyed blonde hair that seemed to pop up everywhere even weeks later.

That pretty much summed up her mother. Regardless, she was still the only parent Elle had. She would feel a pang of jealousy from time to time over her friends, including Ami, whose parents were still happily married. She was certain that after her father up and left when she was five that he had happily started a new family. She could understand why he had left her mother, but to abandon her as well? She most likely had half siblings and would sometimes wonder if the random red haired girl or boy she saw was related to her.

Elle sipped her melting iced coffee, preparing for the plunge. "I'm good, really good," she said, this time really meaning it. "I just took a spin class and had a quick coffee with a friend and yeah... I'm doing well." She considered telling her about Asa but decided there was no point. She would only say something negative and disparaging. "How are you?" She stirred her coffee awaiting her dramatic reply.

"Oh that's great, honey. I'm glad to hear you are staying active. The weight started to be harder to keep off in my early thirties so it is definitely something you always will need to be proactive about. And when I saw you after the accident you seemed to already be getting a slight, what do they call that? Muffin top. Yes. That's it. I didn't want to say anything at the time of course but just be careful. We aren't spring chickens anymore. Well, hopefully the spin classes are helping." Elle took another satisfying bite of her zucchini bread.

"I've never done spin, it seems far too sweaty for a woman," she continued without response. "But I've really been into my Pilates classes lately. Of course now I'm really watching my figure because... I'm getting married!" her mother cheered. "Can you believe it? Walter finally, finally, asked me to marry him! I mean, Jesus, what was he waiting for?! Guys can be so completely blind. Here I am, this attractive and attentive woman, who has been by his side this entire time, even picking up and moving across the country, away from my only daughter. And it's not like I haven't had men here give me their numbers. I mean, I still have options."

She sighed, looking for validation but Elle simply continued to finish her zucchini bread. "But to give him credit, he did make it romantic, and the ring, well the ring, was worth the wait."

"Oh wow, that's great, Mom," Elle said finally, adding all the enthusiasm she could muster. She had never met Walter but he seemed nice enough. And obviously oblivious to her mother's self-centeredness, which was beyond her. "So when is the wedding?"

"We are thinking about this November but I'm pretty sure we will just elope. I'm tired of the whole wedding thing—been there, done that." She snorted whole heartedly. "But of course I want you to meet him and Walter has never been to the States, so we were thinking of coming there afterwards for our honeymoon."

"That would be nice," Elle said. She was at a loss for words. She pretty much always was when it came to speaking with her mother.

"Yes, so that's the latest and greatest for me! So I assume you are still single? Elle, you really aren't getting any younger...

"I actually met this really nice guy," she started, taking a deep breath to alleviate her rising defensiveness, but then her mother abruptly cut her off.

"Glad to hear it is a man at least. Wait, I'm so sorry sweetie but I need to take this call. I will call you back though!"

She switched over even before Elle could say goodbye. Well, that would be the most she would hear from her for about a couple months, which was just about all she could tolerate. She took a few more deep breaths, gathering herself. Sometimes it was extremely hard to be unphased by her mother as much as she told herself she didn't care. She would never change. All Elle could hope for was that she would never be like her. So far she felt she had done pretty well making a conscientious effort not to adapt any of her mannerisms. The biggest insult Ami had ever said to her was in ninth grade when she nonchalantly announced that Elle made the same facial expression as her mother when she was upset. Elle had to restrain herself from hitting her. In hindsight, she was glad she had pointed this out to her.

Outside, an attractive-looking man walked past in a perfectly tailored suit as Elle took her last sip of coffee. Her mind immediately went to Asa. Speaking of which, she had waited more than the appropriate amount of time to respond to him, even by Ben's standards. She reread his text and without overthinking she texted him back.

I had an absolute blast with you, too, and can't wait to see you again soon. Let me know what works.

Screw it, she wasn't going to hide the fact that she had plenty of time on her hands. He already knew she was on her summer break.

He responded back right away.

Great, how does tonight sound? Dinner at 7pm? I can pick you up and we can decide where then.

Perfect, I can't wait… see you then :)

She beamed. The rush of excitement hit her all over again. It had been so long since she had felt this excited about anything, guy or girl. Probably since she was a child when everything was still inherently exciting. And finally something other than anxiety, which had become her shadow these past few months. She sat a few minutes longer, relishing in this novel, long overdue feeling. Perhaps this year could end on a good note after all.

Chapter 8

At exactly 7 p.m., Elle watched as Asa pulled up on her street and expertly paralleled parked as she sipped on her first glass of wine. She decided to go casual yet classy in white jeans, wedges with cute polka dots and a sheer blouse that revealed just the right amount of skin. She wore her hair down in its full curls, untamed and unapologetic.

"Wow, you look amazing," Asa said, coming up the stairs as she opened the door.

"You, too," Elle replied, noting how his muscles permeated from underneath his tight, but not too tight shirt. He kissed her cheek as she stepped back to let him in.

"What would you like to drink?" she asked. "Red, white, water?"

"I'll do whatever you are having." Asa touched the small of her back as she poured another glass of white wine, instantly setting her cheeks on fire. She handed him one of her better wine glasses.

"Cheers to the most beautiful redhead there ever was," Asa said as he reached out to touch her hair with his free hand.

"I'll take it," Elle said. "Cheers." They clinked their glasses and did not let go of eye contact as they sipped. His eyes were like a maze she could easily get trapped in.

"So how was your day?" He finally asked, breaking the staring contest.

"Good, good. Just went to spin, met a friend for coffee and mostly spent the rest of the day painting. How about you?"

"Oh you know, work. Stressful as always but nothing overly significant. I couldn't stop thinking of you all day either. So I guess I was more distracted and not nearly as productive as I usually am." He smiled.

"Well, I'm sorry to have made your work day more difficult," Elle replied and stepped forward to kiss him, something she felt compelled to do. "Perhaps I can make it up to you." There was no holding back with him.

He kissed her slowly and smoothly and then retreated all too soon with a huge smile on his face. "There will be plenty of time for that."

She nodded her head and beamed.

"Now let's see some of your art before we eat," he said. "I can't handle the suspense any longer." He would rather see her art than hook up with her again? She didn't know what to make of that. But she couldn't be disappointed that he was taking an interest in her beyond sex.

"Ok, but don't get too excited." She took his hand to lead him into her overwhelming explosion of color and design.

He let her hand go and slowly walked the perimeter of the room, analyzing her paintings and random art pieces without comment. She felt a tingle of nervousness at his close inspection and flat expression. He finally turned to her. "These are spectacular, Elle. Truly amazing. You are an exceptional artist."

"Thank you," Elle said, relieved yet also slightly taken aback by his sincerity. She was more accustomed to critique than compliments when it came to her artwork. She mostly kept her pieces private, except for Ami and Ben's eyes, who of course had nothing but praise to give. With their encouragement, she had attempted to start an Etsy account at one point, but after not having any sales in a couple months, she grew frustrated and took the site down. Some of the kid appropriate ones she had donated to the hospital that had cured her cancer, but otherwise she kept most of her art in storage.

"Seriously, you need to open up an art gallery. These are just too good to not share."

"Ah, maybe one day," she deflected.

"What's holding you back?"

"Well, cost for one thing. And I don't know, I guess it's hard to judge your own art when you see it every day, you know? I really just do it for fun and peace of mind."

"Well, I'm telling you it is that good, and I would definitely buy a piece, more than just one, and I know others would, too. Now tell me about this one here, it looks like you are still working on it." He pointed to the canvas sitting on the easel where her golden locked girl remained in her unfinished dreams. She had felt an urge to work on pottery today instead.

"I just, well, I guess I was drawn to paint this because sleep and dreaming have been, I guess you could say, a focus of mine lately."

She decided to cut to the chase. "I was in a bad car accident about seven months ago, along with my best friend Ami, and well, the driver of the Uber died."

"Oh my God," Asa said, his face looking aghast. "That's terrible."

"Yeah, it was awful. It was New Year's Eve. Drunk driver. The driver had a wife and two kids. Just so tragic and unfair. And Ami and I got off completely unscathed." She couldn't help but feel a swarm of guilt as she said this. "The most we could do was start a Go Fund Me for the family." Asa squeezed her hand, encouraging her to continue.

"Anyways, ever since then I have been a bit anxious and have had trouble sleeping. So I started seeing this psychiatrist, who prescribed me some sleeping medication and I don't know, sometimes I wish I had never started taking anything. It definitely helps me sleep but it's almost like waking up from a coma every morning and my dreams can be so odd and intense." She declined to add the sleepwalking and drinking aspect as well.

"But now, I can't seem to sleep without it." She sighed, annoyed with herself for even bringing up the accident and her sleep issues. It wasn't exactly something that she wanted to be talking about on a second date.

But Asa only looked at her with concern and pulled her into his strong arms, where he held her for longer than their previous kiss. "I am so sorry you went through all that and I am so happy you and your friend are OK. And I am also really happy that I am able to just hold you right now. I feel so lucky." She breathed in his scent and felt all the hard ridges of his body that encompassed her. She felt safe.

"Thank you, I am so glad to be here with you, too," she finally said. He continued to hold her without words, the strength in his embrace saying everything. It felt so natural just to lean into his body and do nothing else.

Finally he kissed the top of her head and said, "now how about I take you on a date you deserve?"

---

45 minutes later they sat at Killen's Steakhouse, their bodies brushing each other as if they did not have an entire large booth to themselves. Elle had never been to Killen's before and felt underdressed but she

really didn't care. All she was concerned with was this gorgeous man beside her. She didn't feel all that hungry when their sizzling steaks arrived, she had such butterflies just being next to him. But as soon as she had a bite, the tender meat falling apart in her mouth with a punch of flavor, her appetite instantly came back.

"Wow, this could seriously be the best steak I have ever had," she said between bites.

"Oh good, I was just going to ask you if it was prepared to your liking." He winked at her, obviously knowing how much she was enjoying herself.

She laughed. "Yeah, I guess I did not realize how hungry I was either."

"I'm glad, eat up. You certainly don't look like you need to watch what you eat. Have you been this thin since high school?"

She grimaced thinking of her mother's muffin top remark from this morning. "I mean I don't think I'm all that thin, I'm just tall and carry the weight well. I am trying to eat healthier though and drink less," she motioned to the wine. "But hell, you got to enjoy your life."

"Cheers to that." Asa clinked his glass to hers.

After a repeat of last night's tryst in her bed, (God she could do this on repeat every night for the rest of her life and it would never get old), she fell asleep just as peacefully next to Asa, smiling, his gentle fingertips on her back, practically electrifying.

The drink hit Pierce even faster than he expected. He came out of his bedroom in his tux, profusely sweating. "Oh God!" he ran to the bathroom and without even closing the door, proceeded to vomit violently.

He sat up on his bed with a smile and crossed the hallway to the bathroom, his brother on his knees, vomit already streaming down his starched and pressed shirt. He wrenched again and again.

"Pierce, are you OK? Can I get you anything?" he asked. The display of concern came so easily to him. He had perfected his acting over the years.

Pierce looked up at him pathetically, and even more pathetically squeaked, "Mom."

"Sure thing." He turned down the stairs to where his mother was prepping the video camera for her son's precious pre-prom moments. It was disgusting how everything about his brother was so overly documented. As if he were some rare specimen.

"Oh shoot! This darn thing. For goodness sake." It was so annoying how his mother never swore. Even when Pierce caused her to almost slice her finger off when he was demanding her attention for the millionth time. As if they were still in kindergarten.

"Hey Mom, it looks like Pierce is sick," he announced feeling a sudden jump of glee.

His mother looked up at him wide eyed. "What do you mean, sick?"

"He's puking, puking his brains out actually," he clarified.

"Oh no! For goodness sake!" his mother exclaimed again, nearly dropping the camera. She immediately went to the medicine cabinet in the kitchen, stocked with an array of carefully aligned medications. Quickly, she identified the Pepto Bismol, grabbed it like ammunition and skipped every other step up the stairs to her ailing son. He lingered downstairs, his adrenaline pumping.

"My poor baby!" he could hear his mother shriek between Pierce's heaves.

He went into the downstairs bathroom and checked his face in the mirror. He'd showered right before Pierce and was freshly shaven. He had even spritzed himself with his brother's cologne. But his damn acne protruded from his face like his inner anger. He had the urge to slam his fist in the mirror but he resisted, staying calm with his plan at the forefront of his mind. It wasn't all about looks he reminded himself. While Pierce clearly existed with nothing else, he actually had something to offer.

"You look beautiful this evening," he practiced in the mirror. "You look absolutely beautiful this evening." He smiled at several levels of intensity, assessing which was most appropriate. No teeth. He didn't want to overdo it.

He crept upstairs and loomed in the hallway where his mother was holding his brother, on his hands and knees, next to the barf ridden toilet, like he was a fucking baby. The smell nearly made him throw up.

"Oh man, I'm sorry you're feeling so bad," he said. "Could it be something you ate?"

His brother shook his head, too exhausted to speak or even look up on him. He convulsed a couple more times but nothing was expelled except for a long line of drool. He was like a completely helpless animal. He wanted to hold onto this degrading scene in his mind forever.

"Oh honey, let's get you into bed." His mother stood up and he attempted to help her lift Pierce off the floor. After a couple failed attempts Pierce snapped, "I got it!" and slowly rose to his feet, vomit plopping from his tux.

He stumbled over to his bedroom and aggressively ripped his shirt off, the buttons splaying over the floor. He undid his belt and threw it so hard on the wall that his mother screamed again. He watched in delight as he finally stripped his pants off and got into his unmade bed, throwing a blanket over his head like a little boy trying to hide.

His mother's next layer of despair came to realization. "Oh no Pierce, you won't be able to make it tonight!"

"No shit, Mom," he said gruffly and threw a pillow on the floor.

She went over to the bed to stroke his cheek but he brushed her hand away. "Let me get you a cold wash cloth," she offered.

"I just can't believe this," she whispered harshly. "His senior prom just ruined!" She spoke to him as if he were one of her girlfriends. He was always the one his parents turned to for everyone's respective drama. Never was he the one to be fussed over.

Just then, the doorbell rang. "And ruined for sweet Maddy, too!" She opened the linen closet to retrieve the washcloth, which she put to her cheek to brush a tear dripping down her face. So fucking ridiculous.

"I got this Mom," he said, putting his hand on her back. "I got the door and I will let her know."

"Thank you," she replied deflated.

He slowly descended the stairs again, popping a piece of gum in his mouth, his heart starting to race. He could already see Maddy's auburn hair shining brilliantly in the late afternoon sun through the top of the door's window in some perfect time consuming configuration. He took a deep breath as he opened the door. This was his opportunity at last.

"Hey Mad-mad-Maddy," he said immediately. God damn it! His stutter was coming out. "You look beautiful this-this evening." He sounded like such an idiot. He smiled a closed mouth smile and exhaled strongly, trying to get a hold of his damn stutter.

"Thank you." She smiled. "Um, where's your brother?" She shifted on her heels, attempting to peer past him.

"Unfortunately he's really sick, Maddy. He was just th-th-throwing up, violently th-th-rowing up."

"Oh no! Can I see him?" she edged closer to the door.

"I don't, I don't think that's a good idea. He's in bed now."

She eyed him suspiciously.

"He feels terrible. He ob-ob-obviously still wants you to go to prom and have fun. So I was th-th-thinking that we, that we could go together," he shot out.

"What?! Are you serious? No way!" She looked at him incredulously, her face contorting in a look of pure disgust.

He felt his heart drop and fury rush through his body from his gut up to the top of his head.

"I mean, it just wouldn't be right, you know? She added a little more softly. "I mean people would think that's super weird." She laughed out loud and smacked her gum.

He joined her. "Yeah, yeah, you're right, what a st-stupid idea. Sorry, I mean I just didn't want to leave you hanging."

"Oh it's totally fine. Claire and Brittany don't have dates either so I can just tag along with them. I should get going then. But please tell Pierce I hope he feels better and that I will call him tomorrow. And that I love him very much."

"Of course." He rather she just slapped him in the face.

"Well, um, bye." She gave him a sad pitying smile as she turned to leave, her red dress twirling around her like a princess. He automatically envisioned her dress twirling around her while he spun her on the dance floor, laughing and touching her. Then he would hold her close to him as they danced to a slow song. Afterwards, she would lean in and kiss him without hesitation.

She would say that she had made a mistake, that she had been with the wrong brother this whole time. That he is the one. But he only watched her walk away, get into her car and take off without a second glance. He might as well be dead.

Chapter 9

Elle woke up to find Asa gone again.
She checked her phone.
8 AM.

Good morning and hope you slept well. Had a wonderful time again last night. Didn't want to wake you of course. Have a great day and I will be in touch soon.

She immediately liked his text and responded.

Me too :) Can't wait. Have a great day as well.

She stretched lazily in bed, her legs tight and sore from yesterday's ride. Doing some yoga today would be a good idea. Since it was midweek, maybe Ami would be more willing to actually take her lunch break and join her for a class.

Yoga at noon?

Aw, wish I could but I'm meeting Clay for lunch. He's performing tonight in Wisconsin. But maybe we can grab lunch or dinner this weekend?

Of course. Just let me know. BTW, I hung out with Asa again last night and it was amazing. I am falling for him. Hard.

Good for you! Can't wait to meet him. Gotta go but talk soon xox

Xox

Elle forced herself to get up and have a normal morning. She was proud of herself for not taking any meds again last night. Perhaps it was just all in her head that she needed it. Or perhaps Asa was the drug she needed. She tried to force herself from constantly looking at her phone to see when he would text her next. She secretly hoped that he was just as distracted thinking of her. But then of course she didn't want to affect his job performance.

She spent the morning finalizing the details of Ami's bachelorette party which was coming up in exactly one month from today. She reserved dinner at a couple of Ami's favorite restaurants and found a group deal for the grand opening of a spa that looked to be in the realm of Ami's taste.

However, with the group deal came a down payment guarantee. She used her emergency credit card to book it. She sighed as she entered in her credit card information. It would be all worth it though. She was excited to have some much needed girl time and knew that Ami would be so happy with everything most importantly. And she still had a couple hundred dollars left on her Target card.

She made it to her noon yoga class 15 entire minutes before it started. After having been locked out for being two minutes late once, she had since made an effort to arrive at least ten minutes before. Fortunately her favorite instructor was teaching. She bent and stretched her tight muscles, trying to focus on her movement and breathing rather than the pain.

She was somewhat successful in shutting off her brain for 45 minutes, even with thoughts of Asa, but could feel herself growing increasingly impatient during the last 15 minute meditation, which was typically her favorite part. As soon as everyone came back to reality, she was the first out of the room to the lockers, checking her phone.

Hey gorgeous, how does dinner sound tonight? Something a bit casual followed by some drinks? Pick you up at 7 again?

Her face smiled in delight as she responded.

Absolutely. I have a few spots in mind. See you soon. Heart.

She felt like she was walking on air as she went down a couple blocks to her car, her yoga mat slung over her shoulder. She smiled at the people she passed even if they did not acknowledge her. Everything seemed brighter, especially the trees and flowers. She noticed all the details she normally would gloss over, feeling a renewed sense of appreciation for the world.

She stopped to pick up the bottle a chuberic baby threw with gusto on the sidewalk, squealing with admiration at his achievement, as their annoyed and tired mother, in a stain filled t-shirt, thanked her. She spotted a pair of young male teens, holding hands and then stopping to kiss, so intently focused on each other. She felt happy for them. And especially happy that they felt comfortable enough to demonstrate their affection so openly, and that nobody passing, even some elderly persons, gave a double take. The world was good. No, the world was wonderful actually.

She got into her car, about to head home, when she decided that she should get a few things for tonight since she was already out. She would do a simple spread of cheeses, crackers, nuts, apples and the like. So back to Whole Foods she went. Inside the freezing store, she made her way to the deli, debating if she should go with the cheaper or more expensive selections.

As if the type of cheese she picked out would impress or disappoint Asa. As she was throwing their 365 name brand cheese into her cart, the one employee that she had desperately hoped that she would not run into, approached her with a cart of yogurts to be stocked. There was no way she could act like she did not see him without being rude. She gave him a slight head nod and a half smile. He appeared so excited to see her that he almost dropped the bundle of yogurt he was holding.

"Oh hi hi hi there! Gooooood to see you again! You def-def-definitely are an an avid Whole Foods shopper! Th-thank you for being a loyal cu-cu-customer!"

Her half smile turned into a full smile. She felt herself relax, seeing more of an innocent and endearing perspective of this awkward yet persevering man. She needed to stop being so judgmental. To stop being like her mother. The thought felt like a punch to her stomach. He was just trying to be nice and helpful.

"Yes, I am here way too much," she laughed. "But as many times as I have come here, I do stick to the same things really. What would you recommend as far as cheeses go?"

He smiled wider and stood up taller at the fact that she had just elicited his opinion. "I-I def-def-definitely would rec-recommend this one and this one. They are our bestsellers," he finished flawlessly and beaming.

"Great, thank you. I will take you up on both." She grabbed the couple he pointed at and he moved out of her way as she squeezed past.

"Have a good day now. I hope to see you again soon," he chirped.

"You, too," she responded warmly.

"By the way, you have the prettiest hair I have ever seen," he said as she was already past him.

"Thank you," she said slowly, confused as to how his stutter had instantly disappeared.

Asa arrived at exactly 7 p.m. again, looking even more handsome than yesterday if that was possible. He came bestowed with gorgeous flowers and a bottle of champagne.

"Why thank you," Elle said, inhaling the bouquet deeply before finding a vase to put them in. When she returned, Asa was already trimming the stems with her kitchen scissors. It was nice to see a man take initiative without even asking. She filled the vase with tap water and deposited the flower food packet while he placed the tips in the trash and rinsed the scissors before putting them back in the knife rack. She could envision them being a good team together.

She placed them on the kitchen table admiring them. "They really are beautiful."

"Not as beautiful as you are," he responded and drew her in for a much anticipated kiss.

"Hmmmm" she murmured as they eventually drew apart. He fed her a grape from the appetizer platter she had put way too much time in configuring, slightly choking on it. She laughed at herself.

"I'm so sorry," Asa laughed, too. "That didn't go as planned! How about we wash that down with some champagne?"

"Yes, please," she said, coughing. "That sounds great."

He popped the bottle he brought with the opener she handed him and poured two full glasses using the flutes that she removed from the cupboard.

He handed her the slightly fuller one. "Cheers to us and possibilities," he said.

"Cheers." They clinked their glasses once more. "I like that." She took a solid sip to wash down the remnants of the grape in her throat.

"You definitely like your toasts," she laughed.

"Yeah, I guess I do," he smiled. "But I also really mean it. I'm excited for us."

He grabbed her hand and kissed the top, something nobody had ever done to her.

"Me, too," she said. They both put their glasses down and started kissing again, becoming increasingly aggressive with each other. But then he stopped abruptly and pushed her back, looking at her with those hypnotizing eyes.

"Wow, just wow," she whispered.

"That was just the appetizer," he winked. He handed her glass back and took his.

"Let's finish these and get some food in us and hurry back for the real show. How does that sound?"

"Yes, please," she sighed, still quivering.

She took him to The Dearborn, one of her favorite casual spots, where they split a salad and burger and a bottle of red wine. He had her laughing almost the entire dinner as he recounted his crazy high school and college near calamities. She was open with him about some near arrests she and Ami had almost been in, too, something she had never told anyone, leaving him shocked and in disbelief. She was so comfortable with him, so drawn into him that everything else seemed to stop, as if they were the only ones in the restaurant. They lingered there easily for over an hour and a half.

After a desert he insisted upon ordering even if she had only one bite, (they ended up demolishing the banana hazelnut crunch cake without pause), they went out for a couple more cocktails at some trendy new bars Elle had not even been to.

But it felt too crowded and all she wanted was to be alone with him, which she clearly indicated to him. So back to her place they went, stumbling out of the cab, laughing and giddy, barely making it in the door before their clothes were off. As she drifted off to sleep on his smooth chest she felt like she was floating and never wanted to come down.

His eyes glazed with tears but he aggressively wiped them. He refused to cry. He was done feeling sorry for himself and would no longer live his life like a little bitch in the shadow of his brother. He marched back up the stairs and slammed his door, not bothering to check back with Pierce and his mother. His mother sat on the edge of his bed, scratching his sculpted back. Her cherished and favorite son, missing out on another opportunity to be admired and wanted. How absolutely devastating.

Anyways, he should have known that Maddy would turn him down. She was too blinded by his brother to see his worth, to see what she really could have. He felt bad for her. She had no idea how good she could really have it. She didn't truly love Pierce. She was just obsessed with him. Like everyone was in this stupid town. But it was all the assurance he needed to go through with his plan.

He sat at his desk and wrote. He wrote so furiously that his hand began to ache. He put all of his anger and hate on the paper. His hand couldn't write fast enough, pressing so hard that he was leaving indentations on the desk's surface. It definitely wasn't enough to distill his rage but it was something. His mother finally left his brother's side, knocking softly on his door. Her face was grief stricken.

"So how badly did she take it?" She asked, wincing, as if preparing herself for physical pain.

"She was fine. She was actually happy to just be able to go with her single girl friends," he answered gruffly, closing his desk drawer.

"Oh, sweet Maddy, always trying to make the best out of the situation." She shook her head. "Don't you just love her? She really is the perfect combination of sweetness and beauty."

"Yeah, she is." He could feel the heat boiling to the surface of his head again.

"One day you will find your Maddy, too." She looked at him sadly. He had never wanted to full on pummel his mother until now. He wrung his hands under his desk. "Probably not as pretty of course, but as they say, looks aren't everything. I mean look at your dad. I fell in love with him for his personality and his hard work ethic, for his promise to be able to provide for a family. You will be that man for one lucky girl someday." She bent down and gave him a slight kiss on the cheek, the only one who had ever kissed him, as he gripped his fists tightly.

Chapter 10

She rolled over to find only the imprint of his head on the pillow and felt a sudden pang of disappointment. But then she inhaled the aroma of bacon and eggs and smiled. She got up and quickly brushed her teeth and splashed some water on her face. She attempted to cover up her dark under eye circles and cleaned up the mascara she had not gotten around to washing off last night. She was about to start changing when he came into the room, proudly presenting a tray with a breakfast spread.

"Get back into bed," he said. "It's called breakfast in bed for a reason."

"Wow, this is a first." She plopped back down and positioned the pillows to prop herself up.

"Seriously?" he asked, a look of concern crossing his face.

"Yeah, seriously. I've never had breakfast in bed. Well, except for at a hotel once when I was a little kid."

"That doesn't count." He grabbed her hand and kissed it. "My lady, I present to you your first and well-overdue breakfast in bed, made with only the freshest ingredients." He placed the tray carefully on her lap. She beamed.

"Thank you so much, this looks amazing." He had even put a small flower from the bouquet in a shot glass on the side of the tray.

"It's my pleasure." He kissed the top of her head.

She bit into the eggs and hashbrowns. "Mmmm… this is so good! You are quite the cook!"

"My mother taught me many things, including how to impress a woman with food. "Just wait until I cook you dinner."

"Oh wow, I can't wait" she said, not caring that her mouth was full. "Aren't you going to have some, too?"

"Nah, I mean I had a few bites but I am not much of a breakfast person."

"Your loss."

"It's better watching you enjoy it anyways. I could watch you all day long, you know."

"You would be bored out of your mind."

"No, I wouldn't. You fascinate me."

She could feel her cheeks redden.

"And I wish I could spend the day with you but I'm actually golfing with an old buddy of mine I met in college."

A wave of disappointment hit her again. "Oh that's nice. Yeah go enjoy yourself and have some guy time."

"Thank you," he said. "I actually should head out now. Our tee time is in 45 minutes and I still need to grab my bag. But I cleaned up the kitchen best I could."

"Thank you, this was all so sweet of you."

"Of course. You enjoy the rest of your breakfast in bed and I will see myself out. Call you later," he leaned over and pecked her on the cheek.

"Have fun," she said, giving him what she hoped was a sexy grin before he left.

After nearly cleaning her plate, (damn he really was a great cook on top of everything else), she poured herself another cup of coffee and returned to bed. She might as well make the most of her first breakfast in bed. She turned on the TV and began to submerge herself in another mindless episode of The Bachelor. She felt content, knowing that she would have the day to herself and then Asa would return to her. Hopefully tonight. She would have him all to herself unlike these other women, all pinning after this one man, who paled in comparison to Asa.

Suddenly her doorbell rang, shocking her enough to spill coffee on her T-shirt. She jumped out of bed, assuming it was Asa having forgotten something.

She answered the door with a huge smile. A small but extremely in shape Asian man greeted her with an equally enthusiastic smile. "Ms. Emerson?" he asked.

"Yes, that's me," she answered with uncertainty.

"Ms. Emerson, your Peloton bike has arrived." He motioned towards the large truck behind him. Elle was completely confused for a second but then she realized that Ami's brother had gotten her the bike even after she had turned it down. She felt a surge of revulsion and anger.

Did he really think that buying her a bike all these years later would take back or make up for his complete disregard of her? She was about to tell the nice man that she would not be taking it after all, but as he ran down to the truck where another man jumped out to help him unload it, she decided that she really did want the bike. Who wouldn't? Regardless of the circumstances it was still a Peloton bike that she couldn't buy on her own otherwise right now.

She decided to place the bike by her open bay window in the front room. There really wasn't much other choice, unless she wanted it in her bedroom, but she wanted the open view. After the men gave her a tutorial on how to use the bike, she was beyond excited. She tipped them both $10 that she conveniently remembered she had in her junk drawer and immediately called Ami as they left.

"Hey lady, so I just got my bike!"

"Me, too! How excited are you?!"

"Super pumped."

"And my brother is paying for the first year of classes, too!" Ami said. "So neither of us have any excuses. Tight asses here we come!" She laughed.

"Wow, this is all so generous of him," Elle said.

"Right?! The best bro a girl could have. I'm going to send him an Edible arrangement from both of us as a thank you. I'm actually trying to order it right now."

"Oh perfect." She felt relieved that she would not have to personally thank him. "Yeah, I can Venmo you however much."

"Don't worry about it. Just can we please meet up for lunch today? I have been jonesing for some sushi all week. Really the only downfall I can say about Clay is that he does not share my love for Sushi."

"Of course. My treat then." Elle was not crazy about sushi but she tolerated it, knowing how much Ami enjoyed it.

"Oh yay! I didn't think today could get even better. Noon at Juno then?"

"That works."

Elle and Ami spent some time before hanging up setting up their profiles on the monitor, naming themselves "Climb for Wine" and "Sweat for Sweets" respectively. They played around with the monitor, browsing through all the classes, live and recorded. Elle became increasingly excited as she explored all the bikes' features. Any initial anger she had felt had almost completely subsided. Perhaps she should be more forgiving. He was at least making an effort for the sins of his past, when he was still in fact a child.

On her way out the door to meet Ami for lunch, freshly showered, her still damp hair falling every which way, she almost turned back inside when she realized that Mr. Jensen was retrieving his mail. She didn't want to be late though and she also didn't want to feel like she needed to hide from him. So she strode confidently down her steps and greeted him before he could.

He looked up from his mail and eyed her slowly, a smirk forming on his face. "Sounded like you had some company last night."

She whisked by him, too in shock to respond.

"Have a nice day," he called out as she walked briskly to her car and peeled away. She wished she could have taken her gesture back. And her wine back, too.

When she arrived at Juno, saki bombs were already ordered and waiting. Elle immediately took hers, attempting to calm her nerves. Ami was aghast as Elle recounted both encounters with Mr. Jensen.

"What a nasty old man!" she nearly screamed, hitting her palm on the table, prompting an older couple to turn and look at them.

"Yeah, I could kick myself for trying to be nice to him. I just thought I would attempt to get on his good side. After that party I threw last year got a bit out of hand and all. I always suspected he was creepy and, well, obviously it's confirmed now."

"You should just completely ignore him. If he makes another inappropriate comment, tell him you will go to the police."

"I don't want to start anything," Elle said matter of factly. "I love my home and have no desire to move. I will just do my best to avoid him."

Ami continued on about how she could make a lawsuit against him, as she was prone to do when she really got going. Elle half listened as Ami presented possible options to split, agreeing to whatever Ami thought sounded good. Ami ended up ordering edamame, chicken satay, shrimp tempura rolls and spicy tuna rolls, none of which Elle could really enjoy as she was still full from her breakfast in bed.

The women excitedly discussed Elle's new romance, Ami's upcoming bachelorette party and more details about her wedding. Although Elle was happy to be with her best friend she found her mind wandering to thoughts of Asa and had to remind herself to refocus.

"I can tell you are super distracted," Ami finally said, smiling. She used her chopsticks to expertly grab another roll. "I really can't wait to meet him! Or rather see him again. And now you will have a date for my wedding!"

"Yeah, hopefully you're right. I didn't even think about that," Elle said. "And I'm sorry for being so distracted. I guess I really am head over heels."

"You have nothing to be sorry for," Ami said, putting down her chopsticks and reaching over the table to grab Elle's hand. "You have done more than your fair share of listening to me blabbing on and on about Clay and the wedding. I am happy for you."

"Thank you," Elle said, feeling the surge of possibility once again.

After Ami paid for the meal, indicating that she ate most of it anyways, Elle offered to at least buy her ice cream. Ami protested at first but relented a few seconds later. Her sweet tooth was probably worse than Elle's. They walked a couple blocks to Hagan Daz and waited in the line that was starting to form out the door. Children impatiently complained to their parents and one little girl sobbed as her cone fell from her hands. Elle considered buying her another cone but then what appeared to be her older sister, handed the pretty blonde her own cone, stating that she "didn't really want it anyways." The little girl looked up at her and smiled in delight. The line went more quickly than expected though. Elle ordered her favorite caramel cone in a cup and Ami ordered mint chocolate chip in a cup but with a cone on top as usual.

They sat outside as there was nowhere else to sit. The humidity wasn't as intense today at least. Elle savored the creamy deliciousness of each bite and made a deal with Ami to do their first spin class at 9 a.m. tomorrow morning together and work it off. As they both neared their last melting bites, Elle's phone lit up with a text from Asa.

Just finished golfing. Want to come over to my place tonight for dinner? I can cook for you.

Ami appeared even more excited than Elle, leaning over Elle's shoulder as she responded.

That sounds great. What time are you thinking and what can I bring?

Around 7pm if that works for you. And nothing but your beautiful self. Also, do you like spaghetti and meatballs?

That works and yes, I love spaghetti and meatballs.

Awesome. You are in for a treat then.

Ami clapped as Elle finished the text exchange. "That's so sweet he is going to cook for you."

"He already made me breakfast in bed this morning. I really should be the one cooking for him."

"Stop it. He obviously wants to. And you deserve it. Now go have fun." Ami stood up and Elle followed, tossing their empty cups. After confirming their spin class the next day and exchanging goodbyes, Ami gave Elle a big hug, holding on longer than usual. Elle could sense that she was relieved to finally see Elle happy with someone who had real potential. Someone who gave her a positive focus. Someone Elle could turn to as she inevitably became consumed in her new marriage and her husband took precedence.

Chapter 11

Asa ordered her a limo despite Elle protesting that this was unnecessary. It arrived at 6:45 p.m. as she was changing back into her original outfit, a long, high waisted skirt and bodysuit. The driver, a nice middle aged man, put her at ease, driving cautiously, and distracting her with his difficult to follow stories due to his broken English. Elle laughed and smiled politely at the appropriate junctures.

She was pretty blown away by the elegance of the building as he pulled in. It seemed too flashy and blingy for a straight man's taste. The doorman greeted her with gusto and buzzed her right up to the 10th floor when she announced that she was there to see Asa. However, when she entered his condo, it felt just like him—masculine, modern and minimal. He greeted her wearing an adorable apron and a huge smile.

"Welcome, welcome," he said, giving her a quick kiss on the lips. "You look gorgeous as ever."

"Thank you." She batted her lashes that she had taken the time to apply an extra layer of mascara on. How is everything going? It smells absolutely amazing in here!"

"Oh good. I am just about done cooking. Just got to perfect the sauce and throw the garlic bread in the oven."

"No rush. Take your time." He placed his hand on the small of her back—how could such a small gesture be so electrifying?—and guided her to the kitchen, which was without a doubt, any chef's dream. It smelled so intensely of herbs and spices that her mouth began to water.

"Wow, this is so impressive! And look how clean you are!" All the used pots and pans were already on the drying rack and the counters appeared immaculate.

"I try to clean as I go. Less work at the end. A cooking pointer that has stuck with me." He motioned her to come towards the full range Wolf Gang stove and tasted the sauce before spooning a bite into her mouth as well.

"Mmmmm, sooo good."

"Do you think it needs anything else?"

"Nope, I think you nailed it."

"No, that's for later," he laughed. She pinched his slightly dimpled cheek.

They ate by candlelight in the dining room, already carefully set with ample wine waiting. He pulled her chair out for her and served her a generous portion she knew she wouldn't be able to finish. But as she bit into the first bite of spaghetti and meatballs she figured she actually just might.

"This is honestly the best spaghetti and meatballs I have ever had. Seriously."

"Why thank you but the credit goes towards my mother." He kissed his fork and motioned to the ceiling.

"She certainly taught you well."

"Yes, she did. She is the epitome of a mother in all respects. Tell me about your mom, what is she like?" he asked as he wrapped his fork in spaghetti.

She swallowed slowly, considering how to best answer this question. She decided to be brief but honest.

"Well, she has been living in England for the past couple years. She's about to marry someone from there—her third marriage. I wish I could describe her in a more positive light, but to be perfectly candid, she's a complex and self-centered woman. She has never been especially supportive of me and I have never felt close with her though I have tried. She is someone I tolerate simply because she is still my mother."

Asa put his fork down. "I'm sorry to hear that."

"It's totally fine. I've never known differently so I guess I don't know what I've been missing out on, you know? Kinda like how I felt before you and now that I know…" She felt herself blush. She had gone too far. This was only their third date after all.

But he got up from the end of the table and walked toward her and looking intently into her eyes he said, "I know. I feel the same way." He kissed her deeply. Nothing was so good as this. The spaghetti and meatballs would have to wait.

They languished in bed the next morning, enjoying not being rushed with the entire day looming in front of them. Their dirty dinner plates and wine glasses sat on the nightstands, since dinner turned into dinner in bed. He gave her a new toothbrush and she took her time showering, trying out his Dr. Kiel's products, a brand not feasible on a teacher's salary. Especially when she already indulged by shopping at Whole Foods. His towels were spa material, soft and fluffy and smelling like they were straight out of the dryer. She used the corner to wipe the foggy mirror. Her face was completely washed without a hint of makeup, her eyelashes blonde and seemingly nonexistent. But she didn't care. She already felt comfortable enough with him and didn't feel the need to be self-conscious, something that she had never been free of even in her longest relationship in college.

She put on several different lotions. No wonder he had such great skin. She tousled her damp hair and slipped on the robe he had carefully folded on the counter. She joined him in the kitchen, the trickle of coffee brewing and eggs and pancakes sizzling on the stove.

"Jeez, I feel bad that you have been cooking for me so much." She came up behind him and rubbed his bare back as he stirred the eggs.

"I enjoy every bit of it." He smiled and kissed the tip of her nose. "How was your shower?"

"Amazing. I didn't want to get out. Well except I did because I'm excited to spend the day with you."

"Me, too. I am totally open to doing whatever you like. There is still so much I haven't done or seen in Chicago. The art museum, Navy Pier, The Shedd Aquarium—well I guess we did do a field there in middle school. But I just want to do it all with you."

She beamed. "We totally can do it all. And I'm honored to be your guide."

"How lucky am I? You're the sexiest tour guide I've ever seen." He turned off the burners. "You look so beautiful in your robe with your curly wet hair, so Julia Roberts esque. I'm one lucky man alright."

"And I am one lucky girl." She trailed her finger down the curves of his stomach muscles as he divided the steaming food onto two plates.

He kissed her gently, still holding the empty pan. "Let's actually eat breakfast though." He laughed. "Cold eggs are just the worst and we have a big day ahead of us."

And that they did. After purchasing a $175 outfit, paid for by Asa despite her protests, they headed to the Chicago Art Museum, Elle's favorite icon of the city naturally. She enthusiastically explained several artist's styles and their distinctions and similarities. Asa appeared to soak it all in, with a serious expression on his face that made Elle smile. She was attracted to him all that much more for showing an interest in her passion for art. No one she had dated had ever taken a solid interest in getting to know such an important part of her life.

Nearly four hours later, they headed to Navy Pier and sat outside by the Ferris wheel to eat lunch, famished. They both ordered hot dogs, fries and Diet Cokes from a stand they were so hungry. Elle could not remember the last time she had a hot dog. Or soda for that matter. She had hers plain, while Asa submerged his with every topping, which Elle could not help commenting on. Asa dared her to try it. She wasn't a huge condiment person but in spite of herself she went for it and nearly threw up. Asa got her a huge hot pink cotton candy for being such a good sport, feeding her the first bite of fluff. It instantly melted in her mouth and brought back memories of when she was a child at the fair, getting lost with Ami.

After a few more cavity inducing bites, Asa insisted on riding the Ferris wheel despite the long line. Elle was hesitant to do so. She was not a fan of heights but it was worth it. They shared a magical kiss at the peak of the wheel, one that she would certainly always remember. Even with her fear of heights, she felt safe sitting next to Asa. With him, there was no past or future, just the glorious present.

To top off the day, they grabbed a few beers before heading to the Shedd Aquarium where they mostly sat and watched the dolphins swim in comforting silence, Elle resting her head on his shoulder. She could have easily stayed in that moment forever.

Chapter 12

Three blissfully happy days later, the text came to her like a slap in the face. She had not heard from him all day, which was starting to give her anxiety. She had kept telling herself he was probably just super inundated at work. She had been consuming a lot of his time and energy after all. She could be a reasonable person.

So she attempted to distract herself—going for a bike ride, working on some pottery, scrolling through Pinterest for some new art ideas for her students. As she was saving some Mandala rock art to her "Classroom" board, the text came in.

It was long and she knew immediately that it was over. Her heart raced and her eyes spilled over. She could barely make out the words.

Elle, I am beyond heartbroken to be sending you this text. I know I should have called or told you in person but I don't think I would be able to without breaking down. I went back to Wisconsin yesterday to see my ex-wife and my—baby. Yes, I have a son! He is three days old and perfect. As I told you my ex-wife suffered from multiple miscarriages while we were married. When we broke up, she was actually pregnant but decided not to tell me unless it resulted in a healthy birth. And it did. She called me yesterday and told me. I was in absolute disbelief until I held him. He has my chin and eyes and so much hair. I am so over the moon to be a father, Elle, but I am also so devastated that my relationship with you now has to end. I need to be the father my son deserves and put him first. I am moving back to Wisconsin and am going to try to work things out with my ex because that is the right thing to do. I am so sorry that it had to play out this way. What I had with you was real and beyond amazing. You will always hold a special place in my heart and I wish you all the love and happiness you deserve.

He ended the text with a photo of a dreamy newborn in a blue beanie along with the caption, "My son, Sebastian." Elle stared at the newborn. The baby certainly had his chin and a perfectly symmetrical nose. Actually, his entire face looked like Asa's despite being puffy and pinched. There was no denying Sebastian was his son.

As she continued to stare at the photo, she felt so much joy for Asa but also resentment that this baby had essentially torn him away from her. She knew that this was completely unfair and irrational. She couldn't help thinking that if he really loved her that much, he would still want to be with her. He could have invited her to come live with him in Wisconsin to be near his son. Wouldn't he? She would have put everything aside for him and his son, even if it meant leaving her city so full of life, so full of her life, and moving to Wisconsin. She would have easily done that to be with him. On autopilot and with shaky hands she replied,

Congratulations. He's perfect. I'm very happy for you. Best of luck with everything.

She didn't know what else to say. Her hands continued to shake as she reached for a wine glass. She poured herself a tall glass which then fell to the floor, shattering in a million pieces just like her life had become in that instant.

The sobs ravaged her body. She lay on the cold tile, next to the blood red liquid and all the shards of glass, curled in a fetal position, defeated and pathetic. What if she were to cut herself with a shard of glass and end the pain right now? The crazy thought made her sob even harder, quaking through her entire body, unrelenting and uncontrollable.

She cried until her body was dry and exhausted and she literally felt like she could not move. She simply stared at the disaster on her tile with absolutely no motivation to clean it up. She located a lone Cheerio under the stove. That was her. Alone and lonely forever. Her eyes welled again. But she got herself up from the floor and poured herself a new glass of wine in a plastic cup and gulped it before she could start crying again.

She gulped the entire glass without breathing like she was back in her college days. And then another. Her head started to spin and her body, heavy with grief, instantly felt light and airy. She sipped another glass until she felt numb. Then she cleaned up the mess, grabbing a broom and dustpan, and forced herself to get in the shower.

She would go out by herself. She couldn't be alone and she was not ready to tell Ami about the breakup. She was too shocked. She stood motionless in the shower for ten minutes before she finally washed herself thoroughly, washing herself of him and all the expectations she had for their future. Through the sadness she also felt anger towards him for leading her on so quickly. But mostly the anger was at herself, for letting herself be taken there so quickly. Drying herself with her towel she screamed into it, remembering his ridiculously soft towels. Hers were old and stained.

Though very tipsy, Elle somehow managed to apply her makeup with a steady hand. She applied more eyeliner than she normally did. She wanted to be noticed tonight. She wanted to forget all about him even if it was just for the night.

She blew her hair out slowly, allowing it the time needed to become perfectly straight. She slipped on a short skirt from her twenties that she had not worn since but refused to part with still, and a sheer peacock blue top that was quite complementary with her red hair. She chose some of her highest heels and finished her outfit with some long earrings and a small clutch purse. She admired herself in her full length mirror. She looked pretty damn good especially compared to what she looked like just an hour ago. She forced a smile in the mirror. She could pass for normal.

As she waited for her Uber to arrive she had a beer that she had discovered in the back of the fridge. Walking down her steps she had to put effort into balancing in her heels. She was definitely drunk now.

"You look very nice tonight," the driver commented as she got into the backseat. He was a handsome black man. She simply thanked him suddenly feeling shy and awkward. When he pulled up in front of the bar a few minutes later, she almost told the driver to turn around, her surge of confidence gone.

But no, she would do this.

She refused to just go back home and feel sorry for herself. So she got out, thanking her driver who told her to "have a nice night sweetheart," admiring her legs as she strut up to the front door. A group of men sitting at the bar looked up from their drinks in unison as she came in. They smiled approvingly at her while a few women on the other side gave her a quick assessment and looked away. She went right up to an empty seat between the groups and asked more confidently than she felt if the seat was open. She was back in elementary school trying to find an empty seat on the bus. They nodded and she sat down relieved, flinging her purse over the chair, almost dropping it.

The bartender, an extremely attractive man with dark everything, took her order-an extra dry martini, as a group of women entered, laughing. She admired his biceps, slightly larger than Asa's, bulging through his shirt as he shook the concoction and expertly poured every last drop into the glass, topping it off with two green olives.

"Thank you," she said as he delivered the drink to her with a flash of white teeth.

"You bet." She handed him her card. "You can keep it open," she said before he could ask. He winked at her, highlighting his extremely long and jealousy worthy eyelashes.

She conscientiously made an effort to not spill her martini as she brought it up to her lips, rimming it with a perfect kiss of lipstick.

"Waiting for someone?" the guy next to her leaned over, a wave of his cologne hitting her.

"Actually, no," she replied. "Just wanted to get out for a drink."

"Well, the next one is on me if that's OK with you." She looked directly into his brown eyes, so dark they almost looked black against his pale skin. His smile was sweet and genuine. He was not as attractive as Asa but he was attractive nonetheless. And he did appear to be a bit younger, most likely still in his late twenties, evidenced by his lack of hair recession and lines around his eyes.

"Why thank you, that is a very kind gesture."

"Of course." He smiled, revealing a prominent dimple. "I'm Jake." He held out his hand and she grasped it. He squeezed ever so slightly. "Elle, nice to meet you."

"You as well. Have you been here before?"

"Actually, no. I'm just in town on business. From Ohio. With my business crew here. Trying to let loose a little before our big convention tomorrow." Of course another attractive and unavailable man.

"Oh that's nice. What kind of work do you do?"

"We are in software sales. Nothing fancy or interesting there. Plus I'm more interested in you. Tell me about you." His face came closer to hers. She did not draw back.

"Um, I'm an art teacher. Elementary school. I'm from here. Not too fancy or interesting either."

"I doubt that. Tell me something that you have never told anyone. Or at least that most people don't know about you," he raised his eyebrows in challenge.

"Oh wow, something I have never told anyone to a complete

stranger." She laughed, her mind racing to think of something that would be interesting but not too revealing.

She took another sip of her martini, pondering, and then despite herself replied mischievously, "well, I've never slept with a younger man."

He laughed a hearty and deep laugh that prompted his friend next to him to peer over and knuckle him in the head in good spirits.

"Frank," the man said, holding out his hand to Elle, which she leaned over and took. "Didn't want to interrupt but also didn't want to be rude since this knucklehead probably wouldn't have introduced us."

"I absolutely was going to!" Jake protested. "This is Elle. And this is Steven, Josh and Chris." The other men gave polite waves as Elle said hello. They were older and all wore wedding bands. They definitely seemed like a nice and respectable group of men. Frank turned back to the others allowing Elle and Jake to resume their conversation.

"Wow, that is not what I was expecting," he said, his eyes studying her.

"Sorry, that was too much." Elle regretted her admission but oh well, she would have to own it.

"No, I think it's great. I love your honesty. Would you like to change that?" he asked, peering even more closely at her. She was hoping that he was not inspecting her crow's feet, her self-consciousness returning.

She giggled nervously. "I'm not sure who would be interested in an older woman."

"Are you kidding?!" he asked, looking incredulous. "You are stunning. And here's something most people, well besides my best friend, Joe, don't know about me. I have never slept with a red head, let alone kissed one. And I would love to see that lipstick on my lips," he finished, eyeing her lipstick marked martini glass.

"Wow, so you have slept with a woman older than you?" she asked, now completely brazen.

"Yes, Ma'am," he took her hand and kissed it. "And far older than you."

"Um, do you want to get out of here by chance?" she asked. Obviously fully aware of what she was getting herself into.

"With you, I'd go anywhere," he said with a straight face. "But don't you want to finish your drink first?"

"Nope, I've had enough to drink and I want to remember this in the morning." She was on fire. "I just have to close my tab out and use the restroom."

"Why don't I close your tab and you go to the restroom," he offered.

"Sounds good." She knew she was really entrusting this man. It's Elle Emerson."

"Sounds good Elle Emerson," he smiled a perfectly seductive smile as she grabbed her purse and carefully steadied herself off the bar stool. She felt like she was floating as she walked to the bathroom. She could not believe she just did that, but screw it. Sleeping with someone else would help confuse all the intimate intricacies she was holding onto with Asa.

She walked past a group of girls who were clearly celebrating a bachelorette party. "Congratulations," she said to the pretty and petite blonde wearing the prerequisite "Bride to Be" sash, swallowing a tinge of resentment.

"Thank you!" she squealed, and all the young women cheered.

She was reminded of Ami and her upcoming bachelorette. Ami would not be partaking in any of that cliche bachelorette party hype though. She felt almost rebellious having not shared her breakup and impending hook up with her yet.

And then as if her thought of Ami conjured her appearance, there she stood in her striking splendor next to Clay. He had his arms wrapped around her waist as they kissed deeply, his fingers brushing through her long auburn hair. He had on the same shirt that he wore the night she had them over for dinner, a vibrant and somewhat ugly conglomerate of colored stripes. She slowed her stride, not wanting to burst in on their make out session, but then Ami broke away from him suddenly and turned, laughing, as he attempted to prevent her from leaving.

Her mouth parted to form her name but then her mind caught up and she froze, mouth agape. This was not Ami. This was another woman who looked nothing like Ami with the exception of the long red hair. What the fuck?! She turned around and slipped out the back exit as quickly as she could, stunned. Had she not been so inebriated she would have confronted him right then and there.

She hailed a cab and robotically gave the female driver her address, in complete disbelief. But she knew exactly what she saw. That woman was clearly not Ami, not even close. In just two seconds she could clearly assess that she was not nearly as attractive as Ami.

Her facial structure was not as pronounced and the giant rose tattoo coming out of her cleavage was certainly not something Ami would ever consider getting. And she was at least three inches shorter, even taking into account the extreme high heels she had on. Her heart broke again for the second time that night as she told the driver to keep the change from her twenty and made her way back up her stairs, alone.

She immediately got in bed, only bothering to take off her heels, and cried herself to sleep.

He was desperate to see her naked. All day at school he couldn't stay focused envisioning every beautiful curve of her milky white skin. He waited for her to be done with cheerleading practice in the library where he pretended to do his homework. He waited another ten minutes until the girls left the gymnasium, sweating and oh so delicious in their little skirts that left a pinch of ass hanging out like a little snack to nibble on before the main course.

She would immediately shower when she got home. He knew her parents worked late and didn't even get home until 7 p.m. most nights. If they only knew what their daughter did unsupervised.

He could already hear the shower going when he got inside, her uniform and panties thrown to the floor. Her bed, which Pierce had fucked her in countless times was perfectly made. Obviously, they had a housekeeper. The bathroom door was ajar, steam and the scent of flowers escaping.

He watched as she touched her body. Her long, perfectly sculpted legs, her smooth stomach and ample breasts. She washed her hair next, her beautiful hair that came down to her ass, as if she wanted people to look at it. She arched the curve of her elegant back as she rinsed her hair.

As she reached for her razor and started shaving the little patch of red hair that Pierce thought he only saw, he could hear someone opening the door, the click of heels pounding up the stairs. Shit, shit, shit. He didn't have time. He opened her window, its long lace drapes getting twisted around him.

A flashback of him and Pierce playing on the playground randomly infiltrated his mind. They couldn't have been more than six years old. They were playing on the monkey bars as a young girl in pigtails watched them, hesitant to join. Their father and her mother sat on a nearby bench, his father's face buried in a newspaper.

His hands already felt calloused and burned but he felt compelled to keep up with his brother, who swung himself over the bars with ease. He wanted so badly to impress the girl and prove that he could be just as athletic as his brother.

"Wow, is that your son?" He could overhear the woman asking his dad.

He did not add that both boys were actually his sons. "Yes, that is my son," he clearly said.

"He is going to be quite the athlete," she remarked. "And what a handsome boy on top of it!"

"Thank you. Yes, my wife and I certainly lucked out with him."

And at that he fell from the bars and broke his wrist. His brother's laugh echoed in the background as he screamed and the girl and her mother looked at him wide eyed. His father did not run to him. Instead he took his time, folding his newspaper neatly, before he approached the inconvenient situation.

At that moment he jumped and fell into a bush but this time he didn't break anything. He was indestructible now.

Chapter 13

Elle woke with her clothes still on, her skirt hiked up to her waist. Her pillow was saturated in tears and mascara. Her head was pounding and her entire body ached.

She slowly moved to an upright position and slung her legs over the bed, standing on unsteady feet as she hobbled over to the bathroom and retrieved three Advil from the mirror cabinet. She swallowed them with the tap, on the verge of throwing them right back up, and then retreated to her bed once more.

The memories of last night overtook her along with a flood of sadness and anger, first for herself, and then for Ami. She was too hungover to even put together a sentence but she knew she would have to tell her what she witnessed last night. That man did not deserve even one more second of Ami's time. Of her beauty, intelligence, humor and kindness. The anger she felt towards Clay heightened her anger towards Asa. In fact, she wasn't really sad at all anymore, just beyond pissed with the unfairness of the world.

How could he simply go running back to his ex-wife as if she meant absolutely nothing to him, with no hesitation? And he had the audacity to do it over text at that.

So what if he and his ex had a baby together?

Babies should not be used as pawns to keep unhappy parents together. It was certainly best for the child to know no different than have them divorce when he's older. And she could be a positive mother figure towards him. She was great with kids.

She turned on the TV and watched images flicker across the screen on mute in too much pain physically and emotionally to change the channel. After twenty minutes her headache subsided. She got up and forced herself to drink a bottle of water, eat a banana and take a shower. She brushed her teeth twice, until the disgusting alcohol taste lingering in her mouth was gone. Feeling somewhat more human, she reached for her phone preparing her approach with Ami. But really there was no approach she could take that would make it hurt any less.

Ami answered on the first ring, chipper and bright. She certainly wasn't hungover. This was going to be so hard.

"Hey, how are you?! I just got done riding. God, am I so out of shape! But wow, do I feel so good now."

"Good for you," Elle responded. "Wish I could say the same."

"You sound a bit hungover." Ami could always access her drinking habits accurately.

"I am, although hungover doesn't even begin to encompass it all." She needed to just cut to the chase.

"Oh no, what do you mean?" Ami asked, her voice growing deep with concern.

"Would you rather meet in person?" Elle knew full well that she was not one for suspense.

"No, I mean yes, of course, but tell me now. You know I can't wait. What's going on?"

"Ok, but is Clay there?"

"No, he's traveling to perform this weekend. He left about an hour ago. Why?" Ami asked, her voice exasperated.

Elle sighed heavily. "Ok, well, first off Asa is no longer. He is moving back to Wisconsin and trying to work things out with his ex-wife who just gave birth to his child."

"Wait whaaat?" Ami's voice rose again.

"Yeah, I guess she was reluctant to tell him that she was pregnant again when they divorced because of all the miscarriages she had while they had been married. Wanted to see if it would really come to fruition I guess. Well, it certainly did. He sent me a picture of him holding his boy last night. And it's clearly his child, it looks just like him."

"Wow, wow, wow, that's crazy! I mean, what horrible timing! I'm so sorry Elle. I know how much you were into him."

"I know, thanks. I'm just trying to be happy for him. He wanted a baby so badly."

"Yeah but you could have given him that!" Ami almost shouted. "Sorry, sorry, I shouldn't have said that."

"No, it's OK. I really was hoping things were going in that direction. After some time of course. I really did see a future with him. More than any other guy I have ever been with."

"Ugh, this sucks. I'm coming over right now. Well, after I shower. I'm drenched in sweat."

Elle's heart started racing. She thought that was all there was. She needed to get the rest out before she lost her nerve to tell her.

"Ami, that's not everything unfortunately."

"Oh my God, don't tell me you are pregnant!?"

"No, no, no," Elle shook her head. In that case maybe Asa would have chosen to be with her after all. She quickly reverted her mind back to the task at hand. "It's about Clay."

"Clay?! What about Clay?"

"I um… went out after everything with Asa last night. I just needed to get out of my place, I was so upset." She bit into her fingernails, a childhood habit she had put to rest long ago.

"Oh Elle, why didn't you call me?"

"I know, I would have. But I guess I was just so in shock, you know? So I just went out and sat at the bar for a bit. Met a nice guy…" she was postponing the inevitable.

"Oh look at you! Already meeting someone else, see?!"

Elle ignored her. "And then I got up to go to the bathroom and I saw, I saw…. Clay making out with another girl."

"Wait what? That's not possible at all. Clay was home after playing poker with his friends early at like 7 p.m.!" Ami laughed.

Elle's mind searched for the timeframe to back up her story but she could not think quickly enough for specifics. "It was definitely before 7 p.m. And it was definitely him with another woman, a woman who I thought was you at first because I only saw her long red hair from the back—but they were making out hard. Not just a little kissing. Like they really knew each other." Elle decided to just lay it all out there. Ami needed to know the severity.

Elle continued to bite another fingernail. "And how much were you drinking, Elle?" Ami said in an unexpectedly cold tone. This was not the first question Elle had anticipated.

"I had a few glasses of wine, a martini at the bar when I got there, but that's not the point, Ami. I know what I saw, and I saw Clay making out with another woman. I'm so sorry."

The longest seconds of silence followed.

"Ami?" Elle asked hesitantly. She wished she had waited to tell her in person so she could comfort her while she cried.

"You are such a jealous and sabotaging drunk!" Ami snapped.

Elle felt another slap to her face. "What? No, Ami. I swear I'm telling the truth! I wish I wasn't! I would never want to ruin your relationship or for you to be unhappy!"

Ami came back at her quickly, her lawyer tone taking full effect. "You have always been jealous of my relationships and were secretly happy when I got a divorce. I know it. And now that I'm getting remarried again you feel threatened. I just know it, Elle. I have known you for too long. And now that you and Asa didn't work out, you are that much more bitter and wanting to tear me down. But guess what? You will not succeed."

"No, Ami, that's not true…" she stammered. She could not think straight, could not defend herself, frantic, hungover and pathetic against a lawyer of all people. Her heart was racing uncontrollably, on the verge of a panic attack.

"I am done, done with our friendship. Done, Elle. I wish you the best, I do. And I do hope you get the help you need for your drinking. I just can't be a part of this anymore. I refuse to let you and your issues ruin my happiness." Her voice was flat and distant.

Elle's throat tightened in desperation, fighting back tears. "Please, Ami, please, you are my best friend in the entire world…" she choked.

The phone line died then and she felt herself die with it.

She didn't know what to do with herself. She wanted to scream and break things but instead she sat there on her sofa completely defeated, staring at the clock ticking the time away. Ami had never lost it on her like this. Ever. Which made it feel as if there was no return. She was a matter of fact person, black and white. Guilty or not guilty.

She should have known that Clay would have come first. She should have confronted him last night instead of cowardly walking out, or waited until she had more evidence. Or not have told her at all, though she knew she wouldn't have been an option. She could keep a secret from her as she had done all these years with her brother, but only when it came to what was in Ami's best interest. And it was in her best interest to know that Clay was yet another cheating asshole.

Nearly two decades of friendship done just like that in less than five minutes. Over the desire to help her, to save her from another disappointing and fake marriage. She would have hoped that Ami would have done the same for her. It was shocking how Ami could be so quick to disown her. Obviously she had never valued the friendship, not the way Elle did. The fact that Ami truly believed that Elle was out to get her, was jealous of her and didn't want her to be happy, felt more than she could bear. Even worse than yesterday's surprise.

Now she did wish she could take it all back and just say nothing. Let her figure it out on her own. Better yet, she wished she never had gone out to the bar last night at all. What was she thinking going out like that drunk and alone, inviting complete strangers over?

And then her doorbell rang. Could it really be her? She had calmed down and come to her senses. Thank God. She would hug Elle and Elle would comfort her as Ami apologized to her between sobs. She leapt up with urgent relief and opened the door as quickly as she could, a smile already forming on her face.

"Wow, I didn't think you would be this happy to see me!" Her heart sank. It was the guy from the bar last night. Her brain searched for his name. She had always been terrible with names, drinking or not.

"Oh hi, um... sorry, I was, um… expecting someone else."

He looked at her curiously. "Ah I see, did you order some hangover food? I totally get it. I'm definitely feeling it myself. I actually left my work event early 'cause I felt like I might throw up on someone. Sorry, TMI. Anyways, you left your credit card at the bar last night and I wanted to make sure you got it back OK." He retrieved her card from his wallet and handed it to her.

"Oh, wow, thank you. I totally forgot about that." She took it with a slightly shaking hand.

"You probably forgot my name as well. It's Jake. No offense taken of course." He gave her a cute one sided grin. She couldn't help but notice a speck of something on his nose. A good looking nose, straight, and fitting for his face. She resisted the urge to reach out again and remove the only imperfection on his face.

"Oh yes, that's right. Jake. Thank you. Yes, I am so sorry for leaving so abruptly like that, without even saying goodbye. I had a bit of an emergency."

"No issue at all. I hope everything is alright now?" He looked genuinely concerned.

"Um, well, not really, but I'm sure eventually it will be." She felt like she was going to start crying again and bit her lip.

"I'm sure it will be," he said matter of factly staring intently into her eyes.

She averted his gaze, knowing how blood shot her eyes must be.

"Well, would you like to come in?" she asked, overcome by a sudden wave of loneliness.

"Sure. That would be great," he replied without hesitation.

She stepped back to allow him to pass. Despite her state, physically and emotionally, she let it all go. Fifteen minutes later she let him possess her, allowing her brain to shut off, knowing she would never see him again.

That night, sitting outside on her patio with a glass of wine, she started formulating a text to send to Ami. She was careful in her word choice but honest. After a half hour of debate though, she erased it all. She would allow Ami the time to come to her when she was ready. She would eventually come around. She was too damn smart to just look the other way and put herself in jeopardy again. She would catch Clay in a lie in no time. Obviously last night was not his first rendezvous and it wouldn't be his last.

She felt the first small sense of control she had felt in the past couple of days, confident in her decision to withstand reaching out as badly as she wanted to. Plus she was hurt and wanted and deserved an apology first, as childish as that sounded. She knew Ami was hurt, too, of course.

She finally felt some sort of numbing calm with each sip of wine as a text came through. Her heart jolted. But it was only the last bachelorette invitee finally responding that unfortunately she wouldn't be able to make it as she would be on her long overdue honeymoon. Long overdue. The unnecessary detail infuriated her. As if everyone got to go on a honeymoon in their lifetime.

She quickly sent out a group text to the girls who had committed to the party, which was now three weekends away, and let them know without explanation that she would no longer be facilitating the party. She requested that they should reach out to Ami directly to see what she would like to do as she would be canceling all reservations.

She knew how odd this seemed and expected some questioning but fortunately nobody responded with inquiries. Probably too consumed with their husbands and children to really care. She took a deep breath, actually relieved not to have to be dealing with the whole bachelorette party anymore. She wouldn't cancel the reservations right away though. Ami would come around before then.

She slowly drank her wine, watching the sun slide down the horizon like a slippery egg yolk amongst a fury of intense and convoluted colors. She could not help but think of Asa and how nice it would be to share watching this sunset with him. She wondered what he was doing. Most likely cuddling up next to his ex-wife watching the same sunset from Wisconsin as the baby slept peacefully in her arms.

She topped off her glass and texted Ben to see if he would like to grab lunch or something tomorrow. She could see him replying and then nothing.

She heard a rustling below and peered over her gate to see a couple squirrels coming out from between two bushes. She watched as they nervously fidgeted around and then scampered back into the bushes. The first flicker of fire flies illuminated the sky as darkness began to fall. She and Ami used to always catch them as scabby kneed kids in the seemingly endless days of summer. They would make wishes before releasing them back into the sky.

Of course this was when the beauty of possibility and excitement still consumed her. When she still felt confident that one day she would be a famous artist who would delight the world with her renowned masterpieces. They would be coveted after and displayed in museums and in her favorite celebrities' homes. At the time this would have included her favorite singers, Tori Amos and Alanis Morisette, and all the cast of Friends, Boy Meets World, and Sabrina the Teenage Witch.

Suddenly Elle had a flash of a specific memory. She and Ami were having a rare sleepover at Elle's house, her mother having been on a "good mother" stint for a few weeks since her most recent breakup. The girls had squeezed together in the backyard hammock listening to the chorus of crickets as the fireflies came out. They both reached out to catch them, nearly knocking each other off the hammock, triggering an uproar of laughter that penetrated the peaceful dusk.

As the firefly frantically collided into the palms of her hands, her laughter quickly dissipated as she glimpsed her mother in the bright kitchen window, staring blankly outside into the darkness. In that one glance, she could feel how sad and lonely her mother was. How broken she still was from her father's leaving all those years ago. How she continued to fill this void with endless dating.

Normally they did not share their wishes. But as they released the fireflies back into the sky at the same time, Ami asked her what she had wished for in a dreamy voice.

"I wish my dad never left," she whispered.

"I know," Ami said, resting her head on her shoulder, as if she had already known that that was her wish. "But that's his loss. And you will always have me at least, no matter what."

Nearly two decades later, Elle reached out to grab a firefly and wished for her best friend back.

She took a hot bath, filling the tub with the lavender bath salts Ami had given her for her birthday a couple years ago. They both had never skipped a year of birthday or Christmas gifts for one another in all their years of friendship. It was a tradition that Ami had started their first year of friendship. There were several years where Elle had to scrap the money together to buy her something. If she was really down and out, she just made her something. She had made her countless ceramic platters and mugs. She wondered what would become of these as well as the portrait of her now deceased golden lab, Lucy, Elle had painted her. And the piece of metal art on her mantel.

Well at the very least she would not be responsible for any more gift giving if Ami never came around. The thought of this finality felt like a death. But deep down she knew that this could be a possibility and one she would have to accept. The numbing sensation from her wine made this idea manageable. You couldn't bring someone back from the dead and you couldn't change a person no matter how badly you wanted to.

She soaked in the hot water, relishing in the feeling of weightlessness, thankful that the alcohol had slowed her brain's thinking, until she nearly fell asleep. She would be able to fall asleep easily tonight. But after finally getting her prunny and languid body out of the tub and falling into bed, she lay there for over three hours, her mind instantly awake again, bouncing back and forth between thoughts of Asa and Ami.

At 4 a.m. she desperately reached into her nightstand for her meds but the bottle was empty. Damn it. She had forgotten to pick up her prescription today, she had been so upset. But they did have a 24 hour drive thru. She gave in, throwing on some sandals and grabbing her purse.

The early morning air was actually chilly as she walked to her car. As she fumbled for her keys in her purse, becoming aggravated, she sensed someone walking briskly behind her. There was nobody else out on the streets. She started walking faster. She kept walking past her car, not wanting to stop since she still had not located her keys.

She would walk to the end of the street and cross. She picked up her stride wanting desperately to look back at the figure, whose shadow she could see at intervals between the street lights, looming dangerously close to her.

And then she fell, her flip flops hitting an uneven sidewalk edge, her purse contents splaying everywhere, including her god forsaken keys. She frantically grabbed for everything, throwing it all back into her purse, except her keys, which she gripped tightly, preparing to use them to gauge his one eye ball out if necessary. The figure stopped and came around to her front, where she was kneeling on skinned knees, paralyzed. She slowly looked up to find her neighbor, Mr. Jensen grinning down at her.

"You OK?" he asked her, extending his hand. She reached for it tentatively and he lifted her up with a surprisingly strong motion until she was looking right into his fake eyeball. She quickly moved her focus to his real eye.

"Thank you," she said, mustering a steady voice. She would not allow this old man to intimidate her.

"You know you passed your car already," he said, his one eye looking directly into hers, diverting to her braless chest, and back to her eyes again, clearly wanting to get a rise out of her.

"Oh really?" She feigned obliviousness on both accounts. "Well thanks again. Have a good night—well day—I guess."

"I could walk you to your car if you like," he said abruptly.

She laughed nervously. "Oh, thank you but that's not necessary. It's not far."

"Suit yourself. See you around then." He winked at her and she smiled politely in return.

She turned around praying that he wouldn't grab her. She could hear him clear his throat obnoxiously and spit on the sidewalk as she nearly jogged back to her car. She immediately got in and locked the doors, her heart pounding, though she could clearly see his silhouette disappearing down the road.

Twenty minutes later, after double checking her door was locked, she was back home in bed, the Seroquel having already started to hit her. She was grateful for the exhaustion that overpowered her mind and body. Five minutes later she was in a dead sleep shut off from all feeling.

Chapter 14

He knew his father had a gun but he didn't know the code to the safe. He assumed it wouldn't be that difficult to figure out though. His father was a very simple and predictable man. He tried his father's birthday and then his brother's. And that was it. As if he needed more proof that Pierce was the favorite child.

Now he held the gun and looked at himself in the mirror. He immediately felt strong and powerful. He had the ability to easily take away his brother's life... and then some. Soon he would be getting an overwhelming amount of acknowledgment though. After the initial pity they would realize that they had been admiring the wrong brother this entire time.

He planned to take the gun out that weekend for some practice shooting. He told his mom that he had a group project he needed to work on for his English class. She didn't give it a second thought as she counted out the Gatorades and granola bars for Pierce's team practice tomorrow. He could have told her his plan and it wouldn't have registered. It was all about Pierce still—but only for a few more days.

He slept that night with the gun under his bed, writhing in anticipation. When 6 a.m. came, with the first glints of light sneaking through his blinds, he was up immediately, the most eager he had ever been to get up this early on a weekend. He crept down the basement stairs, undid the lock and retrieved the gleaning gun. He took a couple minutes admiring it, mesmerized, knowing that this object would change so many lives. He carefully stowed it along with several bullets in a duffel bag. A duffel bag that was at least a decade old but looked new, stuffed in the back of his closet, having never been on an airplane or on sleepover since second grade at Dylan Scott's house.

At the time, Dylan had just moved to town and did not realize how unpopular he was considered yet. They had actually hit it off really well but unfortunately his bladder had to ruin everything. He ended up wetting the bed, something he had not done in years. He never said anything but it was obvious Dylan found out. And then learned how unpopular he was on top of it. The next week he passed Dylan in the hallway and neither boy acknowledged the other and that was the end of that potential friendship.

Ironically, he had crossed paths with Dylan at the convenience store last week. He had been grabbing a water bottle on his way home from school, parched. Dylan had walked in with Melanie Mantrose at his side, laughing as the girl looked up at him adoringly. At least Dylan was so enamored with this girl he didn't even notice as he quickly paid for the water and left.

He had to admit that he had turned out to be quite a handsome guy, long and lean. And as a basketball player he was sure that Dylan had ample opportunities with females. Yet another good looking and athletic guy who reaped the benefits of his born traits. The world was so fucking cruel and unfair. But he had the power to balance it out some now in his own hands.

Before leaving he collected several bottles in the recycling for his targets and some sodas and beers from the fridge. It was doubtful his dad would notice just a couple beers missing. He had more important things to be concerned with, like Pierce's upcoming history test he overheard them talking about the other day. If Pierce flunked it, he was in jeopardy of having to sit out his next football game. What another tragedy that would be.

Sipping on his Coke, he walked a few miles, the caffeine hitting his veins, adding to his excitement. The fact that only he knew what was in his duffel bag and what he eventually planned to do with it, exhilarated him. He walked with a confidence and purpose he had never felt before. He crossed the train tracks that seemingly divided the city into class. He was on the blue collar side of course though that did not seem to make a difference in Pierce's status.

On the other side the homes were not only larger but set back with bigger yards. He randomly turned off and walked far out into a wide area of open land, surrounded by a canopy of trees. He lined up his bottles with careful precision. He loaded the gun and stepped back, aiming as level as he could at the first empty beer bottle. The beer his father enjoyed with his brother on the couch, cheering on their beloved sports teams as if they could hear them.

He breathed in deeply and as he exhaled, the bottle shattered in pieces before he even had time to process the shot. Hundreds of obliterated pieces never to be whole again. The beginning of his indelible mark.

When she woke, the sun was shining directly on her face. It was almost noon. No response from Ben. No missed calls or texts from anyone. Deflated, she brewed some coffee, extra strong, the welcome aroma hitting her nostrils. She poured a bowl of Grapenuts and stood chewing and staring at the outdated backsplash, with specks of meals past, and decided that she would redo it today, once and for all. She needed a project to keep her busy. And those stick and peel things she saw at the Home Depot looked easy and cheap enough.

A half hour later, she roamed the aisles of Home Depot, past families set out on their weekend house projects. She walked by an extremely pregnant woman and her husband browsing blue paints and an elderly couple considering swatches of carpet before she and her own companion, her favorite and overly large travel mug, reached the kitchen area. She took her time browsing through all the bright and shiny objects, even testing out the tablet feature on a massive refrigerator.

"Can I help you?" She turned around feeling like a child caught touching a breakable object in a fancy store.

She nearly dropped her coffee. "Oh wow, Henry, hi, how are you?" He looked completely different sporting a baseball cap, shorts and sandals. And a low cut V-neck t-shirt exposing a hairless chest. So unnecessary.

"Good, good." He breathed out excitedly. "Just trying to find a fridge for my condo that can actually keep more than a case of beer cold. Looks like you are in the market as well?"

"Actually, no, I was just browsing." She stopped herself from elaborating on why she was there. None of his business.

He gave her a curious look so she added, "thank you so much for the bike. It's been awesome. Totally unexpected and unnecessary but most appreciated." She forced an appropriate smile.

"Oh you are so welcome. The least I can do." He cleared his throat loudly as if trying to take back his last sentence. But she heard it very clearly and understood exactly what he meant.

"Well nice running into you. I hope you enjoy the rest of your weekend."

"You, too." He gave her a departing wave, reminiscent of the guy at Whole Foods and she slowly waved back. She wanted to get out of this overwhelming store ASAP. She quickly spotted the abundant selection of backsplash tiles, and staring at them through teary eyes, an intense sense of loneliness choked her. She made a random selection, grabbing five packages of black and white tiles to start, and checked out before her tears spilled over.

She managed to drive home and get through the door before allowing herself five minutes—a timed five minutes—to cry. She would not allow herself to spend any more time feeling sorry for herself. At four and a half minutes she started to blow her nose and compose herself. She splashed cold water on her face and took some deep breaths.

There. She felt like she had gotten it out of her system—at least for now. She told Google to turn on some upbeat music and then lost herself in meticulously peeling and sticking tiles for the next couple of hours while singing along to some classic 90's music. A fresh layer over old scars. She was so immersed in the repetition that she felt almost normal.

At three o'clock the sticking and peeling became tedious though and she decided she would finish the rest tomorrow. Plus she was extremely hungry. She randomly felt like a grilled cheese. Well not randomly really. Grilled cheese had always been a comfort food for her growing up.

Along with Campbell's chicken and stars soup, which she did not have to accompany it with, unfortunately, but that was OK. Wine would suffice. Speaking of which, her bottle of red from last night was definitely spoiled from having been out on her patio in the heat all day.

She opened her sliding glass door to retrieve her only sad bottle of wine and realized that she had not wasted any of it. It was completely empty. She was positive she had only had a glass and a half but the evidence was clear. She had drunk an entire bottle with absolutely no recollection. Wow, this must really be rock bottom.

She immediately called Dr. Berkshire and left him a voicemail indicating that she would like an appointment as soon as possible. He called her back as she was finishing the last bite of her grilled cheese.

"Hi Dr. Berkshire," she answered on the second ring.

"Elle, good to hear from you. Thank you for reaching out. How are things going?"

"Well, honestly not the best. I'm still having trouble with the Seroquel. Sleepwalking and having no recollection of what I have done. I was hoping to talk to you about trying a different medication."

"Ah, I'm sorry to hear that. And have you been drinking?"

"No," she bit her lip.

"Good for you. Ok, well how about I make things easier for you and just call in a prescription for you for something else. No need to come in. I was thinking perhaps Trazodone would be a better fit for you. Let's start you on 25mg and move you up to 50mg if needed. How does that sound?"

"That sounds good. Thank you."

"Of course. I will call it in right now. Get a good night's rest tonight. Make sure you are doing some meditation, taking a bath, something relaxing that does not involve a screen before bed, OK? And let's schedule you out for next week to see how you are adjusting to the new med."

She could hear him scrambling around in his planner. "Tuesday at 10 a.m. work for you?"

"Yes, that will work," Elle said without hesitation, feeling slightly pathetic having no plans for the foreseeable future.

"Great, see you then. Take care of yourself."

"You, too. Thanks so much." She hung up and sighed deeply. Hopefully Trazodone would be her new best friend.

Feeling the need to keep moving, she spent the rest of the day washing her floors and vacuuming, (long overdue) and then forced herself to go on a short bike ride. 20 minutes was all she could handle but it was better than nothing. She spent equally as long in the shower and then went to retrieve her new prescription.

That night she limited herself to watching just one Law and Order SVU, always the old standby. She realized that she had already seen it before midway through but finished it anyway. At 10 p.m. she promptly turned the TV off as a text came in from Ben.

Hey, sorry for the delayed response. Work has been nutty and Jonathon is making me a bit nutty as well. Would love to see you though. Lunch tomorrow or Thursday?

She smiled, feeling a slight lift. At least she could still count on him. She wanted to make sure this new med didn't put her into a coma so she decided Thursday would be better.

Thursday sounds great. Looking forward to it. Perhaps Mables? Noon?

Yes to both. :)

:)

At 10: 15 p.m. she was in bed with her "new" book, "The Woman in Cabin Ten." She had borrowed it from Ami close to a year ago where it had sat on her nightstand gathering dust since. She popped open the bottle of Trazodone, avoiding all the horrible warning labels she knew she would only obsess over, and said a little prayer for normal, restful sleep as she swallowed the seemingly innocuous little pill. Less than twenty minutes later, she could hardly keep her eyes open and she was out as quickly as she closed the book.

Chapter 15

He walked home with a lightness in his step, feeling a surge of confidence he had never experienced before. He had obliterated all but one of the bottles on his first try. It was tantalizing to think that he would be obliterating human life in the next few days. More importantly, he would be restoring his own.

When he came home, the door was locked. He grabbed the spare key under the flower pot. So stupidly obvious. But it wasn't like their home had anything worth stealing anyways. He let himself in, relieved to have this time alone to put the gun back just so. His father was meticulous about certain things and he couldn't afford to make any mistakes.

Of course his parents were out watching his brother play football. And his sister was most likely with her boyfriend. He laughed out loud. This perfect little family would be screwed beyond belief. All that would remain of his pathetic brother and his pitifully love struck girlfriend would be a few meaningless ashes on the mantel.

He spent the rest of the afternoon enjoying the house to himself. He indulged in two of his brother's prized ice cream sandwiches and watched Star Treck instead of the inane sports channel that always dominated the TV. After a while he grew restless and went into Pierce's room. His bed was unmade as it often was on weekends. His mom would take the time to make it perfectly during the week but would allow it to go unmade on Saturdays before she changed his sheets on Sunday. As if he wasn't capable of making his own bed and changing his own sheets. He had been doing his own since they were eight years old, his mother donning him the "responsible" one.

He looked in the nightstand. Candy wrappers and chewed gum clung to the sides. Aiming for the trash can on the other side of the bed was too difficult for him apparently. He grabbed a crumpled piece of paper and smoothed it out, curious.

I'm the luckiest girl to be able to call you my boyfriend. Last night was so special for me. And even though I know I was not your first, I hope I'm your last! I love you so much, Pierce, and I'm so excited for our future together!

Xoxox,
Your Maddy

He snickered. She would actually be his last fuck. He remembered the first time Pierce had come home with her so vividly. How they both had been glowing and disheveled. It was so obvious. He had been sitting on the couch finishing "The Catcher in the Rye," when they made their obnoxious entrance. Maddy was giggling profusely and immediately went to the bathroom without even acknowledging him. Pierce had that ridiculous smile on his face. His zipper was down.

"What?" he said, zippering himself up. "Jealous or something?"

He had gone back to his book without reply.

Of course Pierce could not be ignored. "You know, I was about to ask you if you had some condoms on you by chance. I ran out. Apparently one box doesn't cut it for me. But obviously you would have no need for those."

Pierce laughed that fucking laugh he detested more than anything as he had glared at the jumbled words on the page, continuing to try to ignore him. He would not give Pierce the satisfaction of seeing him upset. He wanted to scream and punch his perfect face though. As he had his entire life. Tomorrow he would be doing far more damage. He fished around in the drawer some more.

My Beloved Son,

I love you to the moon and back! Happy happy birthday my amazing son! I couldn't be more proud of you, Pierce. I'm the luckiest mother to have you as my son.

Love you forever and always!

Mom

Wow, she had included "son" three times as if Pierce was her only son. His mother never said anything like that to him. Whatever sentiments she did say to him always seemed pitying or forced. He spit into the note. Next was a balled-up science quiz with a "D" in red at the top followed by:

Come see me after class. I am always here to help you, Pierce. You have so much potential. Don't ever forget that.

:)
Ms. Volpe

So gross. Even Ms. Volpe was infatuated with Pierce. So much potential. Pierce was dumb as a rock. He couldn't even get the definition of an organism correct on a freaking multiple choice science quiz. It was quite impressive that an organism could be so stupid actually. He wouldn't put it past Pierce screwing her to get a passing grade. He had gone through his entire life depending on others to make him successful, to make him feel special. The chosen one. Well, he certainly was the chosen one. His heart skipped a beat as he envisioned the blood seeping from his shallow, moronic brain.

She woke up startled, feeling a sense of urgency but unsure for what purpose. It was 7 a.m. A normal hour to get up. Though she felt a bit drowsy, she felt that she had slept through the night. The birds started chirping louder, vying to be heard. She so wanted to lay in bed a bit longer but after a couple minutes she reluctantly peeled herself from her covers, the pressure on her bladder intensifying. She peed for close to two minutes straight.

Washing her hands she glanced at herself in the mirror and that's when she noticed her lip. It was pretty swollen, and it definitely felt sore. It looked like she had been bit by something perhaps. As she started the coffee she held an ice pack to it, admiring her back splash, eager to finish it later. She made a rough calculation of how many more packages she would need. The tiles did not go as far as she had expected but she had always been terrible with accurate estimates. She was always off by hundreds when it came down to guessing the amount of jelly beans in the jar. She only had one package left. She would grab five more to be on the safe side.

She sipped her coffee greedily, desperate for the caffeine to take over her body. She placed a couple waffles in the toaster and rinsed some strawberries to adorn them with. Cutting the berries she couldn't help but think of strawberry picking with Ami the summer before their junior year of high school out in the country. Ami had just gotten her driver's license, and being a few months older than Elle, she proudly drove them, obeying the speed limit exactly, which added an extra couple hours to the trip. But that didn't matter. They were so excited to have their freedom, just on the verge of adulthood. They sang to all the radio songs they now had the power to control. Together they collected heaps of berries, until their backs ached. After they pulverized them into pulp for jam, they then sold them for $5 a jar at the local farmer's market. Every jar was gone in less than three hours.

They did this for two summers in a row and with the money they earned, they were able to take a trip together for their senior year spring break. They ended up going to Miami. Ami's cousin had just moved there. It was a very blurry trip with copious amounts of alcohol and pot involved. They both came back sunburned and tattooed, with matching daisies on their wrists. She glanced at her wrist as she rinsed the knife off. Her daisy looked slightly wilted and had lost its vibrancy over the years.

Perhaps she would get it removed or do something over it that was entirely different. Something that spoke just to her. She had never really wanted the daisy; it had been Ami's idea after all. In hindsight, a lot of the decisions and outcomes of her life had been contingent on Ami. She had always just done what Ami wanted without fully considering what she wanted. Those days were over.

The berries ended up being bitter so she ate the waffles plain. How fitting. Rinsing her dishes in the sink, she decided she would ride this morning and get it over with. Start her day off right. But as she brushed her teeth she realized that her lips had become even more swollen. Shit. This wasn't even an attractive lip filler effect. What the hell was happening? She must have gotten bit by something. She needed to go to urgent care before her entire face blew up.

Luckily when she arrived at the urgent care she had been to one too many times, for some of the most embarrassing of reasons, there was no wait. The doctor immediately gave her a pitiful look followed with "you poor thing." She felt a bit self-conscious but at least it was a female doctor. She could feel her lips continuing to protrude like a water balloon. After detailing everything she had eaten in the past 24 hours it was determined that the Trazadone was the culprit. The doctor was doubtful that she had been bit by something. Of course she was part of the 2% to have an allergic reaction to the medication. The doctor handed her a prescription for Prednisone and told her to head to ED if she had any trouble breathing. Very reassuring.

She grabbed her prescription through the drive through, caving into also getting the stupid Seroquel prescription with it. She immediately swallowed the Prednisone with the last of a hot water bottle that had been sitting in her car for days. Starting to drive home, she realized she had hardly anything to eat and would be forced to go to the store. Screw it. She would suck it up. She had nobody to impress.

She entered Whole Foods with her head high but it soon sank as heads started turning, including a little girl whom she could clearly hear asking her mother what was wrong with her. Oh so many things little girl. If you only knew.

Elle went her normal route through the store, stocking up on all her staple items. Of course her favorite Marsala chicken meal was out of stock. The one thing that sounded remotely appealing to her other than straight wine itself. She dug around the freezer just to make sure. And then there he was, beaming at her. She nearly jumped.

"Here, here, you go," he said, handing her a couple of her prized frozen meals.

"Why thank you," she slowly replied. She reached out to retrieve them but he appeared resistant to letting them go.

"I-I know how howww much you like the-theese."

"Yes, thanks again." He finally released his grip and she quickly grabbed them and dropped them in her cart. She maneuvered her cart backwards, feeling trapped by him blocking her and proceeded to step back into an elderly woman, who proceeded to fall.

Elle finally made it back to the safety of her apartment, after apologizing profusely to the woman who assured her several times that she was fine. She offered to pay for her few groceries but she declined, seemingly more freaked about by her appearance than anything. Her lips had nearly doubled in size. She popped another

Prednisone and then put her groceries away, aligning them carefully. It felt nice to have some control over something. When she opened up the fridge's bottom drawer she noticed how disgusting it was, covered in some sort of thick sticky substance. She retracted her work, taking out every last item in the fridge, throwing away molded vegetable and fruit lodged back in the drawers and wiped down each crevice of the fridge thoroughly. Soon she was moving on to the kitchen counter and floor, finding every hidden crumb and a small shard of glass from her wine glass disaster the other night.

She continued on with every room in her apartment, a surge of motivation bordering on compulsion overtaking her. At least her place would look presentable even if she didn't. She went through all her clothes as well, finally stuffing most of her skimpy outfits from her twenties into trash bags, which she lined down the hall to be donated later. A fresh start indeed.

Six hours later she showered, made herself a protein shake with extra protein powder and peanut butter and rewarded herself with some mindless TV curled up on the couch. She fell asleep just before she found out the next bachelorette to get eliminated and woke three hours later in the lingering light as the sun was coming down. She could feel that her lip had fortunately gone down as well. More than likely, it would be another Seroquel popping night.

Stomach growling, she popped her catastrophe inducing chicken marsala in the microwave and watched it cook on the freshly scrubbed turntable plate for the entire three and half minutes in a dreamy daze. Her mother would always nag her about how dangerous this was. One of the many dangers her mother had ingrained in her head as if she sincerely cared about Elle's wellbeing. If anything, Ami had been more of a parental figure for her, gently pointing out her concern when Elle was getting too caught up in the party scene or letting her grades slide a little too much. Apparently that concern had all been in vain.

The microwave beeped just as the doorbell rang, stirring Elle out of her revere. She was certainly not in the mood for company regardless of her appearance. She peered out the peephole again. It was Jake. Shit. Well, she was not obligated to answer it. She stood frozen in the kitchen. The microwave beeped obnoxiously again. Probably loud enough for him to hear it. She waited until she could hear him shuffle down the stairs.

Starving, she retrieved the meal, burning herself and biting down on her still tender lip and nearly screamed. As she was about to turn the TV on, she heard him come flying up the stairs again. What the hell? But just as quickly as he came up he darted down again. Curious and annoyed, she slowly opened her front door to find a small note sticking out of her doormat with his name, Jake Crawford, and phone number scrawled underneath in neat handwriting particularly for a guy. At the bottom was a little smiley face with "no pressure" next to it. Elle smiled in spite of herself.

She placed the note under the cheese magnet on the front of the fridge. The cheese magnet that she bought to commemorate her cheese tasting tour in Wisconsin with Ami. Instead, she placed the note under an Eiffel tower magnet Ben had brought back to her from a trip to Paris with Cameron, along with copious bottles of wine, and threw the cheese magnet in the garbage.

Satisfied, she ate her dinner on the couch as she started watching a way too predictable Dateline. She lost interest halfway through. She scanned through the movies on Netflix and settled on a drama that she hadn't seen before. It was poor acting and painfully slow. Normally she and Ami would point out and laugh about such things. But she decided to finish it with the help of (just two) glasses of wine. At 10 p.m. she popped another Prednisone along with her other little pill and retreated to bed eager for deep sleep.

Chapter 16

He could hear Pierce's voice growing exasperated as Maddy attempted to help him with his calculus homework over the phone. He was such a freaking idiot. Of course, it was simply too beneath his brother to ask him for his help. Fine with him.

He was glad he didn't waste a minute of his time trying to help the dumb fuck. As if his calculus homework would matter next week.

As if any of it would. There wouldn't be any more trophies to add to his bookshelf. The trophies perfectly aligned that his mother dusted every other week, would be collecting dust for good.

She woke to the ding of her phone with a text coming through from Ben. It was 6:40 am. Ugh, really?

See you at noon?!

She rolled over without responding, pulling the freshly washed duvet over her head. She was so groggy but also knew she wouldn't be able to fall back asleep. She might just have a normal day. After peeing she immediately checked her face in the mirror. Thankfully she no longer looked like a monster. Her lips had shrunk to a filler worthy size. Certainly Ben would comment on this.

She changed into her biking shorts and threw on a sports bra before she could change her mind and headed to the kitchen to brew her coffee. She added an extra scoop of grinds. As the coffee was percolating, its soothing sound and smell assuring her that she would be less of a zombie soon, she decided to cut herself a fruit salad with the remaining fruit that she hadn't thrown away yesterday but was on the verge of going bad. She yawned as she peeled up an orange and removed all the white strings that annoyed her with a knife, carelessly cutting into her finger.

"Shit!" She immediately ran it under the cold tap, the blood protruding to the surface. It wasn't anything serious fortunately. It was the same index finger that she had purposely cut when she and Ami were twelve vowing to be blood sisters for life. For life. Such an innocent and hopeful girl she had been. At the end of the day, you could only count on yourself and sometimes that didn't even seem possible.

After a rigorous ride, (Elle could not envision spinning ever getting easier), and a cool shower, she felt pretty good about herself as she got ready to meet Ben for lunch. She chose a comfy white wrap dress and some flats that she had discovered in the back of her closet yesterday in her cleaning frenzy, both which she had completely forgotten she owned. The dress still had the tags on it. She had bought it right before the accident actually. It was on clearance at Nordstrom Rack, since it was a summer dress, at Ami's insistence. She saw no point in buying something simply because it was on clearance and especially since she wouldn't be able to wear it for months. But it was a pretty dress and now she was glad she bought it. The dress though comfy was still tight so she scrambled through her underwear drawer looking for her pair of no shows that she really should invest in buying more of. She had done all her laundry yesterday and had even put everything away, so why couldn't she find them? She quickly grew frustrated and threw a bunch of the drawer's contents on the floor. There at the bottom was the black pair. But she needed the beige. She searched through everything again and nothing. Damnit. She must have accidentally thrown them away or placed them in the donation trash bags. Oh well, she needed to buy more anyway. Her underwear drawer seemed surprisingly sparse. She slipped on a pair of jogging shorts instead and left thinking nothing more of it.

Shockingly Ben wasn't there when she arrived at the bustling restaurant at exactly 12:00 pm, always the first to arrive. She gave her name to the frazzled hostess with frizzy hair who told her that it would be "at least a 35 minute wait" in an overly apologetic tone. Elle wanted to give her suggestions on some hair products she used to tame her similarly unruly hair but instead she smiled reassuringly. "That's fine. I'll just have a seat at the bar." At the very least they could eat there. The woman smiled gratefully.

She took a seat in the middle of the bar and pulled her phone out. A text had just come through from Ben.

So sorry to bail last minute but I had a last minute work thing come up. So so sorry. I will make it up to you. Any restaurant you want, I'm paying.

It was a small letdown, but she couldn't help but feel a bigger blow with everything else that had been transpiring.

No worries at all. I totally get it. Just let me know when you're free.

She ordered a double vodka on the rocks and slowly sipped on it amongst all the happy and laughing couples. Enjoying the almost instant buzz she decided on ordering one more in lieu of ordering food. Well, this one she would make a single. She was not in the mood to eat in front of all these happy couples by herself. She browsed through her Instagram feed, sipping on her second drink, randomly liking several photos.

It occurred to her that Ami, who regularly posted, had not posted in days. She searched for her name only to find that her account was private. Wow, she had actually blocked her. The realization felt devastating.

She wanted to leave immediately. She needed to get away from the two girlfriends to her left sharing a salad and the couple to her right, who had turned their chairs to face each other and were now full on making out. Seriously? It was the middle of the day for God's sake. She paid her bill in cash, not waiting for her change. At least her generous tip would be her good deed of the day.

She drove slightly tipsy but extra carefully to a shopping complex not far away, ensuring that she drove a couple miles under the speed limit. She treated herself to her favorite chocolate cake milkshake from Portillos, a vibrantly colored pair of Nike's that she did not need but caught her eye as well as some very overpriced makeup from Sephora. She told herself that she would take up running and finally try some dating apps to justify her purchases.

As she left Sephora, $108 poorer, she forced herself to walk in the direction of her car before she got sucked into going into any more stores. She walked briskly to her Jeep, relieved that she remembered where she parked for once. She fumbled for her car keys as usual, mentally adding "car wash" to her to-do list for this week as she noticed the streaks of bird shit on the back window. As she finally retrieved her keys and unlocked her door, a black Volvo parked uncomfortably close beside her straight on.

What the hell, they couldn't wait a damn second?! She opened her door just enough to squeeze inside and turned on her ignition, hot and annoyed. A man exited the car, almost swiping her door, laughing wildly. Oh my God, it was Clay. He disappeared on the other side of the car, presumably to open the door for Ami or maybe the other red head.

Elle did not care to know. She backed out so quickly that she almost caused an accident. Cars honked at her. She waved apologetically at one large and enraged looking man in his tiny Smart car. Clay and Ami looked right at her like a deer in the headlights. She waved brightly at them, and they both raised their hands tentatively, looking shocked. Ha, who was the deer in the headlights now? She laughed out loud and drove off sipping the last of her now melted, but oh so delicious, chocolate cake shake.

On her way home, she turned off to the Home Depot, remembering to grab a few more packages of the tiles, determined to finish the back splash today. She drove home quickly and immediately started on the tiles. But after going through one package, peeling and sticking the tiles, she grew tired of the repetition. She took a break, pouring herself a generous glass of what she considered to be expensive white wine that she had been saving, for what, she did not know. The crisp and buttery taste was absolute perfection.

She finished the glass and ventured into her studio, buzzed again, inspired to paint. She had the sudden urge to paint something messy and angry, with fierce lines and dark colors. She put on her heavily paint laden apron and allowed her rage out on the canvas, wild streaks and splatters layered on top of each other, burying the pain at the core.

After she had thoroughly doused the canvas, she stepped back to access it. It certainly was her most dark and disturbing work of art to date. She felt satisfied though. Calmer. And physically and emotionally exhausted. She left her accumulating dirty dishes in the sink and decided that she would forgo doing her bills for another day. Instead, she curled up on the couch, too tired to move, and eventually fell asleep flipping through channels trying to find something decent to watch, covered in paint, her second glass of wine still half full on the coffee table.

Chapter 17

He listened intently to the details of their call, covering the mouth piece of the phone.

"So what should we do tomorrow night?" Maddy chirped.

"What do you mean, 'we'? Pierce emphasized in an exasperated tone. "I mean, I was planning on going out with the boys tomorrow night. We haven't had a guy's night in a long time. We've been hanging out like every single day. The boys miss me and want to go bowling. And Eric has planned this after party at his place since his parents are out of town. I guess you could come to that if you really want to."

"But it's our nine month anniversary, Pierce. Which is really a year if you count the three months we dated before our silly break up. It's kinda a big deal, don't you think?" So predictably pathetic.

Pierce sighed loudly. "Fine. What do you want to do?"

"I don't know, Pierce. I don't want to force you to hang out with me. If I'm such an inconvenience just go out with your boys! Go make out with Emily at this after party you weren't even going to invite me to for all I care."

"Maddy, please stop overreacting."

"Overreacting? Sorry I actually care about our relationship! Sorry for thinking that our one year anniversary is worth celebrating!"

"But Maddy, it's only technically nine months since we've been back together. So."

"And I have no idea why I even got back together with you! Go back to Emily. Maybe she will make you happier. I mean I don't know what girl could possibly be better to you! I mean I even lost ten pounds for you! I was perfectly happy the way I was, but no, it wasn't good enough for you! I starved myself for you!" Maddy started to cry. Oh poor, deprived Maddy.

"Maddy, Maddy, please calm down." Maddy sniffled loudly. "You look great. I appreciate all you have sacrificed for me. You are a great girlfriend. I am very lucky to have you. And if I wanted to be with

Emily, well, I would be with Emily. But I choose you. I chose you nine months ago when I broke things off with Emily, and I choose you now. That was a mistake, OK? You're ten times hotter than Emily and way smarter. You can actually help me with my homework, and I can actually trust you to be loyal to me. I don't have to worry about you. We can celebrate our anniversary tomorrow night, however long it's been. I will pick you up, say around five, and we can go out to the lake and watch the sunset? Wouldn't that be romantic? Would you like that?"

"Oh Pierce, that sounds like the perfect way to celebrate our anniversary." Her tone had completely changed.

"Can you wear that one sexy red halter dress though? And no underwear. I would like that very much."

"Of course. Anything for you, Pierce. I love you so much. You know I would do anything for you."

"I know. Me, too, Maddy. You're my girl. See you tomorrow then."

"I'll be waiting with no underwear."

"I can't wait."

How romantic indeed. It would be their last sunset. He hoped they would relish its beauty as much as he would.

The wine had spilled all over her pillowcase and soaked into the pillow as well. Damn it. She promptly popped three Ibuprofen in the medicine cabinet, her head pounding in protest. She reluctantly assessed herself in the mirror. She looked like a hot mess though her lips were completely back to normal at least.

She washed her face thoroughly with a new exfoliating wash she had thrown in with her unnecessary purchases yesterday at Sephora. The smell of pineapple was slightly nauseating given her current state though and she quickly rinsed it off before she nearly puked in the sink.

In the kitchen she started to brew her other favorite liquid. She sat at her kitchen table, which was now clear of clutter for once and stared in a trance as the coffee slowly accumulated in the pot. It was actually quite meditative. She admired her work on the tiles, almost complete, feeling the urge to just get it done after she had her coffee.

She reached for her favorite coffee mug on the drying rack and noticed a small chip on the corner. Well that sucks. She was about to throw it out when it occurred to her that all the dirty dishes she had left in the sink last night were on the drying rack. Had she really drank enough to black out and wash dishes last night?

Tossing the mug in the trash she saw the empty wine bottle, evidence of her drinking binge. Holy shit. Shaking her head in disgust, she turned to the refrigerator for the coffee creamer.

As she reached for the handle, she immediately noticed that Jake's note was moved. It was now placed under a Lou Malnatti's pizza magnet. The Eiffel tower magnet now had an upcoming baby shower invitation for one of her coworkers underneath it. This was becoming way too much. Her heart started racing... in fear of herself.

Chapter 18

Four hours later, she sat trying to get comfortable across from Dr. Berkshire. He looked at her intently through his scratched glasses, which he kept pushing back up his nose every few seconds. It was an unnecessary annoyance and distraction when he could easily afford to just buy a new pair.

"Thank you for squeezing me in," she started.

He smiled at her softly. A smile that was not pity but of concern. Something he had perfected in all his years of practice.

"You look exhausted," he said slowly.

"Yes. Yes, I am." She sighed heavily. "I'm back to taking the Seroquel. The Trazadone—I had an allergic reaction to it. My lips blew up actually."

"Oh my! I'm sorry to hear you went through that. In all my years I only think I've had one other patient have an allergic reaction to Trazadone. That must have been scary for you." He pushed his glasses up again only to fall a couple of seconds later.

"It was certainly not a great experience but I went to urgent care right away and they gave me some Prednisone which helped a lot. The next day I was fine. So I started taking the Seroquel again. But what was actually disturbing was what happened last night."

He cocked his head, his drastically long and untamed brows furrowing. "And what happened last night, Elle?"

"Well, I woke up this morning to find that I had washed the dirty dishes in the sink, which I had no recollection of doing. And I also realized that one of the magnets on my fridge was moved. Or rather a note that I had placed under a certain magnet, a magnet of the Eiffel tower, was moved under a different magnet—a Lou Malnatti's one," she clarified, feeling ridiculous. She sounded insane.

His caterpillar eyebrows raised.

"So you think that you must have done it in your sleep," Dr. Berkshire concluded.

"Yes. There can't be any other explanation."

"And how are you sleeping otherwise?"

"I definitely have difficulty falling asleep without the Seroquel, which I've tried not to take a few nights. I literally did not fall asleep those nights. But with it I am out pretty much right away. And I feel like I sleep soundly throughout the night. I do wake up feeling pretty groggy though."

Dr. Berkshire nodded slowly. "And are you having any nightmares?"

"Yes, some."

"About?"

"Sometimes the car accident. It's been a while since I've dreamed about the accident though. Mostly I just wake up feeling anxious, like I had an unsettling dream, but I can't remember anything specific."

"I see. And if my memory serves me right, you had started to sleep walk right after the accident for a few weeks. Prior to that, you had not experienced sleep walking since you were a child."

Elle nodded.

"And what about the alcohol?" he asked, keeping his face as neutral as possible.

She hesitated and then decided to just be honest. "I'm drinking more than I would like. Not a ton but more than I usually do. I have been going through a rough patch with one of my friends, my best friend, and I think it's affecting me more than I'd like to admit. And then there was this guy I started seeing and well, it ended abruptly."

"I am sorry to hear that. Hopefully, in time your friend will come around. And as far as dating goes, just keep an open mind. You will find your person in due time. The wait will be worth it. I didn't marry until I was forty, you know. She was worth every waiting day and even the pain of losing her thirty two years later. Breast cancer. She held on for five long years. Such a strong woman." He glanced over his shoulder at a photo that was obviously of him and his wife on their wedding day.

"I'm so sorry." Elle felt embarrassed complaining about her insignificant issues in comparison. His eyes glazed over and she felt compelled to hug him. But then he cleared his throat abruptly, uncomfortable that the focus had transferred to him. "Ah, thank you. But like I said, she was worth it all. The love of my life. And she gave me six wonderful children who are now grown of course and have children of their own. I have eleven grandchildren and fifteen great grandchildren who I must keep up with now. That certainly keeps me preoccupied outside of here."

Elle wondered why he wouldn't just retire. He looked deep into her eyes. "Don't you give up on love now. You are too young, intelligent and talented. And this friend of yours—may I ask what happened there?"

Elle did not feel like rehashing everything but of course she wanted to be polite. But twenty minutes later she was still going into great detail about how shocked she still was that Ami could just cut her off. It did feel good to get it out, especially to someone so compassionate and understanding. Dr. Berkshire did not interrupt her once nor did he look over at the clock to signal that she should wrap things up. For an older man with not much time left, he certainly made her feel worth his time.

When she finally got to the end of her tyrant, Dr. Berkshire allowed a pause before he spoke.

"You are a great friend, Elle," he finally said. "And Ami knows this. However, she is at a crossroads now where she has to choose between her best friend and her fiancé. And since she cannot marry you she is choosing him, especially in light of what happened in her first marriage. It is nothing personal against you as hard as that may be to accept. She is simply choosing what she needs for her future. And you, my dear, need to concentrate on your own future. With or without her you will be just fine. As cliche as that sounds. After I lost my wife, I felt that I could not go on one more day. I couldn't eat. I couldn't sleep. I couldn't concentrate on my patients. I wasn't the father my children needed for a long time." He shook his head, seemingly disappointed in himself. Elle resisted the urge to comfort him again.

"But then one day, I forced myself to get out of bed. Well, my stomach did actually. I was starving as I had not eaten a proper meal in six months. And the only thing that really sounded good to me at that time was pancakes. Banana pancakes with powdered sugar on top, just like Anna, my wife, used to always make me. But of course when I went to the pantry there was no pancake batter left. That's when I finally took notice of the sticky note on the fridge with pancake batter, eggs, milk, light bulbs and paper towels listed in Anna's perfect cursive. It was as if she was speaking to me, telling me that I had to go on. And that started with making my own pancakes for the first time."

"So out the door I went right then and there in my pajamas. And I bought my own pancake batter and bananas. And I went home and made some of the crappiest banana pancakes. Nothing like Anna's. But I still ate them, I was so hungry. The next morning, I made them again. I made them for a week straight and each time they got better. They would never be as good as Anna's pancakes, but they were still pretty damn good. And I had my children and my grandchildren over the following weekend and I made pancakes for all of them. And we laughed and ate pancakes together. It was then that I knew I would be OK." Dr. Berkshire ended with a broad smile.

"Thank you." Elle returned a smile. "Thank you for sharing that."

Dr. Berkshire nodded and cleared his throat loudly, signaling a departure from himself. "Now young lady, what I think you need, what you really need is some relaxation—some meditation and perhaps some hypnosis if you are open to it. I think your sleepwalking, if it is sleepwalking, could be a response to your stress level as well as your alcohol intake.

"What do you mean if it is sleepwalking?"

"Perhaps it's not the Seroquel. It could be that you are blacking out from drinking."

"I see." She felt her cheeks blushing.

"It's nothing to be ashamed of but this is dangerous," he quickly added. "If you are struggling, I can certainly recommend some additional resources for you."

"Thank you, but I think I can get a handle on it at this point. If I feel that I can't, I will certainly let you know of course."

"Ok, well let's keep an eye on it. Perhaps you can start by trying not to drink for a week and see if this has an effect at all. It will also be a good test. How does that sound?"

"That sounds like a good plan," she said, more confidently than she felt.

"Alright then, glad to hear. I believe in you." He smiled at her, a smile of pure acceptance and compassion. A smile she had not received in a very long time. She felt like she might cry.

"Now before we end, let's do a ten minute hypnosis if you are open to trying it?"

"Absolutely," Elle said emphatically. At this point, she was open to trying anything.

She left his office feeling beyond relaxed, like she did not have a care in the world. She initially had been doubtful that staring at a swaying pen and telling herself that she is "safe and capable of managing negativity healthfully" could be so impactful. But here she was feeling almost invincible. If only she could stay in this state forever.

This was even better than being in love. She felt as if she was in complete control of her mind, her emotions, and not anyone or anything could interfere with this. She did not need anyone. She was so unphased that she nearly got ran over by a couple teenagers on their skateboards.

"It's totally fine," she said with a smile as they apologized. She started laughing at the thought of herself dying in a skateboarding collision. The two boys looked at each other between their shaggy bangs hanging out of their beanies. Wide eyed, they glanced at one another, confused by this crazy lady. Their expressions made her laugh harder. She walked off still rolling in laughter as they gratefully skated on.

When she walked into her apartment, she had a renewed appreciation for how clean and organized it now was. She made herself an early dinner, deciding to use the stove instead of the microwave for once. And sat at her dining table, which she set with her more expensive silverware, to enjoy what she had put some effort into preparing—pesto chicken, lightly steamed broccoli and parmesan couscous. She even lit a couple candles and asked Google to play some Frank Sinatra. She ate slowly, relishing in this newfound peace.

A peace that was not even close to what alcohol gave her. It occurred to her that she was not drinking wine with her meal. And it didn't bother her all that much. But as she started to eat, she couldn't help but acknowledge what a great pairing a fruity Malbec would be. The thought was fleeting but became more protruding as she finished her plate except for a few broccoli florets. She was full but now the meal felt incomplete without her Malbec. Damn it.

"I am safe and capable of managing negativity healthfully," she said aloud as she rinsed her plate in the sink. She said it again more forcefully as Dr. Berkshire instructed her to do so, even looking in the mirror over her console table, where a framed picture of her and Ami had been displayed since the first day she moved in. It was of her and Ami at age sixteen or seventeen, sunburned long limbs intertwined with each other at Lake Michigan.

She wondered what Ami was doing at this moment. If she missed her or even thought of her. She took a deep breath and stared at herself in the mirror, repeating her mantra. The wonder as well as the Malbec fixation faded as she placed the picture in the drawer. A memory that now escaped her and didn't even matter anymore.

    She took a hot bath before bed, filling the tub until it almost overflowed with bubbles. She was mesmerized by their glistening abundance, of all shapes and sizes. When she finally got into bed, she noticed how pruney her fingers were as she opened her book to the marked page. She could only manage a few pages before her eyes grew heavy. She did not force herself to finish the chapter and closed the book and then her eyes.

Chapter 19

That night he lay in bed unable to sleep, too thrilled for tomorrow. He was going to finally have his long awaited opportunity. He had gone his entire life living in the shadows. Now he would be in the forefront once and for all. It would no longer be about Pierce and his accomplishments, his damn football games and impeccable looks.

He would never have to witness females gawking at his brother again. Or his mother babying him like his solid figure of nearly 200 pounds could fall apart at any moment. Or the way his father only smiled when he was with Pierce or talking about him.

And Maddy. He would never have to hear that stupid laugh of hers again as she drooled all over Pierce. It was so sad that she had become so entranced by him. Not only did Pierce not give two shits about her but it was going to cost her life now. Such a shame. He screamed into his pillow in pure excitement until his lungs and body collapsed.

Elle woke feeling refreshed, the birds chirping her good morning. It was 7:35 a.m. She had slept through the night and had fallen asleep without taking the Seroquel. Wow, maybe she could really do this on her own. She felt eager to get going though she had no plans. She reached for her phone where a message from Ben awaited.

Dinner tonight? Any place of your choice on me.

She smiled and contemplated her response.

Nice. Don't mind if I do. Just FYI, I'm not drinking for (at least) one week. Taking a 'lil break. How does sushi sound?

He responded right away.

Good for you! I will join you in abstinence (at least for tonight). Drinks on me another time then. And yes, sushi sounds perfect.

Awesome. How about Tanoshii, 7pm?

He hearted her suggestion and she replied with a smiley face. Dinner could not come soon enough.

She started her day off with a good sweat on the bike. She almost quit five minutes in, her legs already burning. But she pushed herself the entire 45 minutes, swearing aloud at some points and cursing the instructor for how easy he made it all seem. Afterwards, dripping sweat, all resentment was gone. Her lungs and legs felt stronger and she felt completely energized.

Perhaps she would do a drop in yoga class at a studio she had been to a couple of times before in Lincoln Park. Her legs did feel extremely tight. Dr. Berkshire would certainly approve. He almost felt like a father figure to her. The type of concerned yet encouraging father she would have loved growing up. The type of father that she would have wanted to make proud.

Elle arrived at exactly 11:57 a.m., three minutes before they locked the doors. She felt badly for an overweight woman who appeared hot and heavy at the door a couple minutes late as Elle rolled out her mat. She had definitely been locked out before. She tried to clear her mind and focus on her breath and nothing else as she stretched out her tight legs. A man in front of her removed his shirt revealing a chiseled back while a woman beside her coughed loudly followed by a fit of sneezes into her shirt. Great.

The instructor was an extremely good looking man with a head of heavy looking dreads down to his waist. She had never seen him before. He introduced himself as Shawn and expressed how honored he was to be participating in their practice today.

Several downward dog positions later she finally felt her hips start to open up and some of the tension released from her body. She never felt completely at one with herself, with her breath and mind as she thought a "good" yogi should. But today felt different. Today she felt fully present. She was unconcerned with how deep or stable her poses were, focusing more on her breathing and mind. "I am safe and capable of managing negativity healthfully," she reminded herself with each vinyasa.

As she moved back to downward dog again, she felt hands on her hips gently drawing them further back.

"Very good," the instructor commented, surely looking down at her ass. Immediately her whole flow was interrupted. When she thought he would release his grip, he kept holding on. She could feel her ass brushing against his crotch as he pulled her even closer to him, making her feel extremely uncomfortable. Finally, he slowly released his grip, the feeling of his fingers lingering on her body. She decided that she did not mind the interruption after all. After a ten minute meditation in which she fought hard to keep her mind from wandering, the class slowly came to. Shawn thanked them for allowing him to be a part of their practice again and then hit the gong as the class bowed in their final "namaste."

As Elle rolled up her mat, Shawn went around the room chatting to a few people she knew were devoted yogis. She smiled and said a soft "thank you," so as not to interrupt him but he immediately looked over to her, quickly excused himself and then practically leapt over to her.

"Thank you so much for coming," he said, bright and wide eyed.

"Absolutely. It was a much needed class."

"Well, I hope to see you soon?" he said with a slight intonation.

"Absolutely. When do you teach next?"

"I'm here Monday through Friday at noon now."

"Great. That should work for me at least for the remainder of the summer. Until I go back to school."

"Oh, awesome, what are you going to school for?" he raised his perfect eyebrows in curiosity. There was no doubt he got them waxed or at least plucked them.

"Oh, I'm actually a teacher. Elementary school art. Over at Parkview Academy."

"Good for you! Those students are lucky to have you."

"Thanks. Yeah, I'm lucky to have them too. I definitely enjoy it. Well see you soon, Shawn."

"Awesome, see you soon and take care, Elle."

As she walked out the door, she almost stopped in her tracks. Wait, how the hell did he know her name? She replayed their conversation in her head. She was certain that she hadn't given him her name. What the fuck? Her heart racing, she got to her car as quickly as she could. She would not be going back to another of his classes.

She had never met the guy before. Or had she? Was she really losing it that bad? Maybe she was being too hard on herself. People met people all the time that they forgot. But wouldn't she have remembered meeting him with his distinct looks? And moreover, if she had met him before, wouldn't he have reminded her? The way he just called her by her name felt so personal.

She was surprised when she found herself parked in her usual spot in front of her condo a few minutes later. She needed to stop overthinking this. She decided to check her neglected mailbox, which she had been avoiding for days. She sifted through the mass and dispensed the junk in the trash. Such a waste of paper. She held onto a couple of bills she was certainly not in the mood to open today.

All of a sudden, she felt a tap on her shoulder. She nearly screamed. Her creepy neighbor was the last person she wanted to see. She slowly turned around. Squinting in the sun, she could immediately see that it was definitely not Mr. Jensen, thank God. It was a very handsome man in his late 30's probably but it was hard to tell with the large sunglasses he had on. She relaxed.

"I thought it was you!" he said, taking off his glasses. Oh my God. It really was him.

"It's Ryan! You remember me, don't you? Ami's ex?"

She wanted to run. "Oh, hey Ryan, it's um… nice to see you."

He laughed obnoxiously. "Yeah, I'm sure I was the last person you expected to run into. Do you live right here?" He pointed up at her place.

Mail in hand, it was so obvious she couldn't lie.

"Um yeah, I do." She felt defensive now, it wasn't his fucking business.

"Ah, nice spot. My girlfriend actually lives a block away. Parking is such a bitch though." He glanced over at what must have been his precious Porsche.

"Oh, that's nice," Elle responded, not knowing what else to say.

"Yeah she's a real winner. Don't worry, you actually did me a favor. Getting a divorce from Ami was the best decision I ever made. My girl, Kitty, now she is a keeper. Way hotter. And man, can I make her purr. You know, big boobs, blonde hair, raging curves, every guy's dream. I mean, come on, Ami is hot for a redhead but she's a redhead you know? Oh wait, sorry, so are you! But looks aside, because looks aren't' everything, right? She is actually decently smart. Not like Ami but that's OK. She's able to keep a conversation going with all my friends and business partners at least. Not that she needs to say much, her looks speak for themselves. But hey, I don't want to speak badly about your partner. I assume you two are a couple by now?" He laughed outrageously.

Elle ignored his remark. "I'm happy for you then. Glad it all worked out."

"Yeah me, too. Because if I hadn't met Kitty I was seriously thinking about reaching out to you. That kiss we had, it meant something right?" He looked like he was about to kiss her again. Elle backed away, hitting the mailbox.

"Well, I guess I know where to come a knockin' if it falls through." He smiled and winked at her before putting on his sunglasses again.

"See you around, Elle." He turned and strode away and then over his shoulder he called out, "you were always the better looking one, anyways."

She stood there in shock, unable to move until an elderly woman who lived adjacent to her, rolled up to Elle on her walker, "Excuse me, dear, but I'm trying to get my mail. Would you mind opening my mailbox? It's the last box on the right." She held out the key and Elle grasped it with a shaking hand.

The mailbox was empty. Elle returned the key to her, still having said nothing.

"You alright dear? You look like you've seen a ghost."

Elle managed a smile. "I'm OK, I just feel a little woozy in this heat."

"You need to get inside and drink some liquids then. Put your feet up. That's what I intend to do the rest of the day as well."

"Yes, I will. Thank you."

"Of course, dear. Now you take care of yourself."

Inside, Elle immediately locked the door. She splashed her sweaty face with cold water in the sink. Instinctively, she picked up her phone to call Ami and tell her everything. But she couldn't. She wanted to cry. Get a hold of yourself. "I am safe. I am safe," she said aloud. She slowly sipped on some water and took some deep breaths. She needed to keep moving, to keep her mind distracted.

She placed the remaining bills in her accumulating pile. She needed to go paperless with them once and for all. Environmentally conscious, she was being quite the hypocrite. Finally, she got down to the last piece of mail. It was a letter addressed to her in all capital letters. Curious, she opened it immediately.

Dear Elle,

I hope this letter finds you as well as can be. It's been a very long time. 27 years to be exact. I have missed most of your childhood and your entire young adulthood. I am sad that I do not know the wonderful woman you have become. I have no doubt that you have done extraordinary things in your 32 years. You had that passionate spark about you even as a little girl. I knew from the start that you would be going places and nothing was going to hold you back.

  Not even me leaving you. I know you have persevered and made a beautiful life for yourself without me. I cannot express how selfish I was to just leave you and never look back. If I could, I would redo a lot of things, but this is without a doubt, my biggest regret.

  I am an old man now and I am dying. Bone cancer. They are giving me a few months but I feel it in my bones, (no pun intended), that it will be far less than this. I do not want to pressure you in the least. But if you have it in your heart to forgive me, enough to meet with me before I go, you will certainly give me my dying wish and I would be enormously grateful.

  I know that this is terrible timing and I am also sorry for that. I do not want you to think that I have just suddenly wanted to meet with you because I am dying. I have thought of you every single day since the day I left you and have missed you every single day. But I felt that it would be too painful to just suddenly reappear in your life and I didn't want to cause you any more pain. However, now that I am dying, I wanted to at least give you the choice. Obviously my intent is not to upset you and I ask that you do what is in your own best interest, not mine.

  I look forward to your response and if I do not receive one, I also understand. Just know I have always loved you and will love you forever and always even when I leave this earth. You are my one and only little Gingersnap.

Love,

Your Dad
917.320.8625

Elle read the letter over again, slower this time. She started to read it a third time until she could not make out the words, her eyes blurry with tears. She ripped it in half and then into tiny pieces. Just as he had done over and over again with her own heart since he left. Then she balled it all up and threw it in the trash next to her junk mail and rotting avocado. She wanted so badly to have a drink. Instead, she chugged the rest of her water and got on her bike, her anger and disgust pushing her to another level.

That night she decided on a more conservative dress and a low heel, which felt more fitting for her alcohol free dinner with Ben for some reason. Actually, she felt no desire to drink as she munched on a handful of cashews to qualm her appetite. The letter from her dad had put her in a strange mood and she knew that drinking would only make her more consumed with it. Plus, it would be nice to save money on a Lyft since she could drive herself.

She redid her lipstick in the mirror before she left. Double checked to make sure she had at least a couple pieces of gum, one being cinnamon, the only kind Ben liked. Alcohol would not be their mouth rinse tonight.

As she walked into Tanoshi, she almost fell. So much for wearing low heels and being sober. A few heads looked up and she smiled an embarrassed "I'm OK" smile. She was relieved to see Ben at the bar. His tall stature and high head of thick, dark hair always made him easy to spot even from behind. She made her way towards him through the congregating crowd, taking the most unobtrusive route possible and paying extra attention not to misstep again. She was about to call out his name when his elbow abruptly pushed back a shot and then slammed down on the bar. She waited a second before she made her presence known.

"Elle! So good to see you! You look beautiful." He brought her in for a hug.

"You look nice, too," she said, pretending that she had not seen his sweats as they pulled away. But he always did, even in sweats. To be fair they were still probably $150 sweatpants.

"Ah, sorry, I'm so embarrassed I didn't have time to change. It's been a shockingly shitty day. And I'm sorry you just saw me take that shot. I am in full support of your sobriety this evening."

"Oh, it's totally fine. Honestly. Not a big deal. You do you. If you want to drink, have at it. I won't judge." Her tongue started to water in protest though. She needed to get away from this bar.

"Let me just pay my tab real quick and I will meet you at the hostess stand," he said as more people started to clammer up to the bar. A woman most likely in her forties but with the devotion to her looks to stave off a few years, pushed at Elle with her excessively large Louis Vuitton like a shield. Elle pushed back, growing more annoyed. Oblivious, the woman then banged her with the diaper bag as she turned around and squealed, "Sheila! Oh my god, Sheila! I thought that was you!"

"You know, fuck it," she practically yelled over the obnoxious people vying for their alcohol. "Get me a drink. I've had a shockingly shitty day as well." She might as well join them instead of being jealous and annoyed.

"You sure?" Ben asked, his eyebrows slightly raising in some sort of concerned expression. The Botox was wearing off.

"Yes, I'm sure," she said assertively.

"Alright then. Martini extra dirty?"

"Perfect," she responded without pause. "I'll go check on our table while you order."

He smiled his glamour smile as she turned to disentangle herself from the crowd more aggressively this time. She approached the hostess stand where a very pretty and very young woman, girl really, greeted her with intense enthusiasm. Her fake eyelashes outlined her wide blue eyes and her skin was so flawless she looked like a doll. Elle had a strange urge to touch her to make sure she was real. God, she felt old.

"Just wanted to check on the status for Ben," she said instead.

"Absolutely! Just give me one second here." Her eyes glanced down at the screen, revealing vibrant purple eyeshadow.

"There's just one table ahead of you," she announced with satisfaction as her doll eyes blinked back up at her.

"Ok, great, thank you." Elle took a few steps back in the waiting area, thankful to see that the witnesses to her near collapse were gone.

"Clay! Party for two!" The hostess announced in a surprisingly forceful voice.

Clay? Elle gasped in near horror. How could this be possible? How could she seriously be running into them again? She turned towards the corner.

"Clay, party of two!" the girl announced again with even more gusto. "Going once, going twice…"

Elle bit her lip in anticipation. The longest few seconds later the hostess declared, "Ben, party of two!"

Elle exhaled deeply as she followed the girl's bouncing blonde curls and impossibly tight butt to a small table set in the back. Even if she rode the Peloton every day for the next six months, she doubted her ass could ever look like that.

She waved at Ben as he walked over, carefully balancing their drinks.

"Thank you," she said, as he placed the martini in front of her.

"I don't know if you should thank me for being a bad influence," he replied, smoothing out his shirt before sitting down.

"No, you are absolutely not. I'm a grown woman and I'm lucky to have a friend like you." She decided to cut to the chase. "Elle and I had a falling out of sorts and well, I don't think there is any coming back from it at this point." She almost felt detached from her revelation, as if she was telling the story of someone else.

"Seriously? I can't believe that. How could anyone be mad at you?!" Ben's reaction was over the top as expected. His hand shot up to his open mouth as he inhaled sharply. Then he grabbed her hands across the table.

"When did this happen?!"

"Like over a week ago. I don't know."

"Over a week ago and you are just telling me now?!" He looked even more horrified.

"Well, I mean we were supposed to get together a few days ago…"

"Oh wow, now I feel like the world's biggest asshole, cancelling on you like that when you were going through all this. I am so sorry."

"It's fine," Elle said, smiling. "You had no idea. And I'm fine, really. Of course it was hard the first few days but I feel almost numb to it now to be honest. I appreciate you and your concern though. And I know I can always come to you and vice versa."

Ben nodded his head vigorously. "Absolutely. Cheers to always being here for each other." He lifted his cocktail glass and Elle followed suit. She finally felt a sweet release as she sipped her martini. It tasted especially good. It was meant to be sipped and enjoyed. If only she could move forward with this mindset perhaps she could get her drinking under control without entirely cutting herself off. She could find a way to balance it. And then when she did drink, she would appreciate that bottle of wine so much more. Obviously she had been having a shitty year, but now it was time to get it together. She took another sip as she contemplated her ability to control her intake.

"So can you give me the Cliff notes on what happened? I mean if you want to talk about it. I totally get it if you just want to have a relaxing dinner and not rehash everything though."

Of course she knew Ben was just saying that to be polite. To leave him in suspense would be borderline torture for him. After giving him a brief synopsis, including today's horrible run in with Ryan, his look of shock turned into anger.

"Wow, I really cannot believe them. I can't believe he would talk to you like that, what a fucking creeep! And it blows my mind that Ami could have dated that asshole, let alone marry him! But obviously she has terrible taste. She's totally whipped by this new guy, who's just as bad. And to choose him, a guy she has only known a few months over her best friend of how many years? Her friend that saved her from a horrific marriage and now the prospect of another? It's just sad. And it's her loss honestly," Ben concluded with a shake of his head.

Elle smiled slightly. "Thanks, I appreciate it. I mean not to defend her but this is the second time I've told her that her significant other has been unfaithful to her. It is a hard pill to swallow. Maybe I should have just let it be." She sighed.

"No absolutely not," Ben said adamantly "As her best friend, you are obligated to tell her I think. That's what good friends are for. To have your back and to watch out for your best interest always. And she should know that especially after all these years and how much you both have been through."

"Yeah, you're right. And speaking of so many years, guess who decided to reach out after almost thirty? My dad. I got a letter in the mail today. He tells me he's dying and would like to repair the relationship before he goes."

"Woe, woe, woe." Ben holds his hand up. "Are you serious?!"

"100%. Yep, definitely unexpected to say the least."

"How do you think he got your address?"

"I don't know. Probably my mother I'd imagine. She would have no qualms telling him without asking me first." Elle rolled her eyes.

"So what do you think you will do?" Ben asked, taking a long sip of his drink.

Elle took an equally long sip of hers as well before responding. "Well, I ripped the letter up and threw it away immediately, so I guess nothing."

"I'm sure I would have done the same," Ben says contemplatively. "How are you feeling about it now?"

Elle sighed heavily. "I don't know. The same I guess. I feel like a bitch but I don't think I can suddenly just snap my fingers and want a relationship with him because he's dying and wants to clear his conscience. Again, I feel like it is all about him and what he wants. He left me and decided to have nothing to do with me all those years ago—that was his choice. Well now I have a choice, and just no," she ended on a matter of fact note.

"I support you either way," Ben said. "And honestly, I agree with your decision. I mean, what if you did meet and make up and spend his dying days together and all for what? For him to just die and leave you all over again?"

"Right. I didn't even think of it like that."

"I'm sorry, Elle. I'm sorry you are going through this shit. You're the last person who deserves it."

"Thanks, yeah, but hey at least I have you. And a perfect martini." She laughed.

"I can totally understand why you wanted to drink tonight."

"Yep, fun times. And so what's going on with you? Why the sweatpants look tonight?" She smiled broadly, reassuring him she was just joking.

"Ah, yes, my fashion faux pas is certainly mirroring the week I have had. I am at a fuck it point today. A major, major deal I was working on fell through and at the same time I found out that Cameron tested positive for… HIV." He lowered his voice to a near whisper.

"Oh my God!" Now it was Elle's turn to be in complete shock.

"I know. It's devastating. It really is so unfair. Do you remember when we had that two week break up last year?" Elle nodded clearly remembering what a mess Ben had been. Near suicidal actually. Elle had been seriously worried about him, checking in with him incessantly.

"Well, that's when it happened." Ben shook his head. "And apparently he was too drunk and strung out on cocaine to even put the pieces together to figure out who it was. Which adds another layer of shame for him."

"So, what does that mean for you?" Elle blurted, too concerned to hold back.

"Fortunately, I tested negative, believe it or not. And I did two tests to make sure."

"Thank goodness."

"Right. But I feel like I almost have survivor's guilt over it, you know? There's definitely been the most tension and tears between Cameron and I this past week than we ever have had in our entire relationship. I'm so angry at him for getting it, for putting me in this position. And yet I'm so sad for him. But I'm also hopeful for him as obviously treatment has progressed so much, but at the same time, I am also terrified for him and for me. For what this will do to our relationship. I'm just having so many mixed emotions. It's a complete hot mess right now."

"Oh Ben, I'm so sorry." Now Elle reached her hand out over the table and grabbed his. "But at least he was able to catch it sooner than later. And like you said, medicine has progressed so much…" she trailed off, not knowing what else to say.

"Yes, absolutely. And for that I am very thankful. And luckily we are in a position to afford all the antivirals."

"Right."

"He already started taking them this past week. It's a crazy boat load of pills. And of course he's taking all these crazy supplements he researched for hours on end. He's so determined to get his viral load down to a non-detectable level."

"I bet he totally can," Elle said enthusiastically. "I mean people with HIV are able to do it all the time, right?"

"Yeah, we will see. Just taking it day by day, you know? Trying to stay positive and keep stress out of our lives as much as possible."

"Of course. Destressing is key."

"I'm really hoping to buy a little place of our own somewhere in the middle of nowhere with lots of land. Preferably by a body of water. Someplace we can regularly escape to and just decompress. Our camping experience kinda inspired me I guess. As much as I complained to you, it was really nice to be out in nature and I did return home feeling rejuvenated. And Cameron just had a ball. I love the city and could never completely leave it so this would be the perfect solution."

"You guys should totally do that! And I'd be more than happy to house sit," she laughed.

"Ah, well, you would be more than welcome to do that or come camp out with us."

"I would love to. You deserve this. You work so hard. You both do."

"Yeah, sometimes I wonder if it's even worth it but at a time like this, I realize that it really is paying off."

"Exactly."

Ben cleared his palate with another sip of his beverage. Switching subjects he asked, "Any other dates of note lately?"

"Ha, wish I could say so but no." Elle laughed. "I'm taking a break from the dating scene for now."

"Totally understandable. And hey, that just means more dates with me so I am selfishly happy about that."

Elle raised her glass and they clinked their glasses together again. Things may not be perfect, anywhere near perfect, but at least she could count on good times with Ben.

They lingered long after their meals had been cleared chatting over coffee. Finally, Ben picked up the nearly $200 bill without a second glance, placing his shiny metal credit card down. Elle could only imagine the limit on it. She thanked him profusely and then they hugged extra hard before going their separate ways.

Elle felt happy and more hopeful as she headed back home. Even if Ami never resurfaced, she still had others who cared about her. And she certainly was not the only one going through shit.

Once home she was excited to get in her pajamas and just lay on the couch with every mindless show at her disposal. She was flipping between "The Bachelor" and another new series she started, "Finding Love in Paradise" when her mind started to wander to thoughts of Asa annoyingly. Again, she wondered what he was doing right now. Changing a dirty diaper or perhaps escaping for a much needed night out with the guys? Or a date night with his ex-wife and baby mama? She could not resist the urge to check out his Facebook page. She had been so strong up to this point, but really what would it hurt to see a few cute baby photos?

Instead, she found nothing. Not even a birth announcement. Seriously? So odd. Perhaps he had been too busy or maybe a Facebook announcement was not important to him? Or maybe he just hadn't gotten around to it yet. But it had been several days since his birth and he was a pretty regular poster. Certainly the birth of his child was more noteworthy than the majority of his posts. She studied his profile picture, feeling a deep sense of longing to touch his face and rest her head on his shoulder again in the perfect silence at the aquarium. She sighed deeply and returned to her show, where she was hopeful for others to at least fall in love. Soon her eyes grew heavy and she drifted off before finding out which woman received the prized rose.

Chapter 20

That night he dreamt of the worst day of his life, the summer before 9th grade. He and Pierce were at the community pool, where he unfortunately spent the majority of his summers. Their mother would often drop them there while she would go run errands or meet her friends for cocktails. The community pool was his most despised place in the world but his brother was on the competitive swim team so he was also forced to watch his practices. It was beyond misery.

He would beg his mom to just stay home by himself but that only worked so often. She was adamant that he needed sun and exercise. He needed neither. He burnt to a crisp in the sun even with sunscreen and no amount of exercise would benefit his small frame. And he had accepted that a long time ago. He didn't get it. Why couldn't everyone just see him for who he was? Why was everyone so obsessed with appearances? Eventually looks would fade anyways. But his intelligence wouldn't.

Pierce would always shower in the locker room before entering the pool, so free and nonchalant walking around naked, dick swinging. As if he couldn't have showered at home. But of course he loved to show off his body, already that of a grown man. Other men and boys would look and then avert their eyes pretending not to notice. It was disgusting.

He, on the other hand, would make his way as quickly as he could through the locker room and find a lounge chair in a shaded corner, as far away from the showing off, flirting and screaming as possible. Even in the shade he would still get burned. So he would slather himself as best he could while his brother would simply ask whatever female he felt most compelled to, in their practically nonexistent swimsuit, to do his back. Once, Brittany Bower's mother actually approached him and stated that she would be "delighted" to help. Her boobs were so big that they grazed his brother's back as she rubbed in an excessive amount. "We don't want you getting burned now, do we?" she had laughed.

He would manage to get through the miserable hours laying on his towel listening to his death metal or reading. When he was so hot he couldn't stand it, he would finally be forced to dip in the pool. He would enter as covertly as possible but inevitably kids would turn to glance at his gleaming white, stick thin body. Fuck all of them. He was better than all of them combined.

In his dream, it played out just exactly as it had happened. His brother did one of his crazy flips off the high dive, followed by cheers and applause. He approached the stepladder, reluctant to get in. But Pierce surfaced and grabbed a hold of it first with one hand, whisking back his thick dark hair like some kind of movie star with the other.

"You're finally getting in, huh?" he asked as he pulled himself up with one bulging arm and loomed over him. Droplets of water dripped onto his head.

"Yeah, I was." He managed not to stutter.

His brother stepped closer to him, his big toe crushing his pinky toe.

"So why don't you get into the pool like a real man?" he hissed. "Stop embarrassing the shit out of me you pussy. Show me you actually have a dick for once."

He looked up into his brother's eyes, resisting the urge to give him a black one.

"Fine. I'll do it," he spat at him.

"Good. Finally losing your virginity. We'll all be cheering for you." His brother winked at him and then nearly pushed him to the line. There were only three people in front of them. Two little girls and an older man. They all jumped off without hesitation, the little girl's pigtails and the older man's cellulite ridden abdomen flailing on their descent. He could do this. It was not a big deal.

"After you," his brother pushed him up the first step.

His legs felt like they were going to buckle as he ascended the slippery stairs. He gripped the railing forcefully having lost all of his balance. As he came to the platform and looked out over the pool, all the activity seemed to suddenly stop in anticipation of his dive. They were all looking at him. He neared the edge of the platform. It was a further jump than he had realized. He hated heights. Holy shit. He felt like he was going to pass out. He wanted to scream, "fuck all of you! I hate you!" His rage was overwhelming. But instead, he pissed himself in his dry trunks. Piss trickled down his leg.

He backed away from the edge as faces looked up at him in confusion. With each stair he descended he could hear the laughter become louder. He would have rather died right then and there. His brother was even so humiliated he had no words for him as he slunk back to his chair and gathered his belongings as quickly as he could, keeping his teary eyed face down as they continued to stare at him like a crazed zoo animal. He walked the nearly five miles home in his piss soaked trunks in the blistering heat hating himself for crying, for giving into his fear. But tomorrow there would be no fear or backing out. Tomorrow he would show his brother he could be a real man. That he could be a more powerful man than him. So powerful that he could take his brother's life without even flinching.

The next morning, she woke to the puttering of raindrops on her roof. The soothing effect combined with her Seroquel hangover prompted her to fall back asleep for another hour. She had managed to get into bed after having slept on the couch with her neck angled at a terrible position around midnight.

At 10 a.m. she only got up to feed her growling stomach. The rainy mood reminded her of a cute French cafe she had discovered a few months ago darting through the rain. With Ami of course. They had been roaming around looking for a baby shower gift for Ami's coworker amongst all the overpriced boutiques.

Ami had ended up purchasing a nautical outfit that the baby would probably only wear a couple of times, a teething toy shaped like an anchor he would naturally lose and a stuffed whale that would be forgotten amongst all the other toys for just shy of $150 without even accessing the price tags.

Last minute she threw in a necklace for herself, which the cashier was wearing and indicated that she made herself. It was a beautiful necklace and turned out to be "only" $125. Ami had offered to buy Elle one but she assertively declined.

Even as her best friend, Elle never expected Ami to give her charity. Although sometimes this made things difficult as far as spa days and restaurant outings were concerned. Fortunately, Ami chose reasonably priced restaurants overall in consideration of Elle's financial circumstances and saved the really high end places for her other well off lawyer friends.

That day in particular Elle had been running on fumes and had been relieved to see that the prices at the small French cafe were in line with the paltry eighty bucks she had left in her bank account for the next three days. It was called Merci, yes that was it. A buttery croissant and hot latte sounded perfect.

She brushed her teeth for the requisite two minutes, simply splashed cold water on her face and ran her wet fingers through her frizzy mane. She was in no mood to be bothered with makeup. She changed into one of her go to pairs of jeans and a loose fitting shirt she tucked in her jeans paired with a belt. She even dug into the back of her closet for her rain boots that had been sitting there idly since last spring. It had been an extremely dry spring and summer so far, which Elle did not mind one bit. Chicago winters were plenty enough to deal with.

She was easily able to find her umbrella in the bin under her console table, which she had organized the other day during her cleaning frenzy. She glanced in the mirror above the table and tousled her hair once more before she realized something was not right. The photo of her and Ami at the beach was back on the console table.

In the exact angled position she normally had it placed. Before she had shoved it into the drawer on her way out to see Dr. Berkshire. Fuck. She must really be going crazy. She shook her head vigorously, trying not to accept this conclusion. It couldn't be.

Her heart started racing and she felt the sensation of someone choking her on the verge of a panic attack again. She quickly searched for the emergency Xanax Ben had given her in the depths of her purse. In growing desperation, she finally was able to locate it. She attempted to swallow it but her mouth was so dry, she started to choke.

She ran to the fridge and retrieved a bottle of water. She downed the entire bottle in one continuous gulp until she felt the pill dislodge resuming its journey into her stomach, her bloodstream and finally into her overactive nerves. She could count on relief in a mere ten minutes. But ten minutes in panic felt like an eternity. She sank to the cool tile floor and splayed out like a starfish.

She imagined herself as a little girl making snow angels, armored in her snowsuit, the feeling of panic completely foreign to her being.

"I am safe and capable of managing anxiety," she said aloud in a shaky voice and again more steadily, more forcefully. She imagined sticking out her tongue and catching snowflakes, the feeling of them hitting her eyelids and instantly melting. She imagined her anxiety instantly melting along with them. But it was more like the melting of an icicle on an early spring day before she finally was able to pick herself up from the floor, still shaking.

She found a cozy corner booth, allowing her body to completely disintegrate into its plump pillows, beyond grateful to feel mostly back to normal. She took in the calming atmosphere. Light French music played while the thin and presumably French waitresses shuffled about. An older gentleman sat in the corner adjacent to her sipping coffee and reading the newspaper, an uncomfortable look of concentration furrowing his forehead.

Elle could not recall the last time she had picked up an actual newspaper. Two young boys browsed through some thick hardcover novels on a bookcase near her, laughing as they attempted to read aloud in French accents.

A woman and her identical looking daughter sat near the window on a loveseat, the little girl pointing at the unrelenting rain. Elle had fortunately gotten inside right before the downpour.

She stared at the sheets of rain broken by silhouettes of fleeting passersby, thankful that she was warm and protected inside. The waiter interrupted her trance with his perfect French accent. His eyes were an intriguing greyish color but his unfortunate unibrow detracted from their beauty. Elle ordered a vanilla latte, extra hot, and a warm chocolate croissant. He nodded and indicated he would be right back.

Elle retrieved the novel she had started a few nights ago, turning to the corner she had creased to mark her place. It was quite a bit further than she recalled getting to. She started to read but realized she had no idea what was going on so she went back to the beginning of the chapter. This also appeared foreign to her so she backed up another chapter, finally recalling what she had read. She needed to stop being so hard on herself. She was fine. People did things they forgot especially when they were stressed out and not sleeping properly. It was normal.

She sipped on her latte just as she liked it—so hot it nearly burned her tongue—and immersed herself in her novel. She was so engrossed in it, that when she bit into her croissant it was no longer warm but still delicious. Nor did she notice the figure of a man outside staring at her through the rain-streaked window, his face hidden behind his large umbrella.

When she got home, she almost caved and called Jake. His phone number enticed her from the fridge as she opened it to grab a La Coix. Still placed under the Eiffel tower magnet she noted thank goodness. Though her day of solitude had been very nice, she was craving some socialization. She had nearly gotten halfway through her novel, which she was proud of. She could not recall the last time she had sat for nearly five hours and read, if ever in her life. Nor had she ever stayed long enough at a coffee shop to order breakfast and lunch.

But she decided to keep her productive solo day going instead. After she finally finished sticking the last piece of tile on the back splash, she stood back admiring the finished product. A pop of modern really did make a difference. And for all but $125, she really should have done it long ago. She scrubbed her countertops down for good measure, running her finger over them afterwards to make sure that there were no sticky spots.

Satisfied, she moved on to her art studio. The familiar mess and different pieces of art, each in their different stages of progress, invited and inspired her. She was eager to keep working on her painting of the dreaming girl floating on the cloud. Maybe she would even display this one over her bed.

Hopefully it would encourage her to dream of ice cream sundaes and everything pure and good. She asked Google to put on some old school Dave Matthews that came to mind as she set herself up at the easel with fresh brushes and paint. His voice was all too familiar. She put on her apron and hummed along, contemplating where to go with her painting next.

After an hour in her studio, as much as she just wanted to sit on her ass and do nothing the rest of the day, she still forced herself to get on the Peloton and do a 45 minute ride.

She bounced in tandem to some angry rock music, her instructor,

Roxy, yelling "to pick up the pace!" as if she was in army boot camp. She wanted to exhaust herself enough to stop thinking, to fall asleep on her own tonight. She pushed herself until her nostrils nearly collapsed from breathing so hard and she felt like she might suffocate. She gave it everything she had to make it through the last climb.

Drenched in sweat, she rewarded herself with a long hot shower, scrubbing her skin and washing her hair twice. Famished and even somewhat dizzy from what was probably one of the hardest rides she had endured, she went through the lackluster inventory in her kitchen and was excited to find a hidden box of mac and cheese. She ate the entire box of Annie's right from the pot sitting on her sofa. Followed by her favorite Haagen Daz ice cream right from the carton.

Just what her mother used to yell at her for.

"Get a bowl and be a lady," she would nag. Rebelliously, Elle took a hefty bite with the perfect amount of waffle cone and caramel. Oh the joys of adulthood and living alone with nobody to appease, with nobody watching and criticizing her every move. In fact, she felt like making some brownies to compliment her ice cream. The twenty minute wait was worth the overly indulgent combination. But she had earned it. And at least she wasn't drinking her calories.

She was in bed by 10:30 p.m., the exercise and food coma hitting her hard. She could only manage to read just a few pages of her book. By 11:15 p.m. she was lights out.

Chapter 21

His adrenaline coursed through his body. His heart was beating so fast he was sure they could hear him. But they were so disgustingly engrossed with each other that they wouldn't have even noticed a bear approaching them. He was only about 25 yards from their boat. Of course they had stopped to make out. So much for watching the sunset. He needed to get this done before there was no light to see.

Pierces' hands started to work their way up her shirt and then down her shorts. Shorts so short that her ass cheeks hung out. He couldn't take it one more second.

This was it. He surveyed the area again. Creeping the gun around the side of the tree with a surprisingly steady aim, he pulled the trigger, finally releasing all his anger and resentment in that magical shot. All the years of his brother superseding him were over. It blew perfectly right through the middle of his head. Just like that. It was so easy. An explosion of blood and horrified screaming ensued. She looked over in his direction and froze. His second shot was almost as equally satisfying. After the birds had stopped squawking it was completely quiet and still. Finally, some fucking peace and quiet.

He swam out to the boat, gun in hand, and placed it in Pierce's limp one. The surface of the boat was already pooled in blood. Then he tore a few strands of her thick auburn hair from the back of her head, which was now face-planted on the ledge of the boat.

Her vibrant and youthful hair would forever be stunted in time for his keeping. Before he left, he also took that stupid joke of a ring from her finger and placed it on his own. He dove back in the water without giving a second glance at his twin brother, elated that he would never have to see his fucking face again. When he got back to shore, he grabbed his backpack and ran out of the woods to his hidden bike, laughing hysterically. It had been even more quick and simple than he had imagined and yet the feeling of victory would last for the rest of his life.

She woke up to a text from Ben asking if she wanted to meet for a 9 a.m. class. Besides being the most sore she had ever been in her life, she did not have a Seroquel hangover at least. She sent him a thumbs up.

She grabbed a brownie, noting that she had made more of a dent in the pan last night than she thought. Oh well, she would be working it all off again anyways.

She grabbed a coffee to go and a large water bottle, checked herself in the mirror, relieved to note that the picture of her and Ami was still shoved in the console, and was out the door in her new pair of Lulu's that she had been gifted to her for her 30th birthday by a fitness enthusiast she had seen briefly. Doug, yes, Doug was his name. Very sweet guy but Elle had the strong inclination that he was gay after he gave several men the look over in front of Elle. Needless to say, it fizzled out pretty quickly after that.

She did some squats and lunges to stretch out the material before she locked up and flew down the stairs to her car across the street. Her legs did feel abnormally strong. She was not one to weigh herself regularly, she did not even own a scale, but she was curious to see if her body fat had decreased. Maybe she would use the really high tech looking scale in the locker room, constantly in demand by obsessive women.

As she started her engine, "Mom" popped up on her dashboard interrupting one of her newly favorite songs that had grown on her that summer. She knew exactly why she was calling and didn't want to talk about it. Impulsively she answered on the last ring, deciding to just get it over with.

"Hi Mom," she answered in a flat tone maneuvering out of her nearly perfect parallel park job.

"Hi sweetie," her mom replied, with excessive cheer. "How are you doing?"

"Doing good. I'm actually about to walk into a spin class. What's up?"

"Oh that's good. Sounds like you really are watching your figure after all!"

"Yep. I definitely took what you said into consideration." Elle smiled. She might as well try to have some fun with it.

"Oh that's great to hear. I bet you will find a husband in no time now." Of course she only referred to a man or a husband when it came to Elle's dating life. "Just think—finally you will be able to get out of that crammed condo of yours and buy a house in the suburbs with enough space for a couple of grandkids to give me! I have been waiting so patiently."

"Yep, that's the plan!" Elle chirped.

"Anyways, I was calling to see if you received your father's letter. I gave him your address…"

"I assumed." Elle cut her off. "Yes, I got it. Why?"

"That's great to hear. Your poor father, well obviously he is dying as you know then, and well, he has finally come to his senses by wanting to make amends. And with that, he also indicated that he would like to leave some inheritance to us. If we reconcile. Which I have of course."

Well of course you have when money is involved, Elle resisted blurting out.

"I will always love your father regardless. He has certainly made his mistakes and was not there for you as he should have been but at least he's trying to end things on a good note."

Elle knew exactly where this was going. She sped aggressively through a yellow light, unnerved.

"And honey, I know how much he loves you and how badly he feels for everything in the past. But that's just it, it's all in the past now. He's trying to do right by you now at least. And all it would take is you just flying out to see him in Baltimore before he goes. That one trip could give you—well, us—thousands and thousands of dollars. You could finally get that nose job you've always wanted! Wouldn't that be nice?! You would certainly turn some heads!"

Elle snorted through her "inferior" nose. Her mother was the one who had always been fixated on her nose. Elle had never been bothered by the slight crook in it.

"Right. That would totally make it worth it then!" Elle exclaimed.

Naturally her mother was oblivious to her sarcasm.

"Oh good! I am soooo glad that you will do it then! I knew you would have the sense to. It really will be worth it, I promise dear. You can finally have the life you deserve."

Elle did not feel like arguing with her. She had given up on trying to encourage her mother to see things from her perspective long ago. Instead, she said, "great, well thanks for the call and sorry to cut you off, but I can't be late for my class. I need to burn at least 500 calories to stay on track."

"Of course. I have to get going as well. Oh, excuse me Sir!" she trailed off. Once again, her mother always had to be the first to get off the phone to make it a point of how in demand she was.

Elle simply hung up. She released her grip on the steering wheel, unaware of how tight it was. Her mother unfortunately still had that effect on her sometimes despite Elle's best efforts. She took three deep breaths. "You are safe and can cope with negativity in a healthy way," she said aloud and then again.

As she entered the studio and saw Ben front and center with a seat saved for her, her spirits instantly lifted. He made eye contact with her and smiled. She adjusted her bike just so, finally having gotten it down herself, no longer needing to rely on the instructor to help her.

The instructor started the class off in a booming voice with excessive enthusiasm. Her legs were definitely tired after just a couple of minutes but somehow, she managed to push through to the end, refusing to let herself give up. As if getting herself through the longest 45 minutes ever was a reflection of her ability to get through this challenging time in her life. The built up "fuck you's" she wished she could delve out also helped.

Afterwards, drenched in sweat, Elle had lost any desire to weigh herself. She was getting stronger and that was what mattered. She would not be like her mother.

"Wanna grab a smoothie?" Ben asked.

"Sure," Elle replied, wiping the sweat off of her face. She and Ben slowly strolled the couple blocks to a smoothie joint, her legs nearly trembling.

"You OK over there?" Ben asked, nearly grabbing her as she stubbed her toe on the sidewalk and nearly fell.

"Yeah, I'm OK," she laughed. "Just pretty exhausted after that ride."

Ben had barely broken a sweat and looked like he could easily spin another couple hours. "I feel you. That was a pretty brutal one."

He grabbed her arm and they walked the rest of the way there like a happy couple. If she never got married she would be OK with that. She could always adopt on her own if she really felt compelled to have kids. She could figure out the whole single mom thing. Plenty of women did it and with far less support and resources than she had. But if she never did, that was fine, too. She realized she had become too codependent on Ami over the years and would be fine on her own. Once she got her shit together finally, which she was.

Elle insisted that she pay for their overpriced smoothies. They chose to sit in a sunny corner in metal chairs that did not help her sore ass. After Ben asked her if Ami had been in contact, she attentively listened to Ben as he went off about Cameron again, essentially repeating everything he had said the other night. A half hour later her smoothie was gone and Ben had barely taken a few sips of his.

"Thanks for listening… again," Ben said, snapping back to the present.

"Of course. Anytime," Elle said, meaning it. It was good to get out of her head.

"Thank you. One of the many reasons you are the best." He took a long sip of his smoothie finally. "Wow, this is really good."

Elle laughed. "Yes, obviously mine was, too."

"I owe you," Ben said, his eyes locking with hers. He normally did not look at her so intimately. "Again."

"No you don't."

"Just know I will always be here for you no matter what. Even if you committed murder or something crazy. Not that I think you would," he quickly added and smiled. Elle laughed but her heart started to race. She needed to continue to be careful before she really did something she would regret.

When she got home the first thing she did was lock her car keys in a miniature safe she had used to put all her tip money when she waitressed in college, hidden behind a bunch of art supplies in her studio. Sadly, it was empty now. She spent the rest of the day researching what the hell was going on with her, Googling "alcohol, Seroquel and sleepwalking" and "trauma and sleepwalking," until she was too exhausted and overwhelmed to continue reading about these potentially deadly combinations.

After she locked the Seroquel in the safe with her car keys, she got ready for bed quickly, succumbing to the mental and physical exhaustion building up these past few weeks. She didn't have the energy to even floss her teeth. She slipped under the duvet of her unmade bed and picked up her book, slightly disappointed to realize she was nearly done with it. She could only make it through a couple pages before she turned out the light, leaving the last two last chapters of suspense for tomorrow.

Chapter 22

He was too excited to sleep that night, like he was as a little kid on Christmas Eve. Before he was disappointed year after year with practical gifts like socks and underwear. The knock on the door came sooner than he anticipated. He could hear his father grumbling in annoyance down the stairs, followed by the officer's serious voices. His mother came down the stairs as his father yelled in disbelief.

His mother screamed, his calling to join his parents in their agony. He even managed a few tears. His brother and his girlfriend had been discovered by an early morning hunter. It would be all over the news the following day. Delivered at his front door step with the headline, "All Star Football Player Commits Potential Murder and Suicide," alongside their yearbook photos.

His parents left to confirm his brother's body, his mother still in her nightgown. His brother and his beloved girlfriend were only bloody corpses now. His brother's achievements, his popularity and so called charisma would fade in his followers' memories.

When they returned, completely deflated, his mother sank into the couch, where Pierce normally sat, speechless and as white as a ghost. Her hair was disheveled and makeup streaked all over her face like he had never seen before. He laid a hand on her shoulder playing the part of a grieving brother and stoic son. His father sat opposite them in his worn recliner, repeating "it can't be, it just can't be!" over and over again.

He held his mother's hand though it did not appear to even register with her. The good son, the only son. She stared out the window in a catatonic state. His father rocked back and forth incessantly. Comatose and constantly moving, what would become their different grieving styles.

Eventually the doorbell rang and his father slowly got up to answer it. It was his father's doctor friend. He handed him a prescription bag without words. He then leaned in to embrace his father who awkwardly returned the embrace ending with a pat on the shoulder. The doctor said a few indistinct words, his father nodding in response and then softly closed the door.

"Give this to your mother," he said, handing him the bag of pills. The first words he had said to him since learning of his brother's death. He retrieved a glass of water and placed the pill in his mother's hand but she did not move. He placed it in her mouth and instructed her to swallow.

She finally picked up the glass with a shaking hand as he popped a couple himself. Why not? It was going to be a tortuously long day playing the grieving brother.

He continued to sit there with his mother, her blood shot eyes finally closing. He watched his favorite TV shows that he never got a chance to watch due to his father and brother monopolizing the sports channels. He was eating the rest of his brother's favorite Doritos, when his sister came through the door. She had obviously been crying. He embraced her and she embraced him back. Now the lone surviving siblings.

She bent down and kissed their mother, who snored softly on the couch, glints of remaining sunlight highlighting the wrinkles on her face and the sneaky grey hairs she would never bother dying again. His sister sat next to him as they had never done before, always escaping to their bedrooms. Together they watched the sunset. He felt a glorious sense of calm and peace knowing that he had ended his brother's life at the same time yesterday.

She woke up paralyzed, her heart pummeling through her chest. A figure stood looming in the corner wearing a baseball cap and baggy clothes. His face was only slightly illuminated by her alarm clock but she could not make out any features other than his white skin tone. She could only move her eyelids. She squeezed them shut, praying that he would think she was asleep and leave.

"I am safe, I am safe," she repeated in her mind over and over until it felt like an hour passed. Three minutes later she opened her eyes and the man was gone.

She lay in the same position until the sun was fully up and her bladder was absolutely bursting. She grabbed her phone and dialed

911 so it was ready to go in case. She slowly balanced herself on shaky legs and tiptoed to the bathroom and peeled back the shower curtain before peeing as fast as she could.

She grabbed a baseball bat she remembered she had buried under her bed, covered in dust. She had never anticipated actually using it to defend herself. She tiptoed on the outside edge of the hallway to minimize the sound of the squeaky floorboards to the kitchen. Sunlight spilled in from the window over the sink illuminating the white countertops and a few crumbs, but otherwise there was nothing out of place. Frantically, she threw open each closet door and checked behind every piece of furniture. The door was still locked and everything was in its place.

She even ran outside in her nightgown, still holding the bat in hand, not giving a shit how deranged she knew she must look. She ran over to the rock where she kept her spare key. It was right in its place. A young woman pushing a stroller passed by her on the sidewalk. The baby smiled and waved a pudgy hand at her as the woman picked up her pace. Elle waved back at the baby, taking a deep breath.

Had she hallucinated after all? At this point she did not care what anyone, especially Dr. Berkshire thought of her. She had never felt so desperate or out of control. She ascended her stairs, erasing 911, and went to her "favorites" where he was listed at the top underneath Ami. Why she had not erased her number still was beyond her. A useless cause. Like how as a little girl blowing out her birthday candles, she secretly wished for her father to magically appear.

Back inside she immediately locked the door. The line rang several times before Dr. Berkshire's soothing voice instructed to call 911 if this was a mental health emergency, otherwise welcomed leaving a voicemail, which would be returned promptly. She made an effort to keep her voice from cracking and asked him to call her back as soon as possible. She repeated her phone number twice as if he did not know her number by now.

Feeling the adrenaline depleting from her body, she felt beyond exhausted. She made some coffee, adding an extra scoop of grinds. She wasn't hungry but she poured a small bowl of cereal to even out her blood sugar. As she slowly ate the slightly stale generic brand of Cheerios, she distracted herself scrolling through the news on her phone hoping it would ring at any moment with his call back.

The news was nothing new of course. Shootings, an apartment fire, a child abuse conviction. All horrendous and heart wrenching. Elle could never comprehend how so many, her grandma before she passed included, could so comfortably watch this repetitive horror all day long.

Elle could clearly remember sitting with her on her stiff couch as a child, permeated with the thick stench of smoke, immersed in her plethora of pillows, their respective TV dinners on trays, as killings and catastrophes continued to unfold. Her grandma would shovel the food into her mouth unphased by these atrocities while Elle would force each bite down.

Her grandma passed away on that couch from a heart attack, undoubtedly watching the news, her main attachment to the world since Elle's grandpa passed away before Elle was born. Though Elle missed her grandma and cried for several weeks after she passed, she felt a sense of comfort believing that her grandma was at peace with her grandpa again, no longer needing the distraction of negative news to fill the void.

Elle sighed impatiently, studying her ragged looking nails. She bit off a stray cuticle. She couldn't recall the last time she had a manicure. As if that was a concern right now. She poured herself a cup of coffee and slowly sipped the near scalding liquid black. Ten minutes later, she picked up Dr. Berkshires' call on the first ring.

He listened to her without interrupting as she relayed the events from last night. Her terror, though she attempted to control it, was evident. Finally, Dr. Berkshire spoke in his calming, grandfatherly tone.

"Now it sounds to me that you just experienced a hypnagogic dream, Elle. These are actually more common than you would think, most often in children and adolescents though. As you experienced, they occur right before you fall asleep or upon waking. They can also be accompanied by other sensory hallucinations but visual is the most common. Given your history with sleepwalking and insomnia, along with your anxiety, I'm not terribly surprised you experienced this though I'm sincerely sorry you did. They can be very disturbing as you know."

"Also sleep paralysis as you also described, is quite common after these types of hallucinations. Now if you were hallucinating at other times, then I would be concerned. But this is not the case, correct?"

"Correct," Elle said, feeling some relief.

"Good. And how is the sobriety going?"

"Well, I have not drank in the past couple of days," she replied honestly. I haven't taken the sleeping pills either."

"I see. Well good job for not drinking the past couple of days. And if you can get by without the Seroquel, then that is great, too. Of course I would rather you be able to sleep naturally, but I also want to make sure you are getting adequate sleep. Not getting adequate sleep can also be a trigger for these types of hallucinations. Alcohol use can as well."

"Well, I appreciate the information," She laughed uneasily. "And reassurance."

"Anytime. Keep me posted. And perhaps try sleeping with a night light on. Light tends to alleviate them."

"Thank you, Dr. Berkshire, and thank you for returning my call so quickly."

"Of course. Take care, Elle, and talk soon."

Elle hung up and sighed deeply. There was an explanation. She was not going crazy. Or as crazy as she thought. She sipped the last of her now lukewarm coffee, determined to have an ordinary day beginning with a ride on the Peloton. She could even make a live class starting in fifteen minutes with one of her favorite instructors.

Having gotten behind on her laundry again, she slipped into her least favorite pair of leggings and quickly brushed her teeth. She gathered her hair, twisting it up in a bun. As she searched for a hair tie on her bathroom counter that had quickly lost its organization, she felt a chunk of her hair gone at the end. Immediately she released her wild hair, splaying out over her shoulders and brushed her fingers through it.

"What the hell?" She demanded in the mirror.

There was an obvious chunk of her hair missing, cut clear off in one blunt clip. And on the counter lay the scissors. She wanted to scream. This was not her doing. There was someone fucking with her, someone out to get her. Her anger overtook her fear and she impulsively punched the mirror, cracks spreading and blood seeping through her knuckles.

Who was doing this to her? And why? She refused to be a victim any longer. She had to get to the bottom of it now, before it was too late.

She grabbed whatever clean clothes she could find and for at least a few days, her ready to go toiletry bag and phone charger, stuffing it all in a duffel bag, the fastest packing job she had ever done. She needed to get the hell out of here.

She stubbed her toe on the stupid uneven floorboard in the hallway as she went to grab her car keys from the safe in her studio. "Fuck!" she screamed. But her pain was quickly replaced with horror. As she looked up at her painting. "Holy fuck!" she screamed again.

Her innocent girl was crying and bleeding.

Tears of blood streamed from her closed eyelids and poured from her torso, pooling onto the ice cream sundae below her. She covered her mouth, shocked to her core. Terrified and disgusted she threw the canvas on the floor and stomped on it until it was obliterated. Her peaceful and happy painting was now a complete nightmare.

She was on the verge of a panic attack, her heart racing, her head starting to spin. But she needed to keep going. Her hands shook as she turned the dial on the safe and grabbed her car keys. She made sure all her windows were locked, double locked her door, and remembered to grab the spare key before she threw her duffel bag over her shoulder and ran to her car down the street, her shadow following her in the early morning light like a relentless predator.

She had no plan. She needed to calm down first to think clearly." I am safe, I am safe," she said aloud but it was futile. She could no longer convince herself. She drove aimlessly, trying to get a hold of herself and thinking what she would do next. She drove by a coffee shop and turned around, nearly hitting a car as she parked. She grabbed her Cubs hat amid all the random crap in her back seat.

She stood in the line, her head swarming. Could the well-dressed man in front of her or the twenty something year old guy behind her be the one?

After ordering a decaf coffee, (she certainly didn't need caffeine), she chose a spot in the back away from the crowd. She brought out a notebook from her purse with random grocery lists and "to dos" and the only pen she could find in the bottom of its abyss. With a shaky hand she wrote all the possible perpetrators she could think of, no matter how unlikely.

Guy from Whole Foods

Ami's brother
Ami's ex
Ami
Ben
Dad
Neighbor
Jake
Asa

Starting with the guy at Whole Foods she thought of all the grounds, or rather what her gut instincts told her, for and against him being the culprit. As creepy as he was, she still had the sense that he was harmless. Afterall, he had only been trying to be helpful. She crossed him out.

Ami's brother. He obviously knew where she lived and had already victimized her in the past. But would he really have the balls to again? Especially after he bought her a Peloton as some sort of reconciliation gift? Probably not. She crossed him out.

Ryan, Ami's horrible ex. He did know where she lived unfortunately. But he didn't seem vengeful that Elle had essentially ended his marriage with Ami. In fact, he had said that she had done him a favor now that he was with his hot girlfriend. Kitty, was it? Such a stripper name. He probably met her at a strip club the low life he was. Preying on the vulnerable. She furiously scratched his name out. If it weren't for him, she probably would still have her best friend.

Ami, her ex-best friend. who was fed up with her enough to eliminate Elle from her life, to throw her away like some useless piece of trash. So what would be her motive to continue to hang onto her? To get back at her for trying to ruin her second marriage? Highly unlikely. Ami was nothing but logic and stability.

But she was the only one who knew where her spare key was. Many times, they had stumbled back to her place after a night of partying and Elle would grab the spare key, having no room in her tiny clutch for her full set. But still, no. And most importantly, her "hypnagogic dream," though she could not make out the face, the figure was definitely that of a man. She crossed her off and attempted to drink her scalding coffee, which was still even too hot for her.

Ben. There was just no way. She trusted Ben more than anyone in this world. But hadn't she trusted Ami as well? Still, absolutely not.

He just couldn't be. She felt bad for even considering him and immediately crossed his name out.

Her Dad or biological donner really. What could possibly incentivize him to fuck with her after not being a part of her life since she was five? And if he was angry that she had not responded to his letter yet and crazy enough to mess with her, she had only received the letter just the other day. Crossed off.

Her neighbor. He was certainly outright creepy and lived right below her. But he had always stayed to himself. Plus, he was old. Eliminated.

Jake. She just couldn't see him doing this. He was a young party kid only consumed with getting in as many hook ups as possible. And he did not live here. His coworkers also confirmed that. And again, the madness started before she had met him.

And then there was Asa. Her heart pounded thinking of him. The escalation of the craziness had come after the "break up." At the end of the day, she had only known him for a very brief period and had pretty much let him fully into her life. He may have seen her grab her spare key when he dropped her off at home after their handful of dates though. She had never brought her keys since she hadn't driven.

But why? He had broken up with her. Maybe there didn't need to be a reason. Crazy was just crazy after all. Asa made the most sense to her, especially given how quickly he had seemed to come into her life and then leave. It had to be him. She circled his name three times.

She tried as hard as she could to recall the name of the building complex he lived at. She needed to confirm if he had moved—or not. She went through the alphabet in her mind, her old standby memory trick, and landed on "R." The Regency, that was it. She left her coffee on the table having not had one sip.

Back on the road she headed north in heavy traffic, following the British accented commands of Google Maps. Her head was so flooded with thoughts and her body so flooded with adrenaline, that she nearly rear ended a Mercedes. The old man rolled down his window and flicked her off. She held up her hand and grimaced in apology. Unfortunately, she ended up following him to The Regency. Of course he would be driving there. She parked in an inconspicuous visitor's spot far away from the building to avoid any further interaction.

She waited a few minutes to be safe, tidying up her appearance as best she could in the rear-view mirror in an effort to not look like a crazy and deranged ex-girlfriend. She took off her baseball cap and smoothed out her hair, carefully placing the piece with the missing chunk behind her ear. That was as good as it was going to get.

She surveyed the parking lot 360 degrees before she made her way up to the building. She confidently approached the large gentleman at the front desk, who greeted her with a pleasant smile.

"Hello," she said, matching his smile. "How are you doing today?"

"Doing well, thank you. How may I help you, Ma'am?"

"I was hoping you would be able to give this to a gentleman that lives in this building." She thrust the baseball cap out. "His name is Asa Follet. I believe he lives on the fifth floor. I wanted to return it to him."

"Ah, I would if I could, M'am, but unfortunately Mr. Follet moved out of the building at least a couple of weeks ago." His smile faded and he looked at her somewhat pitifully. The relentlessly hopeful ex-girlfriend.

"Oh, wow, I see." She pretended to look shocked. "And would you happen to have any idea where he would have gone?"

"That I am not at liberty to say, unfortunately." He sighed, knowing how much this suspense would haunt her. Finally, he said, "but I will say, without being specific, that I believe he mentioned moving back home."

Elle smiled at him gratefully and thanked him.

He winked at her. "Good luck, Ma'am. He seems like a nice guy and you seem like a very nice lady indeed."

"Yes," she responded. "He is definitely worth the chase." She placed the hat on the desk. "A token of my appreciation."

"Ah, you don't need to do that."

"I insist. You have been more helpful than you know and you don't seem like a White Sox fan."

"You guessed right." He nodded in appreciation and she waved at him as she pushed through the revolving door, headed back to the safety of her car, eager to do some research.

She brought up his Facebook page to see if there were any updated posts since she last checked. Still no baby announcement, nothing. His "current city" was still Chicago, "from" Madison Wisconsin. His "current employer" was also Goldman Sachs. She googled Goldman Sachs locations in Wisconsin. Not a one. Shit. She racked her brain for anything she could recall that would hint at anything more specific.

She scrolled down his Facebook page until she came across "Amy's Toffee" in cursive. Underneath he had written, "come get your Christmas toffee for 25% off on bulk orders!" with a link to Amy's Toffee. That's right! He had mentioned that his ex-wife's family had a toffee business. She clicked on the link, which displayed an assortment of toffees. A picture of an older and younger couple at the bottom stood proudly sporting aprons and large smiles. She did a double take at the heavily bearded man. It was definitely Asa.

She assumed the pretty younger blonde was Asa's ex. She enhanced her screen, honing in on her face. There was no denying that she really was gorgeous. Well, it looked like she was on her way to Cottage Grove Wisconsin to try the "best toffee in the country" after all.

Chapter 23

Elle drove for an hour and a half straight, forcing herself to hum and sing along to some old time hits to calm her nerves, until she relented to her screaming bladder. She pulled off at the next exit following the signs to the nearest gas station.

She was the only apparent customer. She would make this as quick as possible. She nearly ran to the bathroom, relieved to find that the one stall in the women's was unoccupied. She peed for what was probably two minutes straight and bought a well deserved bag of Cheetos and Diet Coke from an older man with kind eyes and a welcoming smile. But oh how deceiving looks could be she reminded herself.

She drove for another half hour, somewhat relaxed, enjoying the freedom of the open road. This was the longest drive she had been on since the accident. She munched on the Cheetos, licking her fingers as needed. Her phone rang just as she finished the last one. It was Ben. She hesitated for a moment. Should she tell him what she was doing? She quickly decided that she would only give a half truth. She needed more information, more evidence before she started telling people about everything going on, even Ben. The last thing she needed was a mental health petition mandating her to be committed.

"Hey Ben!" she answered brightly. "How are you?"

"Doing good. Just finishing up work for the day a bit early. Cameron and I were thinking of grabbing happy hour. Would you like to join us for some apps?"

"Ah, I wish I could!" She sipped her Coke thinking of an excuse. "But I actually have plans with one of my teacher friends."

"Oh gotcha. That will be nice," Ben said, sounding slightly disappointed.

They said their standard goodbyes and she got back to focusing on the road. She would be there in just twenty minutes. She merged off the freeway and drove past towering trees shielding quaint country homes with large porches and ample, neatly kept yards. She rolled down the windows taking in the smell of clean air with the hint of freshly cut grass.

She approached a small group of children playing with a kickball, no adult in sight. Parents were obviously not concerned for the safety of their children here, or rather they didn't have to be. Goodness still prevailed here.

She diligently slowed down to a crawl as she passed the children. A chubby little girl in pigtails waved at her with a bright smile. Elle waved back, smiling. It reminded her of her own childhood before Ami, running around the neighborhood. She would pop over to her friend's idyllic houses with idyllic parents, who would welcome her with open arms. In hindsight, they probably pitied her, knowing how absent her single mother was. She would often join them for dinner and was always provided a variety of junk food, neither of which she got to experience at home.

She licked the last residue of orange stains from her fingers. She needed to get out of the city more often. Or better yet, maybe she should just move out of the city. Where it was safer, quieter and life was just simpler.

She certainly would be leaving her condo regardless after all this. At the very least she hoped she would be able to take advantage of Ben's reclusive second home.

Breaking her needed trance and reentering her current situation, Google Maps had her twisting and turning at several stop signs. The homes grew closer together and then there were a few displaced modern looking condos. She waited at a railroad track as one of those painstakingly long trains covered in graffiti clipped by. She was so close to Amy's Toffee. Her heart rate accelerated in anticipation.

Finally, the gate reopened and she drove into the charming downtown area with young parents pushing strollers and old couples walking hand in hand. And then out of the corner of her eye, nearly blending in with the rest of them, if not for his exceptional good looks, she spotted Asa. Pushing a stroller. She nearly got into another accident.

She got stopped at a red light as he passed her. Please don't see me. Please don't see me. She wished she had not given her hat away. She held her breath and turned her head the other way. As he strode past her, she glanced over. He appeared all consumed by the screaming infant, whose wails pierced her own ears. She lingered behind him until she was able to pull off into a parking spot on the side of the street.

As soon as she pulled over, she observed an attractive woman rush out of a store about twenty yards ahead. She squinted to make out Amy's Toffee. The woman jogged to the stroller and whisked up the flailing bundle from the stroller. The baby immediately stopped crying. She said something to Asa with a look of concern but started to relax when Asa gave her a quick kiss on the cheek before they entered the store as a family.

So that was that. She drove by, inhaling the tantalizing smell of toffee, her eyes starting to swell with tears at the bitter acknowledgement that not only was she no closer to finding out what the hell was happening to her but her chance with Asa was truly over as well.

She drove back in a daze, the music to just a murmur as she tried her best to focus on the road with bleary eyes. She bit her lip to prevent herself from full on crying. She was fine. Asa was telling the truth. He was a father and she was happy for him. He was not out to get her. He had had true feelings for her. Someone else was out to get her though and she would figure it out. She was savvy, independent and more determined than she ever had been. It was a process of elimination and she would get to the bottom of it because she had to.

At five thirty her stomach was growling and she started to feel light headed. She really had not eaten all day besides the bag of Cheetos and now her blood sugar was plummeting. She got off at the upcoming exit, now back in Illinois, and followed a sign to Randy's Diner.

Old men adorned in cowboy hats glanced up at her from their large plates of hearty food as she strode directly to the bar and took a seat. She ordered a cheeseburger and fries from a pretty bubbly blonde without glancing at the menu. And screw it. A Guinness as well. She definitely needed a drink after this failed trip.

The cheeseburger was exceptionally good. It would probably cost at least double the price in the city. She took her time after being on the run all day, her adrenaline dying down as she drank her beer between bites. She glanced between the two TV screens going, one set to the sports channel, and the other to the news.

The Cubs were playing and sadly losing to the Giants. It was a done game at this point in the 7th inning. Her eyes averted to the other screen as she nibbled on a fry. An older but attractive man gently tapped her on the shoulder. She jumped and nearly choked.

"So sorry to startle you, Ma'am," the man said, tipping his hat in apology, "but I wanted to see if the seat next to you was open."

Elle hesitated. Why the hell would he be asking to sit right next to her when there were several open seats?

The man could obviously sense her confusion.

"I have a few buddies joining me," he clarified. "We meet here every week. Our little old men tradition."

Elle smiled politely. "Of course." The man tipped his hat again and as he sat down next to her, he ordered his "usual" from the enthusiastic bartender who obviously knew him well.

She returned to eating her fries and watching the images flash on the TV. She read the captions as a reporter with aggressive makeup, even for camera, discussed the latest horrors. A tornado in Iowa had destroyed several acres of crops and ravaged hundreds of people's homes and their livelihood. A fire had swept through an apartment complex in Chicago, killing six, including two young children, photos of their chuberic faces radiating so much hope and potential. The latest Chicago shootings were highlighted and then a back to school drive for the city's poorest areas was given brief mention.

School would be starting in less than six weeks. She needed to have her life in order by then. She would not let this madness break her or interfere with her job.

Those children needed her. And she needed the income of course. The prospect of acquiescing to her father's wishes in order to receive his money suddenly crossed her mind. It would be a game changer for sure but no, she had gotten by her whole life without him and didn't need his help now. She would move and get a dog. And cameras.

But first she would make a police report ASAP. Not that they would do much about it. Obviously, Chicago PD had much more imminent danger to focus on. But she would do everything she could to get her life back. In some sense, she felt relief that all this craziness was not her. She had not gone insane. Someone was trying to overpower and instill fear in her. But she refused to be the target for their deranged satisfaction a moment longer.

At the commercial break, she asked for a dessert menu. Might as well top it off. The waitress proudly announced that they had "award winning pies." Elle ordered a slice of rhubarb, which the waitress conceded was her favorite if she was "forced to pick." She ordered coffee as well—she still had at least an hour and a half drive. The waitress placed the pie in front of her and waited expectantly for her to take a bite. Elle bit in and enthusiastically expressed her approval to the waitress though she did have to admit it was not the best pie she had ever had.

The Cubs were now in the ninth inning, no chance of coming back. On the other screen, a different reporter was aired, her makeup slightly less aggressive than the previous reporter, her long brown curls partially hiding her ample cleavage. An old man at the end of the bar, undoubtedly sitting with his wife, was instantly riveted by the screen. His wife was oblivious or simply did not care as she continued to sip on her beer. Funny how old age eliminated jealousy and increased one's not giving a shit.

After a string of commercials, including a Rumba commercial Elle noted she would buy to help control her prospective dog's inevitable shedding, the face of an attractive red headed woman appeared transitioning back to the news. Morgan McCormick. Elle put down her fork, at full attention. For a second she thought it was Ami again. Elle followed the rapid captions.

The woman was missing, having not shown up to work at the Consulate General of Ireland in Chicago nor returning calls from anyone in over a week. She studied her face, leaning over the bar to get a closer look. It was her. It was the woman she had seen Clay with, the woman that had caused her friendship with Ami to end. She looked slightly younger in the photo and more wholesome and professional but it was most definitely her.

Elle suddenly had the urge to throw up everything she had just consumed. Hands shaking, she retrieved her wallet from her purse. She left a fifty-dollar bill and her half eaten pie slice and was back on the road within 30 seconds.

She exceeded the speed limit by twenty miles, her veins pulsing with adrenaline again and her mind flooded with questions. Was Clay the one that had abducted that woman and had also been breaking into her place? Was Ami in danger, too? And why them?

She desperately wanted to call Ami, but she knew it could be detrimental. Especially if she was with him right now, which there was a good chance she was at this time of day. Instead, she called Ben and prefaced the call that she was OK but that she needed a place to stay for a few nights and that she would explain later. Without question he told her to come on over and that he and Cameron would be at home waiting for her.

But first she needed to go home and gather whatever evidence she could to bring to the police station for them to take her seriously. The picture of her and Ami at the beach, the magnet, the pair of scissors. Hopefully they had some DNA on them though she highly doubted it. He was most likely smart enough to wear gloves.

She started to drive frantically, swerving in and out of lanes to bypass the slower cars. Less than an hour later, she was parked outside her place. She took some deep breaths. She should have asked Ben to meet her at her place but it was too late. She could do this on her own. She would be able to get in and out in just a couple minutes. As she pounded up the stairs, she nearly tripped over the woman sitting on the top landing.

She automatically screamed as the woman slowly stood up, holding her hands up in defense. She was very tall and slender, attractive, though slightly disheveled looking.

"I am so sorry to scare you," she said. "I'm Chloe." She extended her hand tentatively.

Elle slowly extended hers still in shock. "Chloe?"

"You sent me a letter last month. About the bachelorette party," she clarified.

"Clay's sister," Elle said.

"Um, yes. I am so sorry to just show up like this, but it's urgent. To get right to the point, I am afraid that your friend may be in danger."

"Come in," Elle said, as she unlocked the door.

"Thank you." Elle held the door open after her. For a moment she regretted her decision. She did not know this woman. What if she was in on it as well? But she needed to take the chance and hear this woman out. Time was of the essence.

The first thing she saw was the letter on the console table written in all capital's with permanent marker.

She grabbed it, and glimpsed over the brief note. "Hope you had a nice drive."

"What is it?" Chloe asked, coming up behind her, alarm in her voice. Elle handed her the note. Chloe's face fell.

"It's his writing," she said matter of factly. That's Jeremy's writing." She reached into her bag and pulled out a journal, which she handed to Elle. Confused, she grabbed it and opened it to a random page.

November 14th, 2003:

Today I followed both of them to the store. I was in the other aisle but I could still hear them. It was obvious they were buying condoms. How romantic. Piere insisted on needing extra-large. Such an egotistical asshole. And of course, Maddy was just laughing the entire time in that ridiculous way she does all the time. It pisses me off because I know how smart Maddy actually is. But she has already gotten sucked in and succumbed to my brother's stupidity. She is completely obsessed with him and jeopardizing her future by putting him first. It's beyond sad. I want to scream.

I hate him so much. If not for him, she would be mine. All mine. She doesn't know what true romance or love is. I could give her that but of course Pierce takes and takes just like he always does. He will see soon enough though. It is about time that I take back what is rightfully mine. She was my first kiss in kindergarten. I kissed her in the tunnel of the playground. She pushed me away but I know she liked it. It will be her first and last kiss. I will make sure of that.

Elle looked up at Chloe, horrified. There was something eerily similar in her facial structure to Clay's. "What the fuck is going on?" she demanded handing the journal back to her.

Chloe gave her a pitiful look. "My brother, Jeremy, who now apparently goes by Clay, is a killer," she said quickly, as if to relinquish herself of the shame. She reached into her bag again and brought out a Ziploc bag with a lock of red hair.

"He killed my brother Pierce, his own twin brother, and his girlfriend, Maddy, when they were in high school. This is a piece of her hair." She held up the baggy to Elle. The lock of hair was the vibrant red color of youth, of a life ended too soon. Elle's own hair color hadn't been too far off from it before she reached her 20's. Elle was horrified.

"And who knows who else he has killed. But I refuse to allow your friend to be another victim."

Elle was speechless. Chloe continued. "I always suspected there was something wrong with him but I never thought him capable of killing, especially his own identical twin brother. Jeremy Steven Harper—that's his real name—was insanely jealous of Pierce. I just didn't realize how jealous. Pierce was better looking, extremely popular, and had always been the more favored brother, that was apparent in the way my parents treated him. And unfortunately I was always doing my own thing. I should have paid more attention to him."

"I lost touch with him soon after his sophomore year in college. He made no effort to engage with the family, not even coming home for holidays. Eventually he just disappeared off the face of the earth. Now I realize he cut me and my parents out so he could continue to lead his psychotic lifestyle."

"When my parents sold their home last year and I was helping them pack up, I found both of these items buried in his drawer." Her eyes darted to the journal and then to the lock of hair in her hands.

Elle felt dizzy, like she was about to pass out. She caught herself on the table. "We need to call the police immediately. I just saw another red haired woman on the news that has gone missing. I saw Clay—or Jeremy—a couple weeks ago with her."

"Please let me try talking to him first without them," Chloe's dark brown eyes looked at her like a deer pleading for its life before the shot. "They will most certainly kill him if they get involved. He is still my brother and I do believe he suffers from mental illness. That's not an excuse but I don't think he wants to be the way he is. He needs help." Elle was disgusted that she was so concerned about the welfare of her murderous brother. "I will go alone. I don't want to put you in any further jeopardy. I won't hesitate to call 911 if I have to. I also have a gun." She patted her purse.

"I will drive you there," Elle said, too exhausted to protest. "We need to go now."

Chloe simply nodded and the women left determined in their quest.

They drove in silence to Ami's house with only the hum of the radio. Elle prayed that Bob Marley's "Every Little Thing is Gonna Be Alright," prophesized the outcome of this unbelievable situation.

Small talk felt inappropriate. But as the song ended, in need of distraction, Elle finally asked, "So I'm assuming you aren't schizophrenic and were never committed to an institution?"

"No, I am not schizophrenic and I was never committed," Chloe responded. I can only imagine the tales Jeremy has spun."

"So how did you get my letter then?"

"I work at the Bloomtree. I'm a nurse, not a resident there."

"And are your parents deceased?" Elle abruptly stopped at a red light she had impulsively wanted to run.

"No, they are very much alive though devastated from losing my brother. They have never been the same since."

"I couldn't imagine." Without thinking, Elle grabbed Chloe's hand and squeezed it. Chloe squeezed her sweaty hand back, staring out the window. She was a complete stranger, yet Elle felt an inexplicable comfort with her. She could only hope that they weren't on their way to further devastation.

Chapter 24

Elle parked a couple houses down from Ami's, to be on the safe side. It did not appear as if there were any lights on but Ami's car was in the driveway along with another car she did not recognize.

"It's that brick home." Elle pointed. "I should go in first. He would certainly know something was up if you did. Ami and I have been in a fight. I will pretend that I have come to apologize and I will ask her to go talk with me somewhere. I will text you if Clay—I mean Jeremy is there."

"Ok," Chloe finally agreed. "Give me your phone number at least. Text me if you need me to come inside or call 911. Here, take my gun. I will keep my mace."

They exchanged numbers quickly and Chloe handed her the gun, letting her know how to turn off the safety. Elle had never held a gun before, but she retrieved it with a steady hand and gently secured it in her purse alongside her emergency trail mix. How ironic. A sudden wave of calm overcame her, as if her body knew she needed to be in order to execute this plan effectively.

The women locked eyes and without saying anything more, Elle turned towards Ami's home as she had done so many times before, bearing wine and appetizers for a fun girl's night. However, this time she came bearing a gun with an uncertain outcome ahead.

The house was dark, the curtains drawn. She took one last deep breath and rang the doorbell. She could hear talking inside. The talking continued and she waited, an urge to flee coming over her. She was no cop, she had never even shot a gun before, what the fuck was she thinking?

But before she had a chance to change her mind Jeremy opened the door.

"Elle, what a surprise!" he exclaimed, only cracking the door enough to reveal part of his face, sweating profusely.

Her heart started pounding so hard she thought she might pass out again. She mustered a smile. "Oh hey, Clay, how are you? I just came by to see if Ami is home?" She used every ounce of effort to keep her voice stable.

"Unfortunately, she isn't at the moment. She um... went to grab some takeout food for us."

Ami's Prius was obviously parked in the driveway. She could hear a muffled howl in the background followed by a loud cough.

"That's OK," she replied nonchalantly. "I can wait for her." She looked Jeremy straight in the eyes and pushed the door open.

Jeremy stumbled back. Time seemed to stop as she took in the scene. Ami was tied to a chair in the kitchen, her red and tear streaked face bound with duct tape. Her wild eyes met Elle's and she attempted to scream again. Then she glimpsed Ami's brother in the corner of the kitchen on his hands and knees, bound, like a crazed animal. His face was beaten and bloody to the point that he was nearly unrecognizable.

And Jeremy was holding a gun, a very legitimate looking gun, especially compared to the tiny pistol in her purse.

"I just told you Ami wasn't home but of course you couldn't wait." He leaned into her, the gun jamming into her ribs. "Just like every other red haired cunt. Well, welcome I guess." He sneered at her, his face contorting into someone entirely different.

She had to be strong. Their lives depended on it. "I'm sorry but I was concerned about my friend. And from the looks of it, I should be. She doesn't deserve this. Why don't you just go and we can pretend this never happened. I'm sure you don't want to spend the rest of your life in prison. That wouldn't be worth it for people whose lives you obviously don't even care about, right"

"Ah, I wish it was that easy," Jeremy pressed the gun harder into her rib forcing her against the wall. "But unfortunately you ruined my plan. You had to go ahead and tell Ami that I was cheating on her and set this whole mess in motion. Now Ami knows about the other stupid bitch I kidnapped. So since you got involved, lucky you, off you go, too. Just because you couldn't mind your own fucking business." He shook his head disdainfully.

"What did you do with Morgan?" Elle demanded. She would not cower down to this monster.

"What the fuck did I just say?!" He leaned in so close to her she could smell his disgusting breath. "None of your fucking business!"

"But it's your business to break into my place and stalk me?" Elle shot back.

Ami squealed, signaling to Elle to back off. Elle needed to break him though, she had no choice. But then he shoved the gun in her mouth.

"Wow, you got it. Good job! Took you long enough to figure that one out." He patted her shoulder and then abruptly slapped her across the face, leaving a hot imprint on her cheek. Elle resisted flinching.

"Could you put your spare key in a more obvious place?" he sneered. "And how dumb are you drinking and mixing pills? But just to make sure, you sitll made it so easy for me to inject you with Proponal or slip some roofies in your wine. Because I can actually use my brain." He punched her in the head so hard she thought she would collapse but she refused to give up now.

"Did you like my addition to your painting? I thought the blood splatter was a nice touch, didn't you? A nice foreshadowing. Thanks for the brownies by the way. They were still pretty good for being boxed." He laughed heartily. "Oh and how about the hair I snipped off? Let me see." He took out her ponytail and brushed her hair back from her face like he was about to kiss her. She wanted to vomit. "Ah there it is. Looks like you will need to chop off all your hair now. Too bad your face isn't pretty enough to pull off the short hair look." He spat in her face, disgusting saliva slid down her cheek.

"But at least you have a nice body. You have been working so hard on those legs, that ass. He grabbed her butt and squeezed. "Hmmm, not as hard as I thought. Well, it doesn't matter now, does it?"

"And in case you still haven't put two and two together by now, I was the camp counselor that you and your little tied up friend over here had in the summer of '06. Both you fucking bitches told on me like the little pussies you are. I was simply minding my own business, jacking off from a distance. I mean why else would little cunts showing off their bodies in little bikinis wear them?" He grabbed her hand and forced it on his crotch. "How sad. You're not even attractive enough to get me hard." He slapped her hand away and pushed the gun further in her mouth. "But since you can take a good mouthful maybe you could actually get me off another way." Elle's eyes welled with tears of rage.

"Did you know I had to register as a child sex offender after that? That I literally could not get a job even as a fucking cashier and had to change my identity? But in a way you also helped me flourish in my killings as I became quite equipped at changing my identities. And ironically you both have this whorish red hair." He yanked her hair so hard she thought her scalp would come off.

It really was the fucking creep. Elle would never forget that repulsive scene she and Ami witnessed in absolute shock.

He relinquished the gun from her mouth and jammed it into her temple. "Being Clay has been my favorite actually. I rather enjoy being a bartender. Bitches don't suspect their bartender would roofie them, right? Especially when they perform in a band. "Oh how awesome! What is the name of your band?" they all say, as if that makes me instantly trustworthy. See you and Ami are not the only ones. You aren't special. Though I do have an affinity for red headed bitches, starting with Maddy, my brother's high school sweetheart. What a fucking joke they were together. I did them both a favor."

"My other three victims were also red headed sluts in case you were wondering about my killing resume. Brunettes and blondes just aren't worth the energy. Regardless, all you bitches care about is getting drunk and getting attention. It's pathetic how easily enticed you are. And if you add a touch of a roofie, it's game over."

Elle couldn't hold back any longer. "You are so pathetic. I actually feel sorry for you. You have no idea what it feels like to care about anyone or anything. Because no one has ever cared about you. You were always overshadowed by your brother. You are evil and worth nothing and you know that."

He glared at her, sputtering and spitting but unable to come up with any retort. She had hit the nail on the head.

He backed away from her then, screaming like a wild animal about to charge its prey. Elle fumbled for her pistol. But she was too slow. The gun went off. She closed her eyes and fell to the floor, screaming.

But it wasn't the sound of a shot she heard. It was the loud, crushing sound of Jeremy's skull being pummeled. The metal piece Elle had made for the "happy couple," the soon to be Mr. and Mrs. Richardson, displayed on the fireplace mantel, crashed to the floor. Henry stood looming over Jeremy's body. His wrists still bound, he retrieved the weapon, ready to strike again. At that moment, Chloe burst through the door and instantly screamed at the sight of her brother, a vast pool of blood already encircling his head.

Henry relinquished the weapon as Chloe knelt next to her dying brother. Her brother who had once been an innocent child, whom she had looked out for. Perhaps if he had been the one to receive more nutrients in the womb, more love and attention, he could have been a normal person. Elle's heart broke for Chloe, for the loss of the actual human he once was. But now the monster was finally dead. The terror was over. Bloody and traumatized but unlike his other victims, still alive.

Epilogue

Elle opened the oven just in time to take out the perfectly done crescent rolls. She had actually taken the time to roll them with precision so they looked like crescent rolls and not some child's play dough project. The house was wafting with all the Thanksgiving smells, the dishes patiently waiting, covered in heavy duty tin foil, which Asa insisted was worth the couple extra bucks, and the table set for seven.

Asa slammed the door per usual and stomped his feet as if he needed to make an announcement every time he entered. He stopped to give Elle a quick kiss, grabbing her face. His lips and hands were freezing from just having finished putting up an abundance of Christmas lights. Elle had told him it was too early for Christmas lights but he had insisted that they should maximize the holiday season. His go big or go home mentality could be frustrating at times but she did truly love that about him. He was always making the best out of every situation. And always so calm and collected when things did get difficult.

Since they bought a home down the street from Asa's ex and their child, Hunter, two months ago, Elle had not heard him complain once or even swear. Not even when the washing machine flooded the entire basement the first time they used it. She was learning to bite her own tongue, which was a great thing. Life was too short to get hung up on the small stuff, Asa would always remind her. And how true that was.

Asa was definitely the stable balance Elle needed. He was her solid rock and alleviated her anxiety more than anyone else or anything. She could now sleep soundly throughout the entire night, waking refreshed in the morning. And without any medication or alcohol. She had come a long way and was proud of herself.

In her final session with Dr. Berkshire, she had shed a couple of tears. Dr. Berkshire would always have a special place in her heart but it was time to move on and leave the past where it belonged. She could tell he felt guilty after Elle rehashed everything that had transpired, his eyes bulging behind those terrible glasses in complete shock and horror. Elle ended up reassuring him that it was not his fault, that there was no way he could have known what had really been going on.

She still felt like she was giving a movie review when she told the story, like it was something she had only watched, not experienced. Not that she had told many people outside of Dr. Berkshire and Asa. Maybe it was her mind's way of protecting itself. And she was thankful for that. It was time to start focusing on bigger and better things.

"Ah, don't touch me," she squealed. "Your hands are absolutely freezing!"

"Well warm me up then!" He attempted to put his hands underneath her chunky sweater, which she had paired with a skirt and tall boots he had insisted on buying for her, ones she would never have bought for herself. He was so thoughtful, always making an effort to show her he loved her, bringing her home a bouquet of flowers for no special occasion or rubbing her feet without her even asking.

He had come back to her and she would never let him go. Once it was clear that forcing things with Hunter's mother just for the sake of being together for their child was not going to work, he had shown up at her new apartment with white roses and the sweetest, most memorable, proclamation of his love for her. She was shocked and speechless, which Asa initially mistook for anger. But her passionate kiss had told him otherwise.

And to top things off, Elle was on great terms with Asa's ex as was he. There was no bitterness or jealousy. Hunter spent half the week with them, and Elle had fallen instantly in love with the mini Asa. He was a ball of endless energy and joy.

Elle loved their little routine in the evenings together. She would often pick him up from his little daycare that he went to for a few hours a day so that she could spend some quality time in her art studio and Asa could log in some uninterrupted time working from home.

Her studio was in the quaint downtown area not far from Amy's Toffee. Elle couldn't have been happier. Her studio was her reprieve, her other dream come true. She missed teaching at times and knew that she would go back to it eventually. But for right now she was content exploring her own potential. She had already sold more than twenty-five paintings in just a couple of months. The hours would go by so quickly as she created and shared her work with the town. She often would leave still plastered in paint to grab Hunter with his own splattered clothes.

He would be all smiles while she put him in his car seat. She had finally gotten the hang of getting him strapped in as he wiggled around with his puffy jacket on. Hunter would babble contentedly as she drove the fifteen minutes home where Asa would have dinner already going. Before eating they would stroll Hunter through the neighborhood, their new puppy, Shiloh, still learning to walk on the leash by their side. She and Asa would talk about their days and plans for tomorrow. It was so ordinary yet extraordinary. Then they would feed Hunter and the puppy and she and Asa would sit at the dining table, eating their own dinner, Hunter, satisfied in his boppy pillow keenly observing them, Shiloh tuckered out by the fireplace.

Afterwards they would do the dishes as a team followed Hunter's bath in the sink. Hunter loved the water and would giggle incessantly as she washed the crevices of his chubby folds. Then they would play, (he was starting to get the humor in peek-a-boo) until his laughter became tearful. Asa would then put Hunter down for bed while Elle chatted on the phone or got in a quick workout. The rest of the night would just be for her and Asa, uninterrupted, except for Hunter's occasional awakenings.

It was all so normal and everything she had never known she wanted. She was ready to not only be a wife but a mother to a child of theirs together. Having Hunter eliminated her doubt that she wouldn't be able to be a "good" mother. Of course she knew she would not be perfect and it would get hard but at the end of the day, she knew she wanted this with Asa, her forever partner and best friend.

After a luxurious minute of kissing she backed away and said, "Our guests are arriving any second."

He gave her a sad puppy dog look and glanced at his watch. "Yep, any minute. Ben called me and said they were about ten minutes out ten minutes ago."

"That's perfect," she said looking down at her incoming text from her dad, indicating that he had just gotten to the airport. "His flight is scheduled to land on time."

She had decided to meet both of her dads. Her dying father, John, whom she had known her whole life to be her father, and her real biological father, Phil.

She had watched another man die in front of her two weeks after

Jeremy. As she held John's limp hand, he told her how much he loved her despite not being her actual father. In a choking whisper he told Elle that her mother had had an affair and that she was not really his. He had forgiven her but she had continued to push him away until he finally left.

It was the hardest decision he had ever made and he could only hope that in his absence her mother would introduce Phil into her life. He decided not to interject even years later to avoid any pain or confusion. But when he reached out to her mother when he found out that he was dying, it was apparent that Elle didn't even know about Phil. He had told her in his raspy voice that this news was devastating to him. This whole time she had grown up without a dad while thinking that he had simply abandoned her.

However, now he could be at peace knowing that she would finally have the opportunity to meet Phil. It wasn't difficult to track him down thanks to Facebook. He had never used Facebook before but was able to set up his own profile, he added with a smile. He wanted Elle to know her real father more than anything before he made his way out.

"I hope you can forgive me, Elle," he had whispered slowly in her ear, his breathing becoming more labored. "I do, I do," she said, her eyes filling with tears, gripping his hand tightly. She wanted him to stop talking, it was painful to listen to. But she also wanted to hear every last thing he had to say, which was, "Thank you, Elle. Thank you for being a shining light in this all too short life."

Elle lost two significant people that night but had gained another. She decided that she could no longer have a relationship with her mother after she had denied her knowing her father until the age of thirty-three. Forgive her, yes, she already had. But she was no longer willing to subject herself to any more pain in this all too harsh and short life. At the end of the day, she had to protect herself.

She had also truly forgiven Ami's brother. Yes, he had hurt her tremendously but he had changed and grown into a good person. He had saved her life that tragic night, all their lives, and for that she would be forever grateful.

She felt especially grateful this Thanksgiving season, breaking down in tears of gratitude the past couple of days. Yesterday she had sold a painting of two figures holding hands in front of an ocean sunset to an old woman. The woman explained that she was a widow and that tomorrow would be her first Thanksgiving without her former husband. Elle had felt so sad for her and invited her to Thanksgiving at their home, but the woman politely declined, indicating that she would be spending the holiday with her sister-in-law for the first time, their mutual loss having drawn them closer. The woman was so happy to bring home the painting and hang it over "their" bed, so she could always have a piece of her husband's presence. As the woman walked out, declining any help to her car, Elle had teared up. She had certainly gone through some stuff in her life so far, but she had also been given so much, which she would never take for granted.

"Everything is ready to go now." She placed the steaming rolls in a bread basket and covered them lightly with a napkin.

"You are amazing! Everything looks and smells wonderful." Asa snagged a roll. "Hmmm, rolls right out of the oven. The best. I cannot wait to indulge. I have only had coffee all day."

"You and me both," Elle said. "I'm starving." She took the last bite of the roll that he gave her. As if on command, the doorbell rang. Elle practically ran to the door. It had been several weeks since she had seen any of them.

"Happy Thanksgiving!" Ben and Cameron greeted in unison.

Elle gave them each a tight hug, followed by Ami and her brother behind them.

"Come inside, please, it's freezing." They shuffled inside, laden with pies and wine bottles. Asa graciously placed everything on the abundant table while Elle took their winter jackets that had already been put into use three weeks ago.

They eventually all got settled near the roaring fireplace, sipping wine and munching on appetizers. Elle was completely in the moment with them, smiling and laughing, just like old times. There was no fear or animosity. Now that Jeremy was gone, and the horrors behind them, they had all been trying to move on as best they could, united by a serial killer.

The horror was over for Morgan, too, the other kidnapped woman. She had been found, hysterical but alive in Jeremy's soundproof basement studio. She had been held there for eight days, with little food and water according to the news reports. Jeremy had tortured her in every way imaginable.

She was now back in Ireland with her family. Elle wanted to reach out to eventually. She wanted to let her know how much she admired her for her strength and courage and would love to meet her someday.

The locks of red hair belonging to Kate Rogers, Bridget Taylor and Annie Charles had also been found in Jeremy's apartment. Their disappearances had finally been solved after years of obsessive searching. Their loved ones could now at least rest from their exhaustive pursuit and feel reassured that the killer who took the lives of their beautiful daughter, sister or friend was finally dead and would never harm again.

Elle was still in touch with Chloe, texting one another from time to time. She was going to make her and Asa's cake for their wedding this spring. It would be a simple wedding in their backyard. All Elle cared about was having the people she loved gathered together and her husband by her side.

She did not want any flashiness involved, however, Ami was still encouraging her to "at least have a little bling." She had scheduled them to go to three wedding dress stores in a couple weeks, a compromise Elle finally agreed to from the initial six Ami had sent her. The dress was the least of Elle's concerns but she was looking forward to spending the time with Ami, especially before she moved.

"Have you closed on the house yet?" Elle asked, trying to keep her tone upbeat. She knew how badly Ami needed this fresh start, just as she had. And she also knew what an amazing victim advocate she would be—her new career path. She was excited to start dedicating herself to helping survivors like herself overcome trauma. Elle could not have been prouder of her. But Ami, as courageous and independent as she was, was still human and vulnerable just like anyone else. Jeremy had left an indelible mark on her and she didn't want Ami to be retriggered at the expense of her career aspirations. However, Elle knew she would persevere regardless and they would both be OK. They had somehow made it this far after all.

"Yup, everything is solidified! I just depleted all my savings and feel like a poor college student again, but that's OK. As long as I have the sound of the ocean waves to put me to sleep and wake up to every morning, I think it will be worth it. So tired of the damn cold." She shuddered for effect. "Sorry," she added. "I know I'm leaving you guys out in the cold, no pun intended."

Elle laughed. "Well, I will definitely be coming to visit lots, especially in the dead of the winter."

"Absolutely! All of you are always welcome to come visit anytime. That's why it was so important for me to find a home with a small guest house."

"That's awesome!" Asa jumped in. "And how long are we all welcome for?" he asked, nudging Elle.

"As long as you like!" Ami said whole heartedly. "I'm going to miss you all so much! I will be banking on you guys to come visit especially since I have no intent of dating-well at least not anytime soon—and not until I do a thorough background check."

Elle laughed even though she had a lump in her throat. She would miss her so much but knew she was so fortunate to have her best friend back, and alive, most importantly. Forgiving Ami hadn't even been a question. Elle had been the one to untie her and peel the duct tape from her mouth. They had immediately embraced and sobbed uncontrollably, relief and gratitude communicated in the tightness of their embrace. But regardless of their physical separation, Elle could truly say without a doubt that they would always be friends after everything they had been through. The trust had been questioned and challenged but in the end, they had each other's backs. Third time's the charm she supposed—surviving cancer, a car crash and a serial killer together.

"Well, that will be no problem for my husband and I!!" Ben said, sneaking his arm around Cameron. Ben was now referring to Cameron as his husband with an emphasis, at any opportunity since they eloped secretly last month in Cancun. As happy as she was for them, not being included had initially been upsetting. But Ben reassured her they would be having a "reception party of the century with a Great Gatsby flair once the shit storm of winter was finally over."

Ben squeezed Cameron closer to him. "My husband and I are always looking for an excuse to get the hell out of dodge!" Elle shook her head, smiling. They had finally bought their vacation home, a condo in the downtown area not far from her and Asa's.

Elle had just finished decorating it. It had been such a fun project having free reign, picking out modern furniture and final fixtures. Along with revamping her home with Asa in a more traditional sense, she had been strongly considering getting into interior design on the side. Despite Ben's eagerness for her to get everything done practically overnight, and her constantly reminding him that she had other responsibilities outside of decorating their vacation home, seeing their eyes light up when they walked into the condo a couple weeks ago had made it all worth it.

"And speaking of solidified," Ben continued, turning his eyes to

Cameron, "Cameron and I just found out that we have been approved to be adoptive parents!"

"What?!" Elle placed her wine glass filled with La Croix down on the coffee table as she pummeled towards them in a joint embrace. Everyone applauded and cheered.

"That is so freaking exciting!" Her eyes started to water tears of joy.

"Yes, we are over the moon," Cameron said with a huge smile. "And we know where you live if we ever need a night to ourselves," he added, squeezing her arm.

More ruckus followed and the fire roared brightly. When the noise had settled down, Elle was unable to contain her own secret any longer.

"And speaking of being parents," she looked into Asa's eyes, who gave her the go ahead, "Asa and I are expecting in April." She and Asa clinked their glasses together and kissed as Ami leapt up from the sofa spilling her wine all over the sheepskin rug.

There were hugs and more cheers followed by hefty plates of food, leaving Elle so full, and so full of happiness, she felt that she could burst. Everything bad and good had all led to this point. She couldn't have been more thankful. And still she knew that the best was yet to come…

About the Author

Shana is originally from New Jersey but has resided in Arizona for the past several years where she attended Arizona State University and ultimately obtained a master's in counseling psychology. Shana has always had an affinity for psychology and writing cultivating *Deadly Deception*. She also enjoys writing poetry when she is not spending time with her family, who encouraged her to publish her first thriller.